Fit
to
Die

Books by Ellery Adams

The Secret, Book & Scone Society

The Secret, Book & Scone Society

The Book Retreat Mysteries

Murder in the Mystery Suite
Murder in the Paperback Parlor
Murder in the Secret Garden
Murder in the Locked Library

Supper Club Mysteries

Carbs & Cadavers
Fit to Die
Chili con Corpses
Stiffs & Swine
The Battered Body
Black Beans & Vice
*Pasta Mortem**
(*by Ellery Adams and Rosemary Stevens)

Antiques & Collectibles Mysteries

A Killer Collection
A Fatal Appraisal
A Deadly Dealer
A Treacherous Trader
A Devious Lot
A Killer Keepsake

More Books by Ellery Adams

The Charmed Pie Shoppe Mysteries

Pies and Prejudice
Peach Pies and Alibis
Pecan Pies and Homicides
Lemon Pies and Little White Lies
Breach of Crust

The Books by the Bay Mysteries

A Killer Plot
A Deadly Cliché
The Last Word
Written in Stone
Poisoned Prose
Lethal Letters
Writing All Wrongs
Killer Characters

Hope Street Church Mysteries

The Path of the Crooked
The Way of the Wicked
The Graves of the Guilty
The Root of All Evil
Fate of the Fallen

Fit
to
Die

ELLERY ADAMS

Fit
to
Die

The only way to keep your health is to eat what you don't want, drink what you don't like, and do what you'd rather not.

—Mark Twain

Chapter One

Eclair

"Would you care for an éclair, sir?"

James Henry stared at the chocolate-covered delight nestled in its crinkled paper cup. He knew he shouldn't even consider eating the tantalizing pastry. He was *supposed* to be on a diet. For the last six months, he was *supposed* to have been on a good-carbohydrate, good-fat diet. And at first he was good—almost a saint—but lately, his cravings for forbidden foods had overpowered him and he'd cheated. Just a little. Just a bite here and a nibble there. But as the months went by, he found himself eating something deliciously unhealthy every day. What began with a slice of pizza once a week had morphed into a jelly donut on the way to work, a small bag of cheese puffs at lunchtime, a tub of buttered popcorn at the movies, and a candy bar during evening television time. It was when he began eating the cheese puffs again that James knew his diet was officially a failure.

All his life, James Henry had had a love affair with cheese puffs. The crunchy, salty, cheesy ambrosia comprised of baked air and addictive, electric-orange dust made James weak in the knees. During the first two months of the diet, in which he was deter- mined to lose weight alongside his new friends and fellow supper club members, James had resolutely avoided pushing his cart down the snack food aisle in the grocery store. If he didn't go near a bag of cheese puffs, he could resist the temptation to buy them.

He had been so strong in the beginning. So disciplined. And the pounds had come off. Slowly, yes. Just a few pounds each week, which was okay with James. He'd read that losing two pounds a week was healthy. Too much more and the dieter might start feeling deprived and would likely take up bad habits again. For James, that would mean eating foods containing high amounts of sugar, salt, butter, and fat.

So he was jubilant that, over the course of two months, he'd lost twelve of the extra fifty-plus pounds he carried on his tall frame. What he'd gained was a spring to his step, a new pant size, and a sense of confidence that he hadn't experienced in years.

This was back in autumn, though. Thanksgiving had then arrived and James had succumbed to turkey, stuffing, garlic mashed potatoes, candied sweet potatoes, and pecan pie. Christmas was even worse because he didn't restrict his indulging to the twenty-fifth of the month. In fact, every time one of the library staff members brought in Christmas cookies, fruitcake, or jugs of eggnog, James found himself sampling each treat. It was during the holiday season that he and the other members of the supper club, who had humorously dubbed themselves the Flab Five, were all sneaking contraband food on the sly.

"This tiny piece of sweet potato pie or one slim little candy cane could hardly count, right?" they reasoned.

At their last supper club dinner, Gillian, the barrel-shaped pet groomer with the nest of wild orange hair and an eccentric taste in fashion, admitted that she had already gained back half of the weight she'd lost during the fall months. Now, here they were in March, and James Henry, head librarian of the Shenandoah County Library main branch, also ruefully confessed that he had steadily been gaining weight instead of losing it. The supper club members had vowed to get back on track and to be fitter and healthier come summertime.

James knew he should be thinking about how he'd look in June should he suddenly decide to mow the back lawn shirtless. Instead, he stared at the proffered pastry and could only imagine how wonderful it would taste. Shrugging his shoulders, he cast aside all thoughts of dieting and accepted the éclair from the woman wearing a green apron and an artificial smile. The moment he did, she began to tell him where the pastries were located in the freezer aisle and how they could be served at his next social gathering.

But James wasn't listening. The second he popped the soft pastry into his mouth and the sweet custard oozed over his tongue, he closed his eyes and surrendered to the blissful taste. He chewed, swallowed, and sighed in contentment. He wanted more. Unfortunately, the bite-sized piece was gone, so he tried to make do by licking a centimeter-sized smudge of chocolate from his left knuckle.

I could do some shopping and go back around, he thought. *That lady might not recognize me or someone else might come to take her place, and I might be able to have a second sample.*

Buoyed by his plan, James pushed his cart up the frozen food aisle. He had no reason to be there, as he didn't have any frozen foods on his grocery list. If he admitted the truth to himself, which he wouldn't, James would have to acknowledge that the only reason he came over to this side of the store in the first place was to get closer to the display of jumbo-sized bags of tortilla chips, potato chips, pretzel rods, and of course, cheese puffs.

James lived and worked in Quincy's Gap, Virginia, a small town nestled in a narrow valley beneath the Blue Ridge Mountains. His town didn't have a large enough population to support more than one grocery store, let alone a mammoth warehouse store, so he made quarterly runs to the discount warehouse in Harrisonburg. He didn't mind, as he enjoyed running errands for his beloved library. He also liked the idea of saving money. The library budget was stretched thin at the best of times, and he derived a simple pleasure from purchasing Scotch tape, printer paper, ink cartridges, and other office supplies. It gave him a sense of industry and purpose. And if he were being completely honest, he'd also admit that he loved the store's free food samples.

With the éclair's sweetness still coating his tongue, James steered a cart the size of a compact car down the wide, congested aisles. He passed the frozen food section and turned down the first of the refrigerated food aisles. Ignoring the shelves of milk, cottage cheese, and yogurt, he paused in front of a case filled with cheerful yellow tubs of chocolate-chip cookie dough.

"Makes seventy-two cookies," James murmured, picturing a heaping spoonful of dough. "Not if I had that tub at home. There just might be enough dough left to make twenty-two cookies."

Tearing his gaze from the tubs, James spied another woman wearing a green apron at the end of the aisle. Pushing his cart a little faster, he swerved around a man squinting at the products in the butter and margarine case and pulled up next to the woman as she was removing a tray of hors d'oeuvres from a small toaster oven.

"Mini pizza bagels!" James said, delighted, and lined up behind her tiny counter. After thanking the woman for the sample, he immediately stuffed a bagel bite into his mouth, ignoring the molten tomato sauce, bubbling mozzarella cheese, and the woman's sales pitch. Chewing manically, he abandoned his cart and hurried over to the juice sampler station on the other side of the aisle. Tossing back the doll-sized Dixie cup filled with sugary berry juice as if he were drinking a shot of tequila at a bar, James blotted his purple-stained lips with a napkin and, seeing as the green-aproned woman in charge of the juice samples was looking the other way, helped himself to a second cup. No sooner had he balled up the cup and deposited it in the trash than he hustled in the direction of what he believed to be a counter of chocolate samples.

"It has to be chocolate. Nothing else would draw the attention of so many people," he reasoned aloud.

This sampling station was incongruously located where health foods and vitamins were displayed. James reclaimed his cart and parked it in a side aisle before elbowing his way through the knot of eager customers. He even dashed in front of a small boy, afraid that all the free samples would be gone before he could get one.

Glancing at the nearby containers of sugar-free gum, unsalted almonds, and protein bars in disdain, James barreled forward until he could see the surface of the white stand being manned by a frazzled elderly lady. The poor woman was cutting squares of chocolate from a shoebox-sized slab as fast as she could, but she couldn't keep pace with the demanding crowd. The luckiest shoppers grabbed a square and retreated, eyes gleaming in triumph. James looked at them and renewed his efforts to reach the front of the line.

"Hey! You cut me!" the boy behind James whined.

Ignoring him, James stretched a long arm through a narrow gap between the hips of two women and snagged a piece of chocolate. As he attempted to retrieve both his limb and what he now realized was a caramel-filled confection, one of the women abruptly swiveled in place. Her purse swung like a thirty-pound pendulum. It smacked James hard in the arm.

"No!" he cried.

He watched in horror as his caramel-chocolate square flew out of his hand and sailed over a tower of granola bars. Taking advantage of James's distraction, the disgruntled boy lunged forward, seized the last square on the tray, and melted back into the crowd.

"Damn it all!" James muttered. He cast a sidelong glance at the old woman with the green apron. "Are you going to cut another piece?" He hated how pathetic he sounded but was unable to stop himself.

The woman fixed a pair of angry blue eyes on him. "No, I am *not* going to open a new bar," she said, seething. "I am going to turn in this apron and go straight home to read the paper."

James was confused. He couldn't see the connection between reading and handing out samples of chocolates. "The paper?"

"The classifieds! I'm going to find another job!" the woman snapped. "I've never seen such rudeness or gluttony in my whole entire life. And my life hasn't been a short one, mind you. For Pete's sake! It's just a piece of candy. I'm not handing out hundred-dollar bills here!"

James flushed, wondering why, out of all the customers in the store, he'd ended up being the recipient of the woman's tirade.

"I'm sorry," James said. And he was sorry that she didn't enjoy her job. However, he still wanted a chocolate, so in a momentary lapse of judgment, he decided to lie. "I don't know about the rest of these people, but I forgot to eat breakfast today. Suddenly, that piece of chocolate looked awfully darned good to me. I guess I forgot my manners in the face of hunger."

Scowling, the woman threw her apron on the counter. "Sonny, that's a bunch of horse manure and you know it." She leaned toward him. "You don't look like you've *ever* missed your breakfast, or any other meal for that matter. Maybe you should try it once in a while." And with that, she stormed off.

Stung by her remarks, James reversed his cart, strode down the main aisle, and practically skidded to a halt in front of the cheese puff display. Just as he was reaching out to pull a bag down from the shelf, he heard a familiar voice.

"James!"

As James swung around, his elbow grazed a row of cheese puff bags, knocking four or five from the shelf. They dropped into his cart with a crinkly plunk. James immediately tried to block the cart with his body and smiled innocently at his friend Lindy.

"Who are those for?" she teased, her brown eyes twinkling.

"Uh . . ." James fumbled for an excuse. "I *was* going to buy one bag, but those others just fell in, I swear."

"Tsk, tsk." Lindy waved a finger at him while simultaneously attempting to block his view of her cart.

Lindy was just over five feet tall, but her curvaceous body was wide enough to prevent James from getting a clear look at what she was trying to hide. Noting the blush creeping into her café au lait-colored face, James stood on his tiptoes and spied three five-pound bags of mixed candy in her cart.

Pink roses bloomed on Lindy's round cheeks, but she swung her long black hair over her shoulder in a gesture of defiance. "They're bribes for my students. Even high school art teachers have unruly students from time to time."

James sighed as he took the bags of cheese puffs out of his cart and put them back on the shelf. "Lindy, you caught me red-handed. Not only have I eaten every sample in this place, but I was going to gorge on cheese puffs on the way home." He looked at the snack display with longing.

"I've eaten everything in sight, too." Lindy glumly pointed toward the checkout area. "Let's get out of this place before we get any fatter."

"Ha! We're going to lose five pounds before we get close to the exit," James said, indicating the long lines. Every shopper's cart was stuffed with loaves of bread, cases of beer, steaks the size of footballs, wheels of cheese, and dozens of rolls of toilet paper.

James and Lindy pushed their carts into adjacent lines. The woman in front of Lindy had a similar body. Like Lindy, she was short and round with large hips and full breasts. James couldn't help but notice that the woman's cart was loaded with cookie assortments, two cheesecakes, potato chips, ice cream bars, a giant-sized box of Frosted Flakes, rice pudding, and several varieties of candy bars. As he studied her, the woman opened a box of Twix bars, pulled out a package, and began to struggle with the foil wrapper. The gold packaging, which was illuminated with an ethereal glow beneath the fluorescent lights, refused to tear.

As James watched, the woman tugged and tugged at the wrapper, grunting with exertion. She even put it down for a moment, wiped her hands on her purple floral dress, and tried again. Just as her line moved forward, she tore the stubborn wrapper apart and one of the chocolate and caramel-covered cookie bars went soaring through the air. It landed in the cart in front of her, which belonged to a thin brunette dressed in workout clothes.

Everyone in line around the Twix Lady watched and waited for the brunette's reaction. Dozens of eyes looked on as she fished the candy bar out of her cart and examined it with disgust. Her mouth compressing into a thin line, she turned and gave the plump woman behind her an appraising stare.

"I'm so sorry!" Twix Lady gushed, holding out a pudgy hand for the offensive candy. If she was expecting to have her treat returned, she was to be disappointed.

"I'd rather stab myself in the heart than give this to you." The brunette eyed the candy as if it were a piece of dung. "This is a disgusting, unhealthy, chemical-filled piece of trash! My dear friend," she cooed as if talking to a baby, "you don't really want this back."

Baffled, Twix Lady retreated a step while James and Lindy exchanged wide-eyed glances. When his cashier asked James if he was ready, he scurried around the other side of his cart and began to unload it, but it was difficult to focus now that he was so close to the brunette.

"Look at the contents of your cart, sweetie!" the slim woman said, her voice rising over the din of the crowd. Without hesitating, she started to rifle through Twix Lady's cart. There was a frantic energy to all of her movements and James found that he couldn't tear his gaze away. "Nothing but sugar, unhealthy carbohydrates, and cleverly disguised lard!" The brunette put her hands to her lips and shook her head. "Honey! How can you put this garbage in your body?"

Twix Lady looked around for help, but the other shoppers only gaped in abject fascination. It was like watching a lioness circle a wounded wildebeest.

"Don't you realize that you are too beautiful to ruin yourself with food like this?" the brunette asked in a deep drawl, her hand held over her heart to emphasize her sincerity. "If I were your friend, and I'm sure you have tons of friends, I wouldn't let you walk out of this store with the contents of that cart."

"I don't . . . I can't . . . ." Twix Lady was clearly on the verge of tears. Finding no allies in her line, she desperately tore open a new Twix bar, bit off a piece of candy, and chewed feverishly, as if the treat's sweetness could stave off further comment from the brunette. "I like the stuff in my cart. It makes me happy."

The brunette smiled in sympathy. "Darling, this horrible stuff posing as food doesn't really make you feel good. For a few minutes, maybe. But at what price?" She let the words drift over the other customers and then took a step closer to Twix Lady. "You are killing yourself. The foods in your cart will kill you. And the thought of that is breaking my heart."

Smoothing back a few wisps of hair that had escaped her ponytail, the brunette took Twix Lady by the elbow and urged her forward. "See what I have in my cart? I'm buying only fruit, vegetables, cheese, lean meats, and sugar-free candy for when I need a little reward. The contents of my cart is why I look the way I do and your cart is why I'm really worried about your quality of life, sweetie. Do you live nearby?"

Twix Lady blinked, clearly overwhelmed by the brunette's concern and startled by her question.

"Not really. I live south of here."

The brunette cradled a bunch of bananas in her hands. "Close to Quincy's Gap?"

Both James and Lindy shot quick glances at each other.

"I live in Hamburg," said Twix Lady. "It's about twenty minutes from Quincy's Gap."

"That'll be perfect." The brunette handed Twix Lady a business card. "My name's Veronica Levitt, and I'm opening a new fitness and weight-loss center called Witness to Fitness in Quincy's Gap. Matter of fact, the grand opening is next weekend. Why don't you come by and I'll help you change what you put in your cart *and* in your mouth. I will save your life, if you give me the chance."

The brunette put a hand on Twix Lady's shoulder and squeezed it tenderly. Twix Lady began to cry, her shoulders and chest jiggling as she wept.

"You can help me?" she sobbed, a trickle of chocolate-colored drool running down her chin.

It seemed to James that Veronica hesitated for a fraction of a second before her lips curved into an enormous smile. "Oh, yes, my dear. It's going to be tough, though. Real tough. But if you stick with me, you're going to be a newer, stronger, *sexier* you in just six weeks!"

"I'd like that." Twix Lady sniffed, holding the business card to her chest as if it were a treasure she might lose. "Thank you." She reached out and hugged Veronica.

"Excuse me!" Lindy called to Veronica from behind Twix Lady. "Did you say six weeks?" Lindy's tone was clearly dubious.

Veronica's bright green eyes fixed on Lindy's figure. "That's what I said. Are you interested as well, hon?"

Lindy hesitated. "I've been on a diet for over six months, actually."

Veronica began unloading her cart. "Is it working for you?" she called back, eyeing Lindy sweetly as Twix Lady turned around to get a good look at the person who might also be transformed by the magical fitness guru.

Shrugging, Lindy averted her gaze. "I lost a few pounds." She then pointed across the way at James. "There are five of us dieting together. We're in a supper club together."

"Good for you!" Veronica cheered. She then pointed at Lindy's cart. "But is that candy a part of your supper club's menu?"

Lindy looked down at her cart and squirmed. "It's for my students. Look, I happen to be a curvy woman," she added defensively. "We don't all have your bone structure. I've always had a very full-figured build."

Veronica finished paying for her purchases. "Of course. We're all different in so many ways. And isn't that wonderful?" She pushed her cart to the side so that Twix Lady could check out and approached Lindy as if she were a lost puppy in need of adoption. Her angular face was a mixture of worry and friendliness. "Wouldn't you prefer Jennifer Lopez's curves to those of Jabba the Hutt? Why, with that gorgeous hair and those big, beautiful brown eyes, you could have men lined up for miles in hopes of getting your phone number! With a little work and willpower, that is."

Lindy's jaw came unhinged and her entire face turned red. Her hands tightened into fists and she balled them so tightly that her knuckles went white.

Veronica seemed oblivious to Lindy's anger and humiliation. "Take my card. I'm giving discounts to the brave and powerful people who sign up for a six-week plan during my grand opening." She bent to retie the shoelace on one of her spotless running shoes. "But I've got to warn you. You won't be eating candy with me as your food advocate, so you may as well get out of this line and put it back on the shelf. That'll prove just how much you want to change your life. Go on, darling, put it back. You don't need that candy to make you happy."

James waited for Lindy's Brazilian half to raise its hot-tempered head and verbally reduce Veronica Levitt into a smoldering pile of ash. Though Lindy was an easygoing and fun-loving person filled with an infectious optimism, she could occasionally give in to fits of rage not unlike a toddler's tantrum. Lindy blamed these infrequent bouts of wrath on her Brazilian mother, a former supermodel. To James's astonishment, Lindy's famed temper remained in check. She didn't lash out at Veronica. Instead, she nodded in silent agreement, scooped up the bags of candy, and left her place in line in order to return them to the shelf.

Dumbfounded, James began unloading his cart. To his horror, Veronica suddenly appeared at his side. She gave him the once-over with her calculating green eyes, placed a pair of tanned hands on her narrow hips, and poked him on the shoulder.

"So you've been on a diet for six months, too?"

James slapped a carton of copier paper onto the conveyer belt. "Yes."

Veronica smiled warmly. "You'd do so well on my program. Men always do." She reached out an arm to lift another carton from his cart, and James stared at the muscular limb. It was sinewy and leathery and looked more like a jungle vine than a part of the human anatomy.

"You know, you have a good frame and a handsome face hidden underneath all of that cushion," Veronica said, tossing the heavy carton of printer paper onto the belt as if it were a box of Kleenex. "I bet you were a looker in high school, weren't you?"

James was amazed by her strength, considering her overall lack of body mass. He was more than a little intimidated as well. He felt more comfortable with less muscular, less angular women. He liked a woman with curves and soft skin and dimpled cheeks. Suddenly, he had a vision of Lucy Hanover, the supper club member who worked for the sheriff's department. Lucy was all softness, like a warm and cozy chair that one longs for at the end of the day. The only sharp trait of Lucy's was her mind. James pictured her sunlit brown hair, eyes the shade of bachelor's buttons, and a pair of full lips that he'd dared to kiss just once a few months ago.

Lost in the lovely memory, James completely forgot about Veronica.

Veronica was not the type of woman to be ignored, however. She shoved a business card into James's hand and then, patted him on the protruding mound that was his belly.

"Let me help you. We can replace that spare tire with washboard abs." She tapped his empty ring finger. "I'll transform you into Virginia's sexiest bachelor."

James shifted uncomfortably. He didn't like being touched by strangers, but Veronica's hand moved upward. She traced the curve of his cheek before hopping back over to her shopping cart. "Hope to see you next week, good-looking!" she called, paid for her purchases, and left.

Seeing that other shoppers were gawking at him, James balled up Veronica's pink business card and shoved it deep into his jeans pocket. Lindy returned to reclaim her place in the checkout line, but James didn't want to talk to her.

"I'll wait for you by the exit," he told her. "I need some air."

James rushed outside and felt instantly relieved when the March breeze cooled his burning cheeks. Lindy joined him a few minutes later and they headed for the parking lot together.

"I thought you needed that candy for your students," James said.

Lindy shrugged. "I'll have to get them something else as a reward. To be totally honest, I would have eaten half of that stash if I had it at school."

James shook his head. "How could you listen to that sanctimonious stick insect? She's part cheerleader, part used-car salesperson, part Dr. Phil."

Lindy paused in the middle of the parking lot and turned to look at James. "Let's face it. We haven't done very well on our own, have we? Maybe it's time to seek professional help."

"But she's . . . she's like Richard Simmons on speed!" James spluttered.

Lindy unlocked her car, a red Chevy Cavalier with a sizeable dent in one of the rear door panels, and began placing her purchases in the trunk.

"Exactly! Veronica will pump us up. She'll have us feeling energized again. Not only that, but she'll force us to be more honest about what we're eating. We haven't held each other accountable, James. When was the last time we even shared our weight-loss progress?"

James fidgeted with his key chain. "At least two months," he said.

"That's because there hasn't been any! I think we're all steadily gaining," Lindy said. "It's time for someone to coerce us to get back on the scale and to get us exercising. If that means Veronica's our new diet cheerleader, then so be it. We need someone to champion us, someone who truly cares about our health and happiness. Tomorrow night, during our dinner meeting, I'm going to suggest that we all go to her grand opening. We need to own up to the fact that we've slipped."

"I guess—" James began.

Lindy squeezed into the driver's seat and shook her car keys at James. "The Flab Five is in desperate need of motivation and leadership. Veronica Levitt is just the woman to whip us into shape. Trust me, you'll be glad we ran into her today."

Picturing Veronica with a whip, James groaned. There was something about the fitness instructor he didn't like. His instincts warned him not to trust her, but he couldn't explain his feelings to Lindy, let alone come up with a good argument as to why they shouldn't join Veronica's program, so he said nothing.

As James drove back to Quincy's Gap, he remembered how Veronica had run her finger along his jawline. Her overly familiar manner gave him the creeps. He was so unsettled by the entire discount store experience that he stopped at a Food Lion on the way home and bought a jumbo bag of cheese puffs.

"I might as well have a happy memory to look back on," he told himself as he tore open the bag.

By the time he reached his house, the bag was empty and James Henry felt calm and content again.

He pulled Veronica's card out of his pocket, effectively covering it with orange cheese puff dust, and thought, *I bet you'd never eat a cheese puff. You might be thin, but you have no idea what you're missing.*

Chapter Two

Chilly Willy's Praline Caramel Kiss

"You got another one of your social dinners tonight?" Jackson Henry asked. He was busy dissecting the tuna casserole James had cooked for him earlier that afternoon and didn't look at his son as he spoke. Instead, he probed beneath the layer of paprika-covered cheddar cheese to see if the pasta James had selected was a shape he favored. "Is this some kind of newfangled noodle? It doesn't look like anythin' I've ever seen before."

"No, Pop. It's not a new noodle. It's elbow macaroni." James sighed with impatience. "It's the same pasta you've had in your tuna casserole for the last twenty years. I followed Ma's recipe to the letter."

Jackson furrowed his bushy white eyebrows. "Except you didn't use that old orange casserole pot. The cheese broils better when you use that pot. Gets all nice and crispy. You could snap it in two like a twig. I suppose you've gone and used it makin' some fancy meal for your friends."

James rolled his eyes. "The pot's in the freezer, Pop. I used it to make you shepherd's pie last week, remember? You said there were too many peas in the pie and that you'd eat it when you were in the mood for peas."

"Well, I ain't in the mood for peas. Matter of fact, I might never be again." Jackson sulked childishly as he flipped through the worn pages of his *TV Guide.*

James refused to be provoked any more by his irascible father. "I'll see you later, Pop."

"Wait just a cotton-pickin' minute," Jackson said. "You gotta stop at Goodbee's first to get my pills."

James looked at his watch. He was already running late and he'd be even later if he had to go to the pharmacy before heading to Bennett Marshall's house.

"Pills for what, Pop?" James asked suspiciously. His father was notorious for trying to put a damper on his son's social life. Jackson never took messages when people called and ripped open all of the mail, even if it wasn't addressed to him. He dumped the bills on the kitchen table, read his son's personal letters, and deliberately crinkled each and every page of the magazines, newspapers, or catalogs he perused while watching game shows.

Recently, he'd "accidentally" smeared peanut butter all over James's treasured copy of the *New Yorker*. Jackson viewed the publication as being unequivocally snobby and written in a manner that made it impossible for "simple country folk" to understand its contents. He even complained about the cartoons, grumbling that not only were the artists unskilled, but they also wrote taglines completely devoid of humor.

"They wouldn't know funny if it smacked them in the face," he'd say and toss the magazine in the recycling bin.

James would have preferred to read the *New Yorker* at the library to avoid his father's tirades on the magazine's short- comings, but the branch's limited budget didn't allow him to subscribe to the magazines he liked best. Instead, he ordered *Better Homes and Gardens*, *Outdoor Life*, and *NASCAR Illustrated*. The publications his patrons were interested in focused on world news, home décor, sports, and cooking. No one had ever requested a copy of the *New Yorker*.

"Pop, I am not going to be late for my supper club meeting unless it's for something important." James tried to adopt a stern tone. "Are these pills a prescription?"

"That's my own business." Jackson averted his gaze. "Can't a man get any privacy around here?"

"You get plenty of privacy. Too much, if you ask me," James said, crossing his arms over his chest. His father was practically a recluse. Ever since his business, Henry's Hardware, had been bought out by one of the country's largest home improvement chains, Jackson had begun to sink into a depression. When his beloved wife had suddenly died of heart failure a year ago, Jackson stopped going out altogether. He was constantly cranky and rarely had positive things to say about anyone or anything.

At the time of his mother's death, James had been a professor of English literature at the College of William & Mary in Williamsburg. James had been living the good life. He had a tenure-track position, a quaint brick town house, and a lovely wife named Jane. But one day, after James returned home from his afternoon lecture on William Faulkner, Jane had announced that she wanted a divorce.

"I'm sorry, honey. Our life is just too dull. I want more," his wife of two years had said.

A few months after this horrific moment, James's mother went to sleep at her usual ten o'clock bedtime, never to wake again. James resigned his position as a professor, the only thing that still brought a fraction of happiness to his life, and moved home to take care of his ill-tempered father.

At first, James viewed his new job as the head librarian of a small-town branch as a step down from his career in academia, but he was pleasantly surprised to discover that his new occupation suited him well. He loved being surrounded by books and he enjoyed his smart, devoted, and amiable coworkers. Most of all, the friendship James had forged with the members of the Flab Five had made his relocation an unexpectedly positive change.

Every time James even thought about one particular member, Lucy Hanover, his heart began to race like a marathon runner approaching the finish line. If only he weren't so shy and insecure, he could tell her that this was how she made him feel. Months after their first kiss, he had yet to ask her out on an official date. Plagued by fears that the dullness his wife had discovered in him would destroy any chance of a romantic relationship with Lucy, James had crawled back inside his shell.

One kiss, and he'd retreated. And Lucy had responded by following his lead. Even though they never discussed the kiss, they still exchanged charged looks from time to time. But it was as if their fall from the diet wagon had also stripped them of the courage to pursue a romantic attachment. So with the exception of his weekly supper club meetings, James had no social life at all. He came home every night to his dilapidated childhood home and his petulant father.

"I thought you were in some kind of hurry. And look at you. You're just standin' there, gatherin' wool," Jackson said, raising one of his bushy eyebrows in amusement.

James snapped out of his stupor, stomped off to his old white Bronco, and tore down the gravel driveway, leaving a cloud of dust in his wake. Goodbee's pharmacy was due to close in a matter of minutes, so James drove fifteen miles over the speed limit and barely paused at the first of the downtown's four-way stop signs to get in the pharmacy door before it was locked for the night.

When James entered the pharmacy, Mr. Goodbee looked up from a pile of paperwork and smiled. James had always liked Mr. Goodbee. He was a kind and patient man with a freckled face and a soft voice.

"Sorry to show up at the last minute, but my father said that he had a prescription waiting here." James paused to catch his breath. "Though I'm not sure how that's possible. He hasn't been to a doctor in years."

Mr. Goodbee laughed. "Oh, he called with a very creative yarn about how his doctor told him he could phone in his own prescriptions from now on. Luckily, when he described his symptoms—bloating, pain, and a feeling of pressure in the lower belly—I knew what was wrong."

Feeling anxious, James leaned over the counter. "Which is?"

"No need for concern." Mr. Goodbee rifled through a box containing prescription envelopes. "Your father has gas. Pure and simple. Now, I know lots of older folks feel better about getting their medicine in old-fashioned, official-looking types of pill bottles instead of packages from the shelves, so I went ahead and dumped a batch of Gas-X in one of my vials and added a Latin name to the label." Mr. Goodbee chuckled and wiped the lenses of his glasses using a corner of his white lab coat. "Works every time."

"You certainly know your customers," James said with admiration as he paid for the pills. "Pop had me thinking this was some kind of emergency."

"Well, he really should see a doctor. Someone his age should be checked out on a regular basis. Try to talk him into booking an appointment with Doc Spratt. He's good with the elderly, and he'll treat your father with courtesy and respect." Mr. Goodbee wagged a finger at James. "Just tell your father it's for his own good, Professor."

Everyone in Quincy's Gap called James "Professor," even though he no longer taught college classes. James knew that vanity prevented him from correcting the townsfolk or suggesting that they simply call him Mr. Henry. He'd worked hard to earn the title of Professor and he was reluctant to let it go.

James shook his head. "Pop would never agree to a physical exam. I'll try to get him to Doc Spratt, but there's a better chance of an iceberg forming in the Sahara than me getting my father to a doctor without him being knocked unconscious."

"Well, you just let me know when you want to take him because I've got pills that can do that!" Mr. Goodbee teased and then walked James to the door.

"There are plenty of times when I could use 'knock-you-unconscious' pills for Pop," James mumbled as he stepped outside. He glanced down at the orange pill bottle in his hands and then caught a glimpse of his reflection in the pharmacy door. His pouch hung over his pants like a hot air balloon trying to squeeze out of a narrow cave opening. The double chin that had shrunk so nicely during the fall was filling in again. James shook his head from side to side and could see an unhappy resemblance between his fleshy neck and a pelican with a bill loaded with fish. Sighing lugubriously, he headed back to his truck. "I wish there were pills to make me thin."

James was the last supper club member to arrive at Bennett Marshall's house. He parked behind Bennett's mail truck and hurried inside after a cursory knock on the front door.

"Oh, here's James!" Lindy exclaimed. "I was just telling everyone about our encounter with Veronica Levitt. I stopped by her fitness center and peeked through the window today. There was a stack of brochures in a display case attached to the glass so I grabbed us a handful. Here, take one." Lindy slid a pink brochure across the table to James. "We can look them over while we eat."

The brochure, which appeared to have been created using an outdated dot-matrix printer, was covered with illustrations of smiling hearts lifting free weights. The text on the front panel read:

Are you ready to grow . . .
Fitter?
Leaner?
Stronger?
More toned?
Sexier?

Are you ready for . . .

New clothes?
Confidence?
A longer life span?
A chance to take control?
Happiness?

Join Witness to Fitness Today!

"I'll take sexier!" Gillian O'Malley giggled, patting her orange cloud of hair. Because Gillian was barrel-shaped, she tried to draw attention to her shapely legs by wearing billowy shirts in a variety of bright colors and busy patterns. A few months ago, she had begun wearing rather form-fitting tops that were more flattering to her figure, but recently she had returned to wearing the blouses James secretly thought of as her "circus tent tops" due to their voluminous shape and brilliant hues.

U.S. Postal Service employee Bennett Marshall examined his brochure cautiously. "I'd like to be stronger, but offering happiness to another person by having them go on a special diet seems a bit pushy. I mean, can a diet make a person happier?" He stood and cleared the remainder of their meal, which had consisted of cheddar burger patties, spinach salad, marinated mushrooms, and ricotta cheesecake. As he cleaned off a water ring left from a glass of diet soda, Bennett cast a suspicious glance at the brochures scattered across the surface of his dining room table.

"I, for one, am pretty sick of eating the food we've been eating," Lucy said as she gestured at the pile of dirty plates stacked next to Bennett's sink. "I love your company, you guys. You have become my closest friends. Because of that, it's time for me to confess something." She took a fortifying breath. "I haven't been honest with you for months. You see, I haven't been following our low-carb meal plan when I'm not with you. I think I got burned out on the limited food choices, so I've just been eating anything that tastes good."

Lindy nodded in agreement. "It's been a challenge packing healthy lunches to bring to school, too. I had to eat the same things week after week. For the last two months, I've been dining on cafeteria food again. Stuff that we shouldn't have on our plan like macaroni and cheese, garlic bread, and those amazing seasoned fries. Just every now and then."

"Stop!" Lucy shrieked. "Please, don't talk about French fries. I'll run right out to McDonald's if I think about them too much."

James cleared this throat and glanced around at his friend. "Did Lindy tell you about Veronica's . . . uh . . . coaching style?"

"Lindy told us that she was really persuasive. A bit bossy, but in a good way. A take-charge kind of person." Lucy flashed her blue eyes at James. "I think we could do with her influence. We'd probably respond well to a caring drill sergeant—someone who won't let us give up on our dreams."

Wondering if Lucy was referring to the group's failure to stick with their diet or his inability to pursue her romantically, James squirmed in his chair. The disappointment in her eyes reminded him all too much of the expression he'd seen, but not recognized, in his ex-wife's eyes.

It's better not to risk our friendship by acting on our yearnings, James told himself.

Still, he found that his desire to impress Lucy hadn't diminished over the long winter. He wanted to make her laugh and to win her approval more than ever. "Do you really think Veronica can get us back on track?" he asked.

"On a whole new road. Look!" Gillian interjected emotionally as she pointed at an interior page of the pink brochure. "She'll even provide us with meals for the entire six-week period. And, praise Buddha, some of the meals are vegetarian. That would make me feel so much better about myself. My *chi's* been completely out of whack since I've been consuming so much . . . meat." Gillian whispered the last word as if she had used an expletive.

"Where do you come up with this stuff, woman?" Bennett stared at Gillian as if she were an extraterrestrial. He pulled on his toothbrush mustache and then clasped his espresso-colored hands together. "I thought I was an educated man, but in all of my forty-one years I have never heard of *chi*."

Gillian inhaled slowly, filling her lungs with as much air as they could hold. This was a sign that she was about to launch into one of her lectures. "Chi is an energy." She spread her arms out into the air theatrically, her polka-dot blouse opening up like an umbrella. "It's all around us. It's very spiritual. One needs to keep one's chi balanced or—"

"So it's like the Force in *Star Wars*," Bennett interrupted, looking pleased. "Cool. I'm down with that. Now, listen y'all. Are we going to sign up for this program or what?"

"Let's vote," Lindy suggested. "Raise your hands if you're ready to try Veronica's method of getting healthy. Who is in for joining Witness to Fitness?"

"Wait a minute!" James waved his hands over the brochure. "Before we vote, I want to make sure you've all read this. Veronica's system seems pretty complicated. Do you think we can figure out how to count all these food and exercise points? Every meal needs to be calculated. Every night, we have to add up numbers. Or subtract exercise points. It sounds like work to me."

"It says here that we'll be 'provided with all the tools needed to achieve guaranteed success,'" Lucy read from the brochure.

James frowned dubiously. "And how much is this going to cost? Meetings, meals, and an exercise program can't be cheap."

Lindy laughed. "Probably not, but if Witness to Fitness can offer us happiness after six weeks in the program, then who cares what it costs? All in favor?"

Everyone raised a hand, including a reluctant James. The supper club members exchanged high fives, finished tidying Bennett's kitchen, and prepared to call it a night.

"It's starting to feel like spring!" Lindy cried as she opened the front door of Bennett's tidy ranch. "Your neighbor's crocuses are coming out. I can see every blade of grass in their yard with the amount of outdoor lighting they have. Are they afraid of rabid deer? Or something worse, like their neighbor?" She nudged Bennett in the side.

Bennett sniffed the evening breeze. "I have no idea. One of their garden gnomes was stolen last year, right around Halloween, and the next thing I know, I can see spotlights out my bedroom window. It's like sleeping next to a disco. Shoot, one day, a small plane is going to land on our road, thinking it's an airstrip. Maybe *I* should hire someone to do it as a joke. After all, April Fools' Day is this weekend. If I sprayed their lights with black paint, I could finally get some sleep."

"It's April Fools' *and* the Annual Brunswick Stew Dinner at the fire department." Gillian pulled on a knit poncho in a pattern with violet and saffron stripes. "We should go. I strongly believe in supporting local causes."

"Shoot, I'd go just to look at the firemen." Lindy grinned sheepishly.

"What about Principal Chavez? Aren't you still in love with him?" Lucy asked.

"Of course, but I don't dare make a move until I've got a little less meatball and a lot more sauce to this body." Lindy patted her round hips. "Does anyone want to ride down to that Asian building they put up where the Dairy Drive-Thru used to be? I saw lights burning when I drove past the place earlier."

Energized by their mutual decision to begin a new weight-loss program, the Flab Five members agreed to extend their supper club meeting a little longer. Dividing themselves into two cars, they drove through the center of their quiet town and headed west to one of the town's two strip malls.

"So Witness to Fitness is located here too?" James asked Lindy.

"Yeah. Veronica moved into that place where Mrs. Peters used to give dance lessons. Her oldest daughter is in my ceramics class this year and she told me her mama's arthritis is so bad that she can't teach anymore." Lindy released a sympathetic sigh. "Bless her heart."

"Hey!" Lucy shouted from the backseat. "There's a sign on that Asian-style building. CHILLY WILLY'S POLAR PAGODA. Pagoda? Is that Chinese architecture?"

"No, it's Japanese," Lindy said.

"Actually, it's both," James corrected. "It's probably an Indian word in origin. A pagoda is a Buddhist building resembling a temple. If I remember what I read in a book about the world's most unusual structures, the pagoda's dome shape was supposed to create balance. I'm sure Gillian could tell you more about the spiritual part of its history."

"No, thank you," Lindy firmly declared. "There's someone washing the glass front door. I wonder if he's the new owner."

"Howdy, folks!" An African-American man with a neat goatee dropped his squeegee into a bucket and waved at James and his two female passengers. A minute later, Bennett and Gillian pulled up beside the Bronco. They got out of their cars and introduced themselves to the man.

"Welcome to Quincy's Gap!" Lindy said.

"Mighty kind of y'all to stop by. I'm Willy Kendrick, but you can call me Chilly Willy. Everyone always does in the end." He laughed. The sound was rich and throaty and filled the night air like a song.

James smiled. He liked Chilly Willy already. Gesturing at the building, he said, "If you don't mind me asking, why the pagoda theme?"

"It's pretty darn eye-catching, wouldn't you say?" Willy chuckled. "Not many pagodas in western Virginia."

"Are you a Buddhist?" Gillian's eyes twinkled hopefully.

"No, ma'am. Southern Baptist born and raised, but I could use all the heavenly help I can get. I lost everything I had in the fall of oh-five. I used to own a restaurant in Biloxi, Mississippi. It was totally wiped away by that wicked, wicked woman known to all as Hurricane Katrina. No offense, ladies, but I've got to call a spade a spade. Katrina took my business, my house—everything."

"You poor thing!" Gillian's lips trembled, and James was afraid she might burst into tears.

"Now, don't you go getting yourself upset on my account." Willy's middle-aged face grew somber. "Lots of folks were hit even harder than I was. My family survived and that's what really matters." He smiled. "Anyhow, I worked a few jobs in Florida and lived through a few more storms until I decided that I was real tired of hurricanes. Figured the mountains of Virginia get their share of snow, but no tornadoes, typhoons, tsunamis, or hurricanes. Besides, I liked the looks of this town and it seems to be filled with neighborly people."

"You might not need to worry about those kinds of storms, but there are other kinds of natural disasters in this town," James said as he watched a BMW pull into the parking lot. "And here comes one now."

The BMW screeched to a stop within a few feet of the small

group and a petite, silver-haired woman wearing a fur-trimmed suede jacket scrambled out of the car and fixed a pair of angry eyes on Willy.

"I suppose this is *your* doing?" she demanded, gesturing wildly at the black-and-red-painted pagoda.

Willy issued a welcoming smile. "Yes, ma'am. Do you like it?"

"Like it?" The woman fumed. "It's an abomination! This town has a two-hundred-year-old history of Southern architecture and then you come along and build this . . . this . . ." She drew in a sharp breath. "Atrocity!"

Willy kept his composure and his grin never wavered. "Yes, ma'am. It *is* different. But you can't get upset with me until you've tried one of my special praline caramel kiss sundaes. Come on in and you might feel a little friendlier toward the world once you've had a taste. I'm Willy, by the way." He stuck out his hand.

"I am Savannah Lowndes, President of the Shenandoah County Historical Society," the woman snapped, ignoring Willy's out-stretched hand. "And I'd rather see this place burn to a cinder than consume anything from inside such a despicable eyesore!"

"Suit yourself, ma'am." Willy shrugged. "Not everybody's got a sweet tooth. How about the rest of you? I've got some coupons for next weekend's grand opening. If you'd like a few, come inside."

"We'd love a sample!" Lucy exclaimed, and the supper club members turned to follow Willy inside.

Savannah Lowndes snorted in indignation and climbed back into her car. She then raced out of the parking lot, her face clouded with anger.

Suddenly a peppy, singsong voice that was oddly familiar to James hailed the group. "Hi, there! I hope you enjoy your ice cream!" Veronica Levitt called from outside her storefront, which was four stores down from the Polar Pagoda. "I expect to see you all here next Saturday. And then you" — she wiggled a skinny finger at Willy — "can kiss this particular group of customers goodbye! If I have my way, they'll be lean, toned, fruit-and-vegetable-eating gods and goddesses by June!"

"Oh, dear." Willy sighed as he held open the front door. A bell tinkled merrily as the Flab Five entered the ice cream parlor, but their host wasn't quite as cheerful as he'd been before seeing Veronica. His bright smile had slipped from his face and his eyes were dark with worry. Turning to the supper club members, he said, "I believe that woman's going to be bad for business."

24

Chapter Three

Fat-Free Popcorn

During the grand opening of the Polar Pagoda, Chilly Willy appeared to be serving frozen delights as fast as his two arms would allow. Due to the unusually mild Friday night, a long line of townsfolk snaked out the front door of the ice cream parlor to stretch the entire length of the strip mall. The patient customers, most of whom had just finished supper or had come straight from the local movie theater, eyed all the colorful cones, cups, and sun- daes mounded with candy toppings being enjoyed by their friends and neighbors. Willy's first-time customers were practically drooled in anticipation. They also exchanged waves, offered tastes of their frozen desserts, and chatted as if they were guests at the town's big- gest cocktail party. The evening air brimmed with an infectious vivacity and fellowship that made James Henry feel like a kid again.

And there were plenty of kids around the Polar Pagoda. Some waited in line with their parents, others raced up and down the sidewalk, and a pack of preteen girls giggled on a bench outside the ice cream parlor. Close to the bench, a band of high school boys sat on the curb. Having already consumed extra-large cones of chocolate-chip cookie dough ice cream and bottles of root beer, they occupied themselves by flirting with any pretty girl who tried to read the menu board containing the day's flavor specials.

After waiting in line for over twenty minutes, James Henry finally made it inside the pagoda's front door. He peered over the heads of the customers clustered around the counter and was hailed by Willy as if he were a long-lost friend.

"Hello, there, Mr. Henry!" Willy's voice boomed through the compact space. "So glad to see you. Are you here for something sweet to eat?"

"Absolutely!" James called back and smiled warmly at Willy. Upon reaching the front half of the line, he watched in fascination as Willy folded a glob of gummy bears into a slab of white ice cream using two tools that resembled spackling knives. "It sure looks like your grand opening is a success," James said when he was close enough to talk in his regular voice.

"I hope so, my man. It's because of this fine March evening and my even finer homemade frozen custard. This here is sweet cream mixed with gummy bears, Red Hots, and rainbow sprinkles. I call it the Kid in the Candy Store mix."

James was hypnotized by the way Willy scooped up the concoction and folded it neatly into a foam cup. "Who's next?" the grinning proprietor shouted merrily.

"Me!" cried a woman. James recognized the trim form and shimmering brown hair of Murphy Alistair, reporter and managing editor of the *Shenandoah Star Ledger*, the county's small daily paper. "I'd like chocolate custard with peanut butter cups, please. Oh, and top it off with chocolate sprinkles. Do you mind if I take some photos for the *Star* while you work?"

"I'd be much obliged to you if you would, pretty lady. And don't you even think about trying to pay me, ya hear? Anyone who might get Chilly Willy some free business gets her lovely little self a free frozen custard."

Murphy grinned. "Are you attempting to bribe me with ice cream?"

"Absolutely, miss, absolutely."

After taking a few pictures of Willy with her digital camera, Murphy turned to James. "Hello, Professor. Are you here for the frozen custard or to buy what will soon become the most infamous T-shirt in all of the Shenandoah Valley?"

James craned his neck in order to view the cobalt T-shirts hanging above the menu board. The white text on the front of each shirt read, *HAVE YOU GOT A CHILLY WILLY?*

"That's an attention-getter if I ever saw one." James laughed. "Every teenager in Quincy's Gap is going to be advertising your shop, Willy."

"Lord willing!" Willy handed another customer an ice cream float. The next customer ordered pumpkin custard covered in hot fudge sauce while James desperately tried to decide which of the flavor varieties he craved most.

"Aren't you cheating on your diet?" Murphy asked, nudging James playfully. Her hazel eyes sparkled and James wondered if she was flirting or simply being friendly.

"I'm joining Witness to Fitness tomorrow," James said in a low voice. "I've been slipping on my own, so I'm hoping to get back on track. My plan is to follow their program until I can figure out how to do it independently."

Murphy was listening closely. "You know, this subject would make a great article. I could track your progress, kind of like one of those TV reality shows, and print before and after photos. The readers would love it, especially because you're such a likeable guy. I bet lots of people would be inspired by you."

James cleared his throat. "I don't think I'd care to share my weight with the entire town."

"Now, would I do that to you?" Murphy teased, but James believed she would print anything to sell more papers. "I wouldn't write anything you weren't comfortable with. No, it would be more about your experience at Witness to Fitness. I think our readers need to hear an unbiased, first-hand account of this new business before they all spend their hard-earned money there, don't you?"

"What'll it be, my friend?" Willy asked, holding his trowel-type tool above the mounded containers of custard.

"Peppermint with hot fudge and marshmallow, please," James said.

"What do you say, Professor?" Murphy pleaded. Still smiling, she licked a dollop of chocolate custard off her plastic spoon.

Dazed, James watched her tongue while his brain struggled to form a reply. "I guess . . ."

"Thanks, Professor. I knew I could count on you." And with that, Murphy patted him on the arm and sauntered outside to interview a few of the Polar Pagoda's satisfied customers.

Just as James received his bowlful of heaven, a troupe of middle-aged women pushed the patrons in line aside and began shouting at Willy in unison. From what James could make out, they were furious about the T-shirts and wanted them taken down and destroyed without delay.

"They should be burned!" shrieked a mousy woman wearing a heavy wool jacket despite the mildness of the evening. "I am Mrs. Gloria Emerson. I am a minister's wife." She gestured to the group of heaving bosoms behind her. "And these are all leaders of our church's youth group. We will not have our impressionable youth clad in this disgusting, indecent apparel."

Willy was nonplussed. "Indecent? It covers up everything, doesn't it?"

Several onlookers chuckled. Mrs. Emerson ground her teeth until James thought they might crack.

"Don't you mock me, sir! I am well known in these parts, and I will use my considerable influence to make sure that no decent folk come here until you remove those offensive shirts from sight. And I have other demands!" She raised her finger heavenward as if she, and not the Reverend Emerson, was accustomed to preaching from the pulpit. "I want you to give full refunds to those innocent boys who have already purchased those filthy rags."

"They're not dirty, ma'am. They're fresh out of the box," Willy said with a grin.

The crowd inside the building gave him a cheer. It was obvious that the customers were on his side.

Mrs. Emerson reddened. "This is not the last you'll see of us. We're going to get those shirts gone. This, I swear to you!"

"At least have some ice cream before you go!" Willy called after the huffy women, and even though he continued to serve cups and cones in a jolly manner, his eyes betrayed a hint of worry.

Not wanting to hold up the line, James paid for his treat, thanked Willy profusely, and went outside. He saw Murphy interviewing Mrs. Emerson and her mob of angry women. Next, Murphy took a photograph of a teenage boy proudly wearing one of the controversial T-shirts.

"I am totally *not* getting rid of my shirt!" the boy shouted at Mrs. Emerson and her posse. "It's not like it's covered with curses or satanic symbols or anything. You biddies need to lighten up."

"See the disrespect that kind of garment produces?" Mrs. Emerson demanded shrilly, and several members of the crowd nodded in agreement. Murphy scribbled wildly on her notepad as the teenager strutted up and down the parking area. Within minutes, two of his friends jumped to the end of the long line to purchase T-shirts for themselves.

James watched Mrs. Emerson get into her car before strolling to where Murphy was standing. "Poor Willy. This makes three threats on his new business. All three were from women, too."

Murphy's eyes narrowed. "Is that so? Who else threatened him?"

James instantly regretted mentioning anything to the reporter. Scooping custard into his mouth, he stalled for time and then shared only a few details about how Savannah Lowndes had tried to pick a fight with Willy. Next, he briefly described how Veronica Levitt wanted to sweet-talk Willy's clients into choosing her business over his.

"It's hard to be a newcomer in this town," Murphy said, surprising James with what sounded like heartfelt sympathy. "Too many people in these parts are uncomfortable with change."

"Can't say I blame them," James said, remembering how he hadn't wanted to move back home. "Unless it's the kind of change that brings people like Willy to our town. We could all use more of his energy and optimism."

"Isn't that the truth? You're all right, James Henry." Murphy suddenly stood on her tiptoes and kissed James on the cheek. "I'll give you a call tomorrow to see how your inaugural Witness to Fitness meeting went."

As a stunned James pivoted to watch Murphy walk away, he touched the spot on his cheek where she'd brushed his skin with her sticky, custard-covered lips. And then he blinked and found himself being glared at from across the parking lot. Lucy Hanover was obviously angry. James waved, but Lucy pretended not to have seen him and disappeared inside the Polar Pagoda.

James finished his dessert while debating whether or not to explain to Lucy that he and Murphy weren't an item, but he didn't see much point since he and Lucy were just friends. And yet the anger and hurt in Lucy's eyes made it clear that she still had feelings for him. Warmed by this thought and the giant bowl of custard filling his stomach, James decided to talk to her. He'd ask Lucy out for coffee and finally come clean about why he'd succumbed to his fears and insecurities after they'd shared that wonderful kiss. Then, he'd pray that he still had a chance to become more than her friend.

Before he could take a step in the direction of the Polar Pagoda, Veronica Levitt appeared on the sidewalk and began turning a series of cartwheels to the great amusement of the crowd.

"Hey, everyone!" she shouted brightly after the final cartwheel. "I'm Veronica Levitt, the owner of the brand-new Witness to Fitness weight-loss program. We're just a few stores down. I know that you all are here tonight to enjoy a delicious dessert, but by the morning, you're going to regret making this choice. That fat is going to stick on your thighs" — she pointed to a woman in tight jeans — "your waistline" — she gestured at a man with an impressive spare tire — "and your rear" — she jerked a thumb at a woman who had bent over to retrieve a set of dropped keys. All three of these people looked horrified and tried to shrink into the background. "But you are all too, too beautiful to do this to yourselves!"

Veronica put her hands out as if embracing the crowd and continued her sales pitch. "Wouldn't you rather have the energy to do a cartwheel, dance with your husband or wife, or live ten years longer?" She fanned a stack of pink brochures in her hands. "Come to my grand opening tomorrow and I'll give you a whole new life — one that will be so sweet that you won't even need desserts anymore."

"Ha! That's not possible," someone mumbled, and several people snickered.

"Yes, it is!" Veronica sidled up to the dissenter. "You can be slimmer, stronger, younger-looking, and more energetic. No surgery. No pain. My program provides a different way of eating and offers a range of easy exercises. You can have a whole new body and a whole new outlook by beach season!"

Several people murmured and nodded their heads. Hands reached out to take brochures from Veronica.

"This looks expensive," a man pointed out.

Veronica glided like a cat on ice to the man's side. She offered him a dazzling smile, grasped his shoulder, and whispered intimately, "Darling, I think your life is worth the cost, don't you?" The man said nothing. Veronica moved away and the man looked blank for a long moment and then began studying the pink brochure intently.

By the time Veronica had reached the front of the line, Willy must have heard about her giving her sales pitches to his first customers. He propped open one of the front doors and spoke loudly, but politely.

"Do you mind letting my customers be *my* customers tonight? Your day's coming up tomorrow."

Veronica thrust her angular chin in the air and swept her arms in a wide arc to indicate her rapt audience. "I'm trying to save the bodies of these lovely people while you're trying to send them to an early grave. Look at all of this potential standing here in front of us! I won't lose a single opportunity to help someone live a longer, healthier life."

"Sometimes folks need something that's just plain fun, too. Now, scoot and do your business in your own time, at your own place."

"I'll just finish handing out these brochures." Veronica turned her back on Willy and bounced farther up the line, her ponytail bobbing enthusiastically.

In a flash, Willy caught up to her, jerked the brochures from her hand, and stuffed them in the nearest trash can.

Veronica's fists clenched in rage. She took a step toward Willy, and James scuttled sideways in order to get out of her way, but not far enough to avoid hearing her hiss, "That was not very nice, ice cream man. You'll learn to be nicer to me in the future."

• • •

On Saturday, as James stood outside the Witness to Fitness storefront gathering the courage to start a new diet and face a disgruntled Lucy, Bennett appeared and put his hand on James's back.

"Man, let's just get this over with," he muttered.

Inside, the space was divided into an office section in the front —four cubicles constructed out of sleek gray plastic—and the exercise room in the back. Here, Veronica had arranged rows of folding chairs in the middle of the floor. Gillian waved James and Bennett over to the two seats she had saved for them. Lucy and Lindy smiled and greeted both men, and though James could sense no animosity coming from Lucy, he still felt anxious. Other than the Flab Five, at least twenty people had gathered in the room. Avoiding their own reflections in the wall-length mirror, the men and women fidgeted nervously or attempted to strike up conversations with their neighbors.

Suddenly, the lights in the room dimmed, flickered, and then returned to their brightest setting. Upbeat dance music began to play from a boom box set up in the rear corner of the exercise room.

The crowd immediately fell silent.

Once again, Veronica displayed her gymnastic talents by doing two cartwheels and a roundhouse on the empty space of hardwood floor. Her future clients clapped, and Veronica beamed and gave a stiff bow.

"Welcome to Witness to Fitness!" she exclaimed. "I'm Veronica Levitt, but since you and I" — she pointed at random people as she spoke — "are going to be *very* close in the next few months, you should call me what my friends call me, and that's Ronnie."

"I wonder how many friends she has. I mean, who could tolerate all of that judgmental perkiness?" James muttered under his breath and Gillian shot him an admonishing look.

Ronnie ran a hand over her hair, which was pulled back so tightly into a high ponytail that it seemed like the woman had just had a brow lift. "All of you are brave and intelligent people. You have made the choice to live a better, healthier life and I plan to reward you for the decision. You see, right now you are all like a bunch of caterpillars. You are overweight. You also spend too much of your time eating. But *inside*!" She reached out to an overweight teenage girl in the front row. "Inside of each and every one of you is a butterfly. Something beautiful and new is just dying to be let loose. *You* are holding *you* back!" Ronnie pointed to Lindy next.

James was surprised to see Lindy nod in silent agreement. Gillian was dabbing tears from her eyes with a pink and purple tie-dyed scarf. Lucy's face was blank while Bennett looked amused.

"Quite a show," he whispered to James as Ronnie skipped around the room.

"It sure is," James agreed.

"Over the next six weeks, I am going to get a little bit tough with you, because that's the kind of help you need." Ronnie grabbed the shoulder of a fleshy man sitting near the aisle. "But you'll have lots of loving support, too. How many of you out there have tried other diet plans?"

A dozen hands rose into the air. Ronnie stared down a man who refused to meet her gaze until he finally raised his hand.

"And here you are, back where you started. Out of shape and unhappy. After six weeks on my plan, I will have taught you how to eat and exercise so that you can continue changing your life on your own. I will help you break out of your shell!" She threw out her arms and flapped like a bird. "My friends, you will fly like butterflies and begin living the life that has always been confined to your dreams!"

Several women to the right of James broke out in sporadic clapping. One of them was Twix Lady from the discount ware- house. She sat with a look of rapt fascination and watched Ronnie's every movement. Her hands were clutched together as if in prayer.

"That's the spirit," Ronnie said. "Now, you can't do Witness to Fitness as a piecemeal plan. You must eat my food, keep a food journal, come in every week for counseling and weigh-in sessions, and attend at least three exercise classes a week." Ronnie clasped her hands over her flat breasts. In a dramatic stage whisper, she pronounced, "If you cheat on any of these items you will be removed from the program and *not a cent of your money will be refunded!*"

Several people twittered in concern.

"Oh, dear. No refunds?" someone behind James whimpered.

"This is for your own good, my friends. You must place your *complete* trust in the program. Paying us up front will motivate you to show up for your required sessions." Ronnie surveyed her future clients. "I have two assistants I would like to introduce to you. The first is Phoebe Liu. Phoebe is in charge of counseling and finances."

Phoebe stood up from where she sat in the front row. She was a petite Asian American with attractive, exotic looks and a demure smile. She raised a small hand and waved shyly at the crowd. "Please don't hesitate to call me if you need any extra support during your time with Witness to Fitness," she said in a whisper-soft voice. "I'm here to help."

The sincerity of her simple statement made more of an impact on James than Ronnie's cartwheels or butterfly analogies.

"Next, we have Dylan Shane." Ronnie's mouth curved into a secretive grin. "Dylan is our primary fitness instructor."

A door in the rear of the exercise room opened and the women in the room issued a collective gasp. A man of average height with white-blonde hair, sparkling brown eyes, and limbs that looked like they were sculpted from tree trunks offered the crowd a dazzling smile. His aquamarine workout shirt strained against his chiseled pectoral muscles and a whiff of his musky cologne drifted over the first two rows of seats.

"Hey, everybody. I'm Dylan." His voice was very deep and very manly. "I live in Harrisonburg, but I'll be commuting to Quincy's Gap every day except Saturdays. I volunteer at a rest home on Saturdays. Don't worry; I can be a little late today. They know how important it is for me to be here for you."

The women turned to one another and murmured their approval.

"How many twenty-something hunks would spend every Saturday helping the elderly?" a woman behind James asked the man seated next to her.

"I'm sure he's gay," the man stated matter-of-factly. "No one who looks that perfect can possibly be straight."

"Dylan made you a special snack to celebrate your decision to join our team." Ronnie winked at her coworker. "Didn't you, Dylan?"

Dylan bounded back into the room where he'd been waiting to make his entrance and returned bearing a tray laden with paper bowls. James smelled popcorn and immediately perked up.

"Here's a sample of the kind of snack you'll be enjoying as a Witness to Fitness member," Ronnie said as she and Phoebe helped Dylan distribute the popcorn. "It's ninety-eight percent fat-free and is garnished with a butter substitute spray to give you that movie theater taste."

James grabbed his bowl and hurriedly stuffed a handful of popcorn into his mouth. His taste buds were disappointed by the cardboard texture of the popcorn, and even though he could smell the butter-flavored spray, he couldn't taste it at all.

"Movie theater popcorn?" Bennett scoffed. "This tastes more like the popcorn tub than the popcorn."

James laughed, but Lucy scowled and said, "I think it's just fine."

"I don't care what we have to eat as long as I get to come in here and feast my eyes on Dylan three times a week!" Lindy declared cheerfully.

"Amen to that, sister," breathed Gillian, who was eyeing the male fitness instructor appreciatively.

"We're now going to divide up into three groups in order to discuss how many food points you'll each be allowed." Ronnie pointed at Phoebe. "Phoebe will take the lovely ladies weighing between one-fifty and one hundred and eighty-five pounds in this corner. Dylan will take the ladies weighing above one eighty-five in this corner. I will meet with all of our fine gentlemen in the front of the store."

As James stood to join the other men, he noticed that several of the heavier women seemed torn between pretending they weighed less than one hundred and eighty-five pounds and the chance to bask in the glow of Dylan's beauty. As if reading their minds, Ronnie added, "And don't worry if you're unsure of your weight, we've got very accurate scales that will provide us with an exact number."

As the men huddled around Ronnie's Spartan cubicle, James detected a pungent odor coming from a man standing to his right. The scent was so powerful that James was unable to focus on Ronnie's lecture about choosing next week's meals and snacks based on their current weight. James sniffed and grimaced and Bennett did the same.

"Some of you might be feeling a bit depressed over your current weight, but on my program, those of you weighing over two hundred pounds are given more food points. More food points means more food. Now, let's share what the scale said. That will bring you closer together as a group." Ronnie gazed at each of them in turn, a patient smile fixed upon her face.

One by one, the six men began to quietly admit what they weighed. The only man who refused to answer turned out to be the source of the ripe smell. James was pretty certain it was a mixture of whiskey and unwashed clothes and flesh.

"Come now, Mister . . . ?" Ronnie prompted. "We're all friends here."

"Name's Vandercamp, Pete Vandercamp." The man coughed repeatedly and then spit into a foul-looking handkerchief.

James suddenly recognized him. Pete was the former night janitor from Blue Ridge High. He'd been a young man when James was in high school and all the students had dubbed him Mr. Vandercough due to the constant wet hacking noises he made while cleaning the floors at the end of each school day.

"Why don't we get to know each other a bit?" Ronnie suggested, ignoring Pete. "Tell us what you do for a living."

James and Bennett already knew that one of the men named Leo worked for Shenandoah Savings & Loan. Another man, Dane, was a plumber, and Pete Vandercamp announced that he had come out of an early retirement in order to work nights at the Polar Pagoda.

"That's some mighty good ice cream," he wheezed and Ronnie clucked her tongue in disapproval.

"Did Willy send you here to spy on me?" she teased, but James detected an undercurrent of tension in her voice.

Pete shrugged. "It's a free country, lady. Folks can eat ice cream if they want."

Ronnie took Pete by the arm and pulled him toward the front door. "Honey, if you're not here to join Witness to Fitness then let's not waste the time of those who've come to change their lives." Under her breath, James heard her mutter, "And you might want to take a bath before your shift starts tonight."

Pete, who seemed to be in no rush to leave, stared at her. "I know you from somewhere, lady. Weren't you on TV a few years ago?"

Trying to mask her impatience, Ronnie turned to find the entire group of men watching her. It was evident that her clients were enjoying themselves, so she quickly tried to guide Pete outside but he refused to budge.

"Well, I *have* been told I look like Hilary Swank, the actress," Ronnie said with false modesty.

Pete's eyes narrowed as he struggled to remember. "Nah. It was you, not some other lady."

Ronnie opened the front door and practically shoved Pete through the doorway with a nervous giggle and a powerful thrust of her right hip. Following him outside, she said something no one could hear and the rest of the men began to talk among themselves. James didn't join in. Instead, he kept his gaze riveted on Pete Vandercamp, who reached into his pocket, removed a tin of Skoal chewing tobacco, and put a wad inside his left cheek.

Suddenly Pete brightened and it was obvious that he'd just remembered something. He pointed at Ronnie and began to laugh.

His whole body shook as he mocked the fitness instructor. James saw all the color drained from Ronnie's face. Whatever Pete said had shocked her, but she quickly recovered. Raising her fist, she took a step toward Pete in an unmistakably threatening manner. Guffawing now, Pete spit a thin stream of brown tobacco juice on the ground at Ronnie's feet. He then turned and casually strode away.

Ronnie stood motionless, staring at the tobacco stain in disgust. She raised her head and calling angrily after Pete, but he ignored her. When he was out of sight, she took a moment to compose herself and then reentered the store.

When she returned, a wide smile was once again plastered on her face, but James noticed that her hands were shaking in uncontrollable rage.

Chapter Four

Brunswick Stew

Brady Gerhardt was the newest member of the Quincy's Gap Volunteer Fire & Rescue Station. Even though he knew as much as everybody else did about putting out fires, the veterans of the department called him "rookie" and forced him to do all of the menial tasks around the station, such as stocking the pantry and cleaning the restrooms. Brady didn't mind. He was an affable young man in his mid-twenties and felt proud to be among the grizzled and seasoned men of Fire & Rescue. He also knew that as soon as someone else signed up to volunteer, he, Brady, would be able to call that person "rookie," regardless of the newcomer's age or station in life.

At the moment, Brady couldn't dwell on rising in status within the department. It was the annual charity dinner and he was incredibly busy ladling steaming spoonfuls of homemade Brunswick stew into deep ceramic bowls in the station's kitchen.

"Come on, rookie!" Dirk Maguire shouted gruffly. "We got paying customers out there and they're starving!"

Brady wiped beads of perspiration off his brow with the back of a potholder and carefully pushed a tray filled with delicious smelling stew in Dirk's direction.

"Keep 'em coming. We'll be able to keep the lights on for another few months after tonight's dinner." Dirk hoisted the tray high on his shoulder, looking like an experienced waiter in a four-star restaurant. Brady was impressed. Dirk worked at the landfill and was known for his strength and direct manner, but he was clearly graceful as well. "We might even be able to buy that secondhand pool table we've been wanting for so long."

Other members of the department came into the kitchen, instantly filling it with laughter and boisterous conversation. Several men clapped Brady on the back, told him he was doing a fine job, and offered him a Solo cup of beer. Brady turned the beer down. As a rule, he didn't drink alcohol.

"This dinner's a record breaker!" bellowed a jovial Chief Lawrence to his youngest volunteer. "Get on out there and enjoy yourself, boy. I'll spot you for a bit. There are plenty of pretty women who'd just love to meet a handsome firefighter like your-self." The chief winked and took the ladle from Brady's hand.

"Thanks, Chief!" Without hesitation, Brady stripped off his white vinyl apron bearing the text IF YOU CAN'T TAKE THE HEAT, GIT OUT OF MY KITCHEN! He darted out of the second-story kitchen and slid down the fire pole leading to the station's garage where rows of tables and folding chairs had been set up to accommodate the din-ers. From the looks of it, every able-bodied person in Quincy's Gap was either sitting and enjoying their meal, waiting in line for a bowl of stew and a piece of homemade corn bread, or flanking the makeshift bar, where dollar bills were being exchanged for cups of cold beer.

"I sure hope there aren't any fires tonight," Brady heard a bar-rel-shaped woman with bright orange hair quietly remark as he made his way toward the bar. "I think the firemen will all be too drunk to drive the truck."

Her friend, a plump woman with glossy black hair and kind brown eyes smiled and said, "I'm sure they've got people who are abstaining in case there's an emergency."

Brady walked past the women in search of a Coke and a piece of warm corn bread. As he sat in one of the few empty chairs and watched a golden pat of butter melt on the surface of his corn bread, he thought about what the woman with the orange hair had said. Looking around the room, he could see that nearly every member of the Quincy's Gap Volunteer Fire & Rescue Station had a red plastic cup in his hand. Ruddy cheeks, twinkling eyes, and hearty belly laughs indicated that the men of Station Seventeen had consumed a goodly amount of beer. With a start, Brady realized that he might be one of the few people able to drive the ladder truck. The problem was that he had never driven it before.

As he bit into his homemade bread, pausing to lick a rivulet of butter from the back of his hand, a cute blonde seated at the other end of his table smiled at him. He returned the smile, suddenly for-getting his concerns over being one of the only sober firemen in Quincy's Gap. When the girl coyly waved him over, Brady leapt to obey.

• • •

James Henry had the misfortune of being stuck in line behind three of the most formidable women in Quincy's Gap. He'd arrived late to the fund-raiser because his father refused to let him leave until James looked over a brochure on roofing materials.

Ashamed to admit that his savings account was nearly depleted after paying the steep Witness to Fitness enrollment fees, James feigned great interest in the brochure until his father told him that he'd already hired a roofer and that the job was slated to begin next week. Panicking, James bolted to his feet.

"We can't, Pop. The roof project will have to be put on hold for another month or two."

"Why?" his father had demanded. "We've already got mold growin' on the bathroom ceilin'. You want to plant a garden in the shower or are we gonna get those leaks fixed?"

Instead of telling his father that the money had gone toward a new diet plan, James promised to discuss the roof some other time and then grabbed his windbreaker and shot out the back door.

"The roofer's comin' on Monday!" Jackson bellowed after him. "And he's gonna want a deposit!"

As James drove through town, his gnawing hunger and the desire to get a seat next to someone he liked had him practically skidding into a library parking space. James was surprised to find the lot, which was across the street from the firehouse, almost full. Trotting across the asphalt, he couldn't help wonder how the Shenandoah County Library could host an event that could draw a similar crowd and raise much-needed funds for his beloved branch.

Winded from jogging from his truck to the firehouse, James burst inside, darted around a lollygagging family of six, and purchased a food ticket from one of the fireman's wives.

"Hey! That fat man cut us!" a child behind him whined. His parents quickly told him to shush, but James had heard the insult and his face burned with embarrassment.

It turned out that James got no closer to the food by skirting around the dawdling family. In fact, the line was at an utter standstill. James craned his neck to see what the holdup was and was irked to observe an elderly couple insisting upon being given a list of the stew's ingredients. They stood, hands on hips, and refused to accept their bowls.

"I'm very allergic to certain foods," the woman said. "It's a very serious condition. I could go into cardiac arrest."

"And I can't eat eggs! I won't let an egg pass my lips," her husband added and shook his cane at the fireman serving the stew for emphasis.

"I don't think there are any eggs in the stew, sir." The fireman looked around for help, but the only other fireman in sight was serving corn bread. Shrugging his shoulders at his colleague, he moved off to replenish his empty tray.

The first fireman held a bowl of stew under the old woman's nose. "Ma'am, it's mostly chicken, corn, beans, onions, and tomatoes and spices. Unless you're allergic to any of those ingredients, you should be just fine."

"What kind of spices?" the old woman demanded suspiciously.

"You know, salt and pepper and stuff."

Fortunately, Mrs. Emerson, the minister's wife who'd been so irate over Chilly Willy's T-shirts, stepped in and coaxed the couple into accepting their bowls of stew.

"You just have to know how to handle people," she boasted to her companion as the older couple shuffled off to find seats.

Mrs. Emerson's friend turned out to be Savannah Lowndes. She cast a haughty look around the hall and said, "I wish you could handle some of this town's more pressing problems that easily, like the existence of that wretched ice cream store."

"We could always pray that the townsfolk get tired of ice cream and that that distasteful owner has to move to another location far away." Mrs. Emerson clasped her hands together. "I'll ask the ladies in my leadership group to pray with me."

"Excuse me." A third woman stepped toward the two matriarchs. James tried to melt back into line as he recognized the heavily made-up stick figure belonging to Ronnie Levitt.

"Hi!" she chirped. "I'm Veronica Levitt, the proprietor of the new Witness to Fitness, and I completely agree with you ladies."

Mrs. Emerson and Mrs. Lowndes smiled widely.

"Welcome to our delightful berg, my dear," Mrs. Lowndes drawled.

"I just wanted to say that once my business becomes a success, no one would be interested in visiting that awful ice cream shop." Ronnie lowered her voice conspiratorially. "People who've committed to diet and are striving to eat healthy foods shouldn't be exposed to such a dangerous temptation as frozen custard, don't you think? But I won't let that man and his sinful treats stop me. I vow to make Quincy's Gap a happier, healthier place!" James half expected Ronnie to shake a pair of pompoms as she uttered this passionate oath. "I might just have to design my own T-shirts. I don't think Willy's send a very positive message, do you? And he's bought enough to outfit the entire town!"

"Those shirts are entirely reprehensible!" Mrs. Emerson cried.

Mrs. Lowndes smirked. "Indeed. It looks like we'll just have to make certain your business succeeds where his does not. We women will put our heads together and take care of this little problem ourselves."

"Yes, we shall." Mrs. Emerson puffed out her chest like a bullfrog. She then turned to receive her stew and the three women moved off to find seats together, feverishly whispering in as they walked.

James had just gotten his own steaming bowl of stew and a generous slab of corn bread when Bennett suddenly appeared at his side. He asked James to join him and a new coworker at a table on the far side of the room. Relieved to have a friend to sit with, James squeezed through the rows of happy diners to a table where Bennett had saved two seats by placing empty letter bags on the chairs. Across from the chairs sat an unfamiliar man in his late thirties. When Bennett and James sat down, the man looked up and gave them a reserved smile.

"Carter, this is my good buddy James Henry. James, this is Carter Peabody. He just moved to town and has taken over Pat Salisbury's route. Pat retired last week."

Carter offered James his hand. The two men shook and as soon as James reclaimed his hand, the younger man gave him another shy smile before averting his eyes.

"Nice to meet you, Carter." James felt immediately comfortable in the presence of another reserved man. James had to assume that was the only thing they had in common because Carter had the looks of a California surfer. His skin was tan, his hair was sun-streaked, and his nose and cheeks were sprinkled with freckles. He was of average build with a hint of a paunch, but overall, James believed Carter would be considered very attractive. James cast curious glances at the newcomer as he ate his stew, while Bennett warned Carter about the more vicious canines on his new mail route.

"I like dogs and they like me," Carter said after Bennett was finished. "Especially big ones like the K-9 units on the cop shows. I've got a border collie named Sergeant."

"If you like big dogs, then you need to meet our friend Lucy," Bennett said. "She has three of the most terrifying German shepherds you've ever laid eyes on."

Carter's eyes gleamed. "German shepherds are the most common breeds to be assigned as police dogs. The New Jersey General Assembly actually tried to get a law passed to give police dogs the same rights as the human officers. If someone were to shoot a K-9 officer, for example, it would be the same offense as if they'd shot a human cop. Isn't that cool?" When neither James nor Bennett acted suitably impressed, Carter studied his empty bowl. "I visit this website about citizens who capture criminals pretty often. I guess it's kind of a weird hobby. Still, maybe your friend Lucy wouldn't find it so strange. I'd like to meet her sometime."

James almost choked on his corn bread. He didn't want Bennett introducing Carter to Lucy. Why, she might fall in love with him, and where would that leave James?

"Have you seen Lucy?" James asked Bennett, doing his best to sound nonchalant.

"She was here earlier." Bennett took a swallow of beer. "I saw her having what looked like a serious discussion with Sheriff Huckabee."

James glanced around the room in hopes of spotting Lucy. He really wanted to pencil in a time for the two of them to have a private talk, but he didn't see her anywhere. As his eyes roved over rows of townsfolk, they came to rest on a young man holding a cell phone to his ear. An attractive blonde was sitting next to him, and though she was batting her eyelashes and nudging his shoulder with hers in order to get his attention, the young man stared straight ahead, a look of horror spreading across his face.

The young man's dread was contagious, and James felt goose bumps erupt on his arms. He stared as the frightened man snapped his cell phone shut, jumped up from the table, and headed directly for James.

"Chief Lawrence!" The young man urgently plucked the sleeve of a man seated right behind James. The chief, who was deep in conversation with his tablemates, ignored his fellow firefighter at first, but when the young man said, "Chief! There's a fire!" he finally turned around.

"Where, Brady?" Chief Lawrence asked. "In the kitchen?" The other firefighters laughed and took fresh swigs of beer from their cups.

"No, sir. It's the Polar Pagoda. That new ice cream place. It's burning like a Fourth of July sparkler!"

The chief frowned. "How do you know? We haven't gotten a call."

"My little brother just rode by the Polar Pagoda on his bike and then called my cell. The alarm will probably ring any second now, sir. We should get ready!"

Chief Lawrence put down his beer cup and studied Brady. "You sure your brother isn't just messing with you, rookie?"

"No, sir. He's a good kid." Brady fidgeted anxiously with his cell phone. "And there's more, Chief," he added, his voice rising in agitation.

"What is it, Brady?" the chief snapped, his eyes taking in the crowded room and his inebriated firemen.

"My brother said he saw someone." Brady's words tumbled out. "Inside the burning building."

At that moment, the alarm sounded.

Chapter Five

Cherry Cola

As pandemonium ensued all around, James grabbed Bennett's elbow. Over the clanging of the alarm he yelled, "Let's go!"

Several firemen shouted and gesticulated wildly at a group of slow-moving attendees who'd thoughtlessly parked their cars too close to the fire truck and ambulance. These vehicles had been left in the nose-out ready position in front of the massive garage doors, and their drivers got behind the wheel and turned on the vehicle sirens. Women shrieked, children cried, and babies wailed as the crowd tried to escape the deafening roar of the alarm. James led Bennett and Carter toward the open garage doors and the waiting fire engine to avoid being trampled.

As he ran, it became apparent to James that at least six of the firemen were sober. These men gathered equipment and prepped the truck for departure with alacrity. James couldn't believe how little time it took before they were boarded and, with set expressions on their faces, prepared to face whatever danger lay ahead.

"You're blocking our truck!" Chief Lawrence roared at a flustered woman, who squeaked and dropped her car keys onto the pavement. "Hurry, woman!" he bellowed, pulling on his jacket and helmet while signaling to the rest of his crew to climb into the truck. "Let's go, rookie!" The chief hailed Brady and the young man struggled to free himself from a petrified matron while attempting to pull on his flame-retardant boots.

"I'm coming!" Brady cried.

Chief Lawrence threw both arms in the air. "Come on, son! I had a beer, so you're driving!"

James, Bennett, and a bewildered Carter threaded their way out of the station house. The last thing James saw before he exited was Chilly Willy. The ice cream proprietor was calmly finishing his stew and watching the frantic crowd. At that moment, one of the firefighters placed a hand on Willy's shoulder and gave it a wordless squeeze as he dashed for the waiting fire truck.

That fleeting touch, which seemed to convey both pity and support, immediately put Willy on high alert. James watched other people shoot the older man sympathetic glances, and it was clear that Willy was well liked, and that the townsfolk were saddened by the thought of this jovial newcomer having to face another tragedy.

Willy stared after the firemen for a long moment before dropping his spoon into his bowl. He stood slowly, as if he'd aged decades since the fireman had squeezed his shoulder and fixed his eyes on the wailing fire engine. The trunk inched out of the driveway, its progress impeded by an old pickup moving out of the way at a snail's pace.

James yearned to call out to Willy, to offer him some sort of comfort, but he knew his voice wouldn't carry over the deafening alarm.

Finally, the yellow fire truck, which had been washed and polished to a lacquer-like shine shortly before the fund-raiser started, shot forward into the street. No traffic blocked its way and the crowd looked on as it headed in the direction of the strip mall. Its departure seemed to snap Willy from his stupor and he forced his way through the crowd and into the March evening.

As James, Bennett, and Carter headed for Bennett's retired mail truck, they spotted Willy in the parking lot next to the station. Apparently, his car had been boxed in by an SUV the size of an army tank.

"Willy!" James called out. "Come on! We'll take you!"

Nodding gratefully, Willy hustled up the sidewalk and jumped into the backseat of the tiny truck. Bennett started the engine and switched off the radio, leaving the foursome to ride in heavy silence down Main Street. As they crested the hill leading to the West Woods Shopping Center and the Polar Pagoda, they could see a twisted column of smoke rising into the night sky. The shape reminded James of a tornado funnel, except that it churned over a single spot—a storm of flames, chewing through wood and plaster and paint.

It took several minutes to reach the top of the rise because most of the people who'd attended the dinner at the station were also heading to the scene of the fire. A long line of red taillights circled around the burning structure. Looking ahead, Bennett swore with agitation and disgust.

"Vultures!" he spat, swerving around a black sports car. The driver had pulled off on the side to get a better view of the action and was now taking photographs or videos with his smart phone.

"It's just what folks do. They don't mean any harm," Willy muttered, his eyes never leaving the orange and vermilion tongues of flame that tore away at the pagoda's wood siding and darkened the red and green paint until the building seemed to be covered in shadow.

James didn't know what to say. He was torn between pity for Willy and the guilty thrill of watching the fire consume the ice cream shop at a voracious speed. A strong breeze sent ashes drifting across the parking lot, and as Bennett turned the truck toward the conflagration, splinters of charred wood and debris still carrying devilish sparks landed on his windshield.

"And here I thought I was safe from disasters," Willy said as he got out of the car and stared at his ruined business. James followed his gaze, noticing that the firemen were doing all they could to control the blaze, but the roof had already collapsed and fresh plumes of smoke belched from the gap. Firemen with hoses aimed arcs of water at the burning structure, while other firemen created a perimeter with caution tape. Chief Lawrence raised a bullhorn to his mouth and barked at the spectators to keep their distance.

Willy, James, Bennett, and Carter watched in wordless shock until the flames were finally extinguished. Thick smoke spread across the ground like a gray fog, and ash fell all around like black snowflakes. James could feel pieces sticking to his hair and skin. He rubbed a piece between his thumb and forefinger. It was warm and gritty. Willy opened his palm to catch some of the minute particles. He stared at them, and James sensed that Willy was staring at the remnants of his dreams.

From where they stood in the parking lot, on a gentle crest above the hustling firemen, the men saw the arrival of two brown patrol cars. The cruisers' red and blue roof light bars blazed, but the sirens hadn't been activated. Three men got out of the cars and conferred with the exhausted firemen. James recognized Sheriff Huckabee and deputies Keith Donovan and Glenn Truett.

At that moment, two cars pulled up next to Bennett's truck in rapid succession. The first was Gillian's environmentally friendly hybrid, followed by Lucy's dirt-encrusted Jeep. As Gillian, Lindy, and Lucy approached, James was pleased to see that Gillian and

Lindy were carrying six-packs of soda. He felt like he had swallowed a mouthful of chalk and couldn't wait to wash away the layer of grime that coated his tongue.

"We saw you standing up here from our vantage point at the other end of the parking lot and we thought you might be a bit parched. Would you like some cherry cola?"

"We'd love some," James answered for his group and Lindy handed each of the men a cold can.

Bennett thanked her and hesitantly introduced the three ladies to Carter.

"Thank you kindly, ladies." Willy raised his can to his lips and took a deep swig. Swallowing the cold drink seemed to break the trance he'd fallen under while watching the fire. "Nothing like a little cherry cola to bring things back into perspective. I reckon it's not all as bad as it looks. I've got cherry cola, I'm among friends, and I have an excellent insurance policy."

"I'm glad your sense of humor is still intact." Gillian put her hand on Willy's arm and smiled.

James continued to stare at the charred structure that had been, for a brief time, a delightfully charming ice cream parlor. The building looked like the skeleton of some great beast. A rib cage of blackened beams jutted into the night sky and melted pipes and partially burned boards stuck out like broken limbs.

Suddenly, James remembered what Brady had said about someone being trapped inside the building. Trying to be inconspicuous, he pulled Lucy a little way down the hill and shared what he'd overheard the young fireman say to Chief Lawrence.

"Didn't you tell me that Pete Vandercamp was planning to work the weekend shifts?" Lucy asked, gripping James by the hand.

Looking down at her soft fingers, James covered them with his free hand. "Yes, but this rumor of someone being inside is just a rumor. A kid on his bike told us. He was reporting what he *thought* he saw. Maybe he was wrong. After all, it would have been getting dark by then. It could have been a shadow cast by the flames or a trick of the light."

"Maybe, but I doubt it. If the kid thought he saw a person inside, then I bet someone was in there." Lucy turned and pointed at the patrol cars. "Anyway, Sheriff Huckabee's here. He's either helping Chief Lawrence decide if this fire is a result of arson or he's here because one of the firemen found a body."

James looked at the charred ruins and shuddered. No one could survive such a fire.

Gazing at the smoldering building, Lucy's face also creased with worry. "I know that Pete didn't always behave like a gentleman. He drank too much, and swore at us when we were kids, and always made lewd comments to the pretty women in town, but no one deserves such a horrible death. I truly hope they don't find anyone inside."

James and Lucy silently made their way closer to the perimeter of caution tape. They watched as the sheriff pulled on a pair of firemen boots and followed an agitated Chief Lawrence into what remained of the Polar Pagoda.

"I'm going to get closer," Lucy said.

"Wait!" James held her firmly by the arm. "You might not want to see what they find. *If* they find something, that is. The remains might look . . ." He trailed off as he noticed Carter, Willy, and the rest of the Flab Five staring at him. He hadn't even heard them follow he and Lucy down the slope.

Gillian leaned toward James. "What are you two whispering about?"

Willy cast anxious glances between James and Lucy. "Do you folks know why Johnny Law is here? Is there more bad news? Is there talk of arson or something?"

James decided that Willy deserved honesty. "Someone might have been inside. Trapped. Unable to flee the fire for whatever reason. But it's not certain, Willy," he quickly added.

Willy shook his head. "No way, man. Nothing in there could have burned fast enough to—" He stopped abruptly. "No. Pete would have gotten out. He's no nuclear physicist, but he's got survival instincts, same as the rest of us. He wouldn't just stand there and watch the place go up in flames around him."

"I'm sure you're right," Lindy said, but her eyes were bright with fear.

"What's the sheriff got in his hand?" Carter asked quietly, speaking for the first time.

Lucy peered through the dark as Sheriff Huckabee moved into

the center of a powerful beam cast by the lights of the fire truck. "They look like our standard plastic evidence bags. I can't tell what's inside."

"From the long neck and the fact that they look like they're made of glass—see how the lights are reflecting on the surface—I'd say they're liquor bottles. One in each bag," Bennett said.

"Wasn't Pete fond of Wild Turkey?" Lucy turned to James. "Remember all the empty bottles he kept in his car when we were in high school? You couldn't pass him in the hall without breathing in the smell of whiskey."

"Yes, I remember." James felt a queasiness spreading in his stomach.

"Well, one's a Wild Turkey bottle. The other's definitely Gentleman Jack," Carter said with authority.

Everyone looked at the new mail carrier in surprise. "Gentleman Jack? Do you mean Jack Daniel's?" Lindy asked, and Carter silently nodded. "How can you tell from this distance?"

Carter shrugged. "I used to work at a liquor store. I could tell you the name of most bottles without looking at the labels. Those two are easy ones. Their shapes are obvious to me." Suddenly he frowned. "That's kind of weird," he murmured to himself.

"What's weird?" Bennett asked.

Hesitating, Carter jerked his thumb at the sheriff. "The different bottles. It's just that most folks don't mix their whiskeys, you know. They stick to one brand pretty loyally."

"Don't look at me." Willy threw his hands in the air with a sound that was part sob, part laugh. "I'm from a dry Baptist household. I wouldn't know whiskey, good *or* bad, from cough syrup. All I can tell you is that neither of those bottles is mine." He watched as an ambulance pulled into the parking lot. "Oh, Lord, please tell me that poor man didn't drink two bottles full of that damn liquor while he was on the job tonight."

Lucy took Willy's hand as two paramedics unloaded a gurney from the back of the ambulance. By this time, most of the onlookers had dispersed. The fire was out and a sudden chill had entered the air. A few teenage boys sat in the rear of a pickup when the sheriff's cruisers first arrived, but eventually they'd grown tired of the scene and motored noisily out of the lot.

Lucy squeezed Willy's hand and tried to lead him away from the scene. "Come on, Willy, let's get you home."

"I know you're trying to spare me pain, friend, but I've got to know." Willy gently pulled his hand free of Lucy's and turned to the others. "I need to see what they found."

James understood. "In that case, we're coming with you."

As the group of seven approached what was left of the Polar Pagoda, Deputy Keith Donovan raced over to stop them from ducking under the yellow tape.

"Hold up there, folks," he said, raising his hand like a traffic cop. "That tape is there to keep civilians like you safe from harm." He looked directly at Lucy as he said this, deliberately reminding her that she was an administrator at the sheriff's department and not a bona fide member of law enforcement.

"This is my place," Willy said calmly and ducked under the tape. "I need to know what happened here."

"We'll inform you in due time, sir. You can't enter." Donovan stepped in front of Willy. He then blinked hard as if something had gotten in his eye. He ran a hand through his unkempt orange hair, which was flecked with ashes and other debris, and growled, "What the hell?" He shook his head violently and black flakes flew onto his shoulders, drifting down to the shoulders of his uniform shirt. While he focused on dusting himself off, Willy walked by him and approached Sheriff Huckabee.

James heard Willy introduce himself to the sheriff. The sheriff's face was unreadable, but he shook Willy's hand in apparent sympathy before pulling him farther away from James and the others. The sheriff spoke to Willy in a hushed tone as he gestured between the ambulance and the ruined building. Suddenly, Willy let out a low cry and covered his face with his hands. Sheriff Huckabee continued to speak in a low, soft voice as he patted Willy on the back.

When Willy seemed calmer, Huckabee looked around and spotted Carter and the supper club members. His brows creased and his walrus-like mustache flared in anger. He bellowed at Donovan, "Get them out of here, Deputy!"

Although Keith Donovan did his best to push and shove the six onlookers well behind the tape, most of them caught a clear glimpse of the gurney as it was being wheeled to the ambulance. A figure lay under a shroud of white. James stared at the form. He was oddly hypnotized by the way the lights in the parking lot turned the sheet a sickly yellow.

"What happened, Keith?" Lucy quietly asked Donovan. "Is it Pete?"

"Give me a break, Lucy," he snapped. "You'll stick your nose into everything soon enough. I'm sure, that by noon tomorrow, you'll have read every single report and you'll have told your friends every detail."

Lucy's brow clouded. "Well, since I have to *type* the reports, I guess I *will* be reading them, but it doesn't take a deputy to know that Pete was scheduled to work in that ice cream shop tonight. If it's not Pete on that gurney, then who is it?"

Her taunting succeeded in confirming their worst fears, because Donovan slapped the caution tape with his baton and spat, "So it's Pete Vandercamp! Good for you, Miss I-Went-to-College. But since *you* can't get near the scene, seeing as it's a crime scene and you don't investigate crimes, I guess you can't deduce exactly how Pete met his fiery end, now can you?"

"I guess I'd have to start by wondering if he drank the contents of both of those two whiskey bottles you bagged and put in the sheriff's car," Lucy said flatly.

Donovan's freckled face grew mottled with anger. "I have work to do! Why don't you and your friends go hang out at the Shoney's buffet and let the rest of us do our jobs?" Having delivered his insult, Donovan stalked away.

The group watched Donovan confer with Sheriff Huckabee. As they spoke, the paramedics slammed the rear door of the ambulance, asked Huckabee to sign a document on their clipboard, and drove off. The ambulance wheels crunched over small pieces of wood and dark shards of broken glass before silently gliding through the empty parking lot, over the top of the hill, and out of view. Huckabee followed the departing vehicle with his eyes while roughly pulling on his mustache.

Then he sighed loudly, checked his watch, and turned toward Willy. After placing a comforting hand on Willy's shoulder, Huckabee steered him over to Donovan's car. He opened the passenger door for him and gesticulated at Donovan, indicating that the deputy should serve as chauffeur. Before closing the car door, Willy looked at his new friends and gave them a small wave and a tight, weary smile. They all waved back, though not one of them could return his brave smile.

Gillian glanced at her watch. "It's getting late. I have a toy poodle coming in at eight tomorrow for the works, so I should get going." She released a little moan. "Oh, how I wish there was something we could do for that poor man."

"I know. It's just awful." Lucy gazed at Willy as he settled in the passenger seat. "What's he going to do now?"

"Lord only knows," Bennett said. "He'll have to find something to keep him on his feet until he can rebuild. Come on, James. Carter. Mondays are always busy at the post office. The mail never sleeps, so we'd better get some shut-eye."

Lindy gave everyone a quick hug and then she and Gillian turned to leave. "I wish our last night out before starting our diet had been more uplifting. As soon as we get the chance, we need to tell Willy that we'll help him in any way we can. We can make him meals, if nothing else. See you all at tomorrow's Witness to Fitness meeting. At least we get to bask in Ronnie's positive energy. She's so sweet and our fresh start is sure to cheer us up!"

"Yeah, I'm sure she'll be turning cartwheels in between counting our money," James mumbled miserably. He didn't think he could stomach Ronnie's chipper demeanor after such a depressing evening. He glanced up at the sky, noticing how the twisting column of smoke had nearly dissipated. What was left was mingling with the silvery clouds. Stars winked in and out of the gray veil as if too weak to burn their way through.

Life can change so quickly, James thought, reflecting on his own life and Willy's recent tragedy. He thought of Pete and wondered what his dreams had been when he was a young man. No one planned on being a drunken janitor, so what happened to him? Did he fail to pursue a higher education? Was he afraid to take risks and had therefore ended up living from bottle to bottle as he searched for just enough part-time work to get by?

James watched Lucy's form recede toward the other end of the parking lot. He was suddenly overtaken by the desire to connect with her.

He glanced at Bennett, who was unlocking the door to his truck.

"You coming James?" he called, preparing to hop in.

"No. Go on without me," James said. He then jogged off in the opposite direction. "Lucy!" he shouted. She stopped and turned, her face a mixture of alarm and curiosity.

"What is it? Are you okay?"

After James caught up to her, he had to take a long moment to catch his breath. "God, I hate running." He put a hand over his aching lungs. "This man's body just isn't designed for that kind of exercise. Listen. Do you have a minute?"

Lucy looked at him in confusion. "It's pretty late, James."

"I know, I know." James inhaled a gulp of crisp air. "Could you give me a lift back to my car?"

Instantly relaxing, Lucy nodded and smiled. "Of course."

James was grateful that she hadn't asked why he wasn't riding back to the firehouse with Bennett and Carter, though he'd miss the cleanliness of Bennett's truck. As usual, the inside of Lucy's car still doubled as a trash receptacle. The last time James had ridden in her Jeep, the passenger seat had been entirely covered by used napkins, clothing catalogues, old newspapers, gum wrappers, and paper bags. Tonight, Lucy swept the debris into the backseat as James sat down, nudging aside a few soda cans as they rolled around by his feet.

They pulled onto the main road and James knew that he only had a few precious minutes with Lucy. It wouldn't take long to reach the library lot. To James, it seemed like he'd parked the Bronco in that lot on a completely different night. He shared this feeling with Lucy.

"You just never know what's around the bend," she said, shaking her head.

James gathered up his courage and finally asked Lucy what he'd wanted to ask her for days. "Lucy, would you have coffee with me at Dolly's after work on Tuesday?"

Lucy's face brightened. "Sure. I'd love to. Any particular reason?"

James felt encouraged by her hopeful expression. "I need to talk to you about a couple of things."

"Sounds good," she said.

As she pulled up next to the Bronco, which was the only car in the lot, she flashed James one of her dazzling smiles. "If you beat me to Dolly's, I'll take a mocha latte."

"That probably won't be on our diet," James laughed, opening his door.

"Ugh, that's right." Lucy frowned. "A decaf with skim milk then. I guess I have to get used to making sacrifices again. I hope this works out for us, James."

James didn't know whether she was referring to their diet plan or to something more important, like their relationship. "I hope so, too," he said as he got out of the car. "Good night, Lucy. Sleep well."

As he drove home, Lucy's smile temporarily banished all thoughts of the fire and of Pete Vandercamp. In fact, James was already fantasizing about how he would look after losing twenty pounds, of a successful date with Lucy on Tuesday, and an altogether brighter future.

Chapter Six

Turkey Sandwich on Whole Wheat

James took a bite of his sandwich and frowned. Two slices of fat-free turkey with lettuce, tomato, and mustard on whole wheat bread wasn't very exciting. He took another bite. It was difficult to enjoy his sandwich because it was missing the dollop of mayo and the three slices of American cheese he would have regularly added. Chewing the mouthful of dry sandwich, he glowered at the sliced Granny Smith apple and microscopic packet of sugar-free chocolate cookie wafers he planned to eat next. At that moment, Scott Fitzgerald, one of the library's four staff members, entered the break room.

"That looks really healthy, Professor," the lanky young man in his mid-twenties said as he grabbed a brown bag from the fridge. Pushing his horn-rimmed glasses farther up his thin nose, he examined his boss's fare while pulling out an enormous hoagie stuffed with salami, pepperoni, and several slices of mozzarella from his own lunch sack.

James glanced at Scott's loaded sandwich, large bag of sour cream and onion potato chips, and package of Hostess cupcakes with envy.

"So how's the new diet working out?" Scott asked, brushing aside a strand of unruly hair before taking a gargantuan bite of his hoagie.

"I just started, so I can't tell just yet," James said. "We have our first exercise class tonight."

"I hate exercising indoors. Francis and I like to ride our mountain bikes in all kinds of weather." Scott took another bite of his hoagie and a trickle of Italian dressing ran down his angular chin. He chewed feverishly, as if someone intended to steal his food. "Guess Francis and I are pretty lucky. Our metabolisms are in hyper drive all the time. Shoot, we try to gain weight but no matter how much we eat, it just doesn't stick. Both of us would love to be bulkier, you know?" Scott tore open his bag of potato chips, unaware that his boss was glaring at him.

"I can't really identify with that issue," James said.

Scott poured the chips on top of his sandwich wrapper. "Did you see the new Robert Jordan book? It's almost eight hundred pages! I can't wait to get it home. I'll probably stay up all night tonight, and Francis won't even notice because he's got the new Neal Stephenson to keep him busy."

James couldn't help but grin as Scott rambled on about his recent reads in the science fiction and fantasy realms. Even though the twin brothers were named after a famous twentieth-century American author, Francis and Scott Fitzgerald had little interest in classic literature. They were savvy mathematicians, adept at solving complex logistical problems, and were both compulsively organized. James enjoyed working with them more than any of the professors from his former department at William & Mary. For one, the twins were the most enthusiastic employees he had ever seen. They worked tirelessly and were completely devoted to seeing that every patron's needs were met. In addition, they were continuously dreaming up new schemes on how to improve their library branch.

However, not even the sharp-minded twins had been able to come up with a fund-raiser idea that would allow for the purchase of several new computers, which were desperately needed.

Wishing a brilliant plan would spring into his head, James polished off his thin cookies. He felt dissatisfied by his meal and knew he could easily polish off three more bags of cookies if he had any. He cleaned up his trash and was just finishing his diet soda when Francis burst into the room.

"Professor," he whispered urgently, jerking a thumb over his shoulder. "Things are getting a little hairy at the computer terminals. Mrs. Hughes claims that Mr. Tuttle has gone way over the thirty-minute allotment, but Mr. Tuttle refuses to budge. She's threatening to sit right on his lap if he doesn't move. I tried to intervene but —"

"That's all right, Francis." James waved at the table. "Why don't you have some lunch? I'll handle this."

Clearly relieved, Francis strode over to the fridge and pulled out a lunch bag twice the size of Scott's. "We have to come up with a stellar fund-raiser idea, bro. I can't take this kind of conflict all the time," James heard him say to Scott.

James couldn't agree more. The computers had become more

and more popular with patrons of all ages and there was rarely a time during the library's working hours when someone wasn't anxiously waiting for one of the two PCs. And thirty minutes didn't turn out to be very long when it took each of the archaic hard drives several minutes to complete even the smallest of tasks. The computers had been a growing source of friction among the patrons. The Shenandoah County Library was supposed to be a place of peace and quiet discovery, but lately, it had been filled with people impatiently pacing around the magazine section or arguing with their neighbors about time allotments.

The two computer terminals were set up in a nook between fiction and nonfiction, and that's where Mrs. Hughes stood, her hands resting on her formidable hips and a deep scowl wrinkling her face. She was normally a cheerful, pleasant lady and James always tried to get in her checkout lane at Food Lion, as she was the speediest cashier and bagger in Quincy's Gap. She could scan and pack a week's worth of groceries in under three minutes.

Mrs. Hughes latched on to James's fleshy upper arm. "Oh, Professor! Thank the Lord you're here! I'm trying to bid on an online auction and Mr. Tuttle here won't get off this machine. I've been timing him since I came in and it's been well over forty minutes since he first logged on."

Mr. Tuttle, a small middle-aged man with a pasty complexion, turned a pair of challenging eyes on James. "Hey, I'm looking for work here. Isn't that a bit more important than something this woman wants to shop for? I have a pile of bills at home as high as the Appalachians, so I need more time on this computer."

James pointed at the sign hanging over the two computers. "You know there's a limit, Mr. Tuttle. You'll have to relinquish your machine until Mrs. Hughes has had her thirty minutes. If no one else is waiting, you're welcome to get back on then."

Mr. Tuttle slammed a fist next to the keyboard. "Damnation, man! I've been out of a job for three months and I can't even use my own library's computer to look for a new one? What kind of public works place is this? I paid my taxes like everyone else. I deserve a chance to sit here as long as I need to!" He stepped away from the computer and gesticulated angrily at a spinner rack containing romance novels. "Instead of buying that trash, why don't you spend our tax money on some more computers? How do you expect the entire town to share two machines?"

As James opened his mouth to reply, a man with a briefcase tapped the young woman using the second computer on the shoulder. James recognized the girl. It was Amelia Flowers, the daughter of Megan Flowers. Megan owned the Sweet Tooth, the town's only bakery and Amelia worked for her mother part-time while also attending classes at the community college. James knew that she was interested in pursuing a career in fashion design.

"My turn, missy." The man plunked his briefcase down on the floor next to Amelia's cavernous book bag.

"Sure. Just give me a sec. I just need to print this article," Amelia said without looking away from the screen. She continued typing as Mrs. Hughes slid into the empty seat next to her.

"Hello, Amelia. I didn't even realize that was you sitting here." Mrs. Hughes squinted at Amelia's screen. "You doing work for school?"

"Yeah. I have a paper due for my History of Fashion course and the books here aren't as up-to-date as some of the articles I found on this website."

Mrs. Hughes smiled. "How nice, dear. I know your mama is awful proud of you for going to college while you're still working at the bakery." She tapped on the computer screen. "I'm going to bid on a Petal Princess Barbie doll for my granddaughter. She's been collecting them since she was five and her birthday's coming up."

"That's just great, ladies," the man with the briefcase said acidly. "But I've got some stock prices to check and I'm on my lunch break, so if you don't mind cutting the chatter and logging off, I'd like to take my turn now."

At that moment, the printer jammed in the middle of the ten-page task it was performing for Amelia.

"Sir." James held out a pacifying hand to the agitated male patron before he tried to physically remove Amelia from her chair. "Let me just fix the printer for this young lady. It will be your turn directly, sir. Amelia? Is this article all you needed?"

Amelia nodded at James. "That's it, Professor. As soon as I have that, I'll be out of your hair." She then cast an irritated glance at the man standing over her shoulder and added, "I couldn't work in this hostile atmosphere for much longer anyway."

James tugged at the crumpled piece of paper blocking the printer. It ripped into several raggedy pieces but finally came free. He then reset the print job and sighed with relief as the machine reluctantly resumed its work. Noticing that his hands were now covered with smudges of black ink, James apologized to all his patrons for their inconvenience over having to share two computers and then headed to the restroom to wash up.

Francis was already in the men's room when James arrived. He was rubbing his glasses with a piece of paper towel without concentrating on his task. In fact, he was gazing straight ahead, as if absorbed by his reflection in the mirror. "Lost in thought there, Francis?"

Jumping in surprise, Francis dropped his glasses in the wet sink. Without bothering to dry them off, he shoved them onto his face and turned to James. "I've got it, Professor!" he exclaimed happily. "I know how we can raise the money we need for the computers."

James began scrubbing his hands with pink liquid soap. "That would certainly be welcome news. If Mrs. Hughes doesn't get that Barbie for her granddaughter before her thirty minutes are up, I think she and Mr. Tuttle are going to come to blows."

Francis pursed his lips in thought. "If I were a betting man, I'd pick Mrs. Hughes to win that fight. I've seen her toss a twenty-pound watermelon into someone's shopping cart like it was a bag of cotton balls."

"Your idea, Francis?" James said.

"Oh, right!" Francis grinned. "Well, Scott came up with it too, so I have to give him credit. Anyway, we thought the library should host a Spring Fling."

James was baffled by the title. "Like last year's Spring Book Drive and Bake Sale? The library only made a couple hundred dollars from that event."

"That's because you weren't working here, Professor. You've got more vision than our former employer. And you're way more adventurous." Francis spoke matter-of-factly, and though James knew that his employee wasn't tying to butter him up, he felt pleased by the praise all the same.

"Go on," he said.

"*This* Spring Fling would be a cross between a book drive and a county fair. We could have it at the beginning of next month when the weather is nice." Francis opened the door and James followed the exuberant young man out of the restroom and behind the circulation desk. Francis produced a piece of paper and set it before James with a flourish. "I made a quick sketch of how things could be arranged in that empty field behind the strip mall. It worked so well for the benefit last fall and we don't need to pay anyone to use it—we'd just need to get permission from the mall owners to allow for parking and we'd be good to go."

James leaned over the drawing and tried to decipher Francis's scraggly handwriting. "Does this say 'Pig Race Course'?" he asked incredulously, pointing to a wobbly oval in the center of the paper.

Francis beamed. "Sure does! We could have two contests. One could be a pig race. That'll appeal to lots of folks, including men. We always have women at our events, but rarely men or children. So if we offer carnival rides and food booths like they have at the state fair, we can attract a huge crowd."

"We'd also have to charge admission." James frowned, mulling over the logistics of running such a large event.

"Yes, sir. We'd also charge people to enter the pig race and the Ladies' Hat Contest. The winners would receive cash prizes. Scott and I think that having a cash prize will encourage more folks to enter."

James looked at Francis in surprise. "Ladies' Hat Contest?"

"We haven't worked out the details yet, but it's a bit different than the usual pie or cake bake-off. Megan Flowers would win any baking contest we held anyway."

James agreed on that point. "Well, we need to remind folks that this event is about the library." He paused to think and then smiled. "What if it was a hat contest with a book-title theme? The ladies could parade in front of a panel of judges and be awarded first, second, and third-place prizes."

"That's good, Professor!" Francis pumped his fist. "Boy, if I were a lady I'd design the coolest *War of the Worlds* hat or maybe a —"

"This is a sizable undertaking, Francis," James interrupted before Francis got lost in fantasies in which he created a dozen hats based on his favorite works. "I think we should limit the number of outside vendors we have for the first year and see how things go. I'm sure Dolly's Diner and the Sweet Tooth would be interested in setting up food stalls, and we could hire a few ride and game vendors, but we don't want to get too big for our britches. We could lose money if we don't sell enough tickets." A slow grin spread over James's face. "But overall, it's a really great idea, Francis. This library branch is very fortunate to have you and Scott. If we could just make enough for two more computer terminals . . ." James trailed off, picturing himself placing the new machines by the windows and then turning to hear the applause of the grateful patrons.

"Two?" Francis pushed the reshelving cart past his boss. "We were thinking of at least four. Maybe even six. We could move those paperback spinners closer to the Children's section and create a whole Tech Corner."

James looked beyond Francis to where Mrs. Hughes sat staring at a computer screen. Mr. Tuttle was close by, flipping the pages of an automotive magazine with unnecessary vigor.

"Six new computers," James whispered in awe. "Our patrons would certainly be better served than they are now. I'd better get on the phone with some vendors." He practically jogged to his office, eager to begin sorting out the details of the first Shenandoah County Library Spring Fling. Throughout the afternoon, he was so busy that he completely forgot about the banana and small bag of pretzels he had brought for a snack. Even when he chatted with a vendor regarding cotton candy, elephant ears, and funnel cake, his mind remained focused on improving his beloved library and not on forbidden foods.

But his hunger wouldn't be ignored for long. When James arrived home a little after five, he was ravenous. He'd eaten the banana and pretzels in the Bronco on the way home from work, but he still felt as if his stomach was totally hollow. However, he forgot all about the grumbling in his belly the moment he pulled up in front of his house.

There was his father, thirty feet off the ground, tool belt strapped around his trim waist, inspecting the newly laid roof shingles surrounding the base of the chimney. As an incredulous James looked on, Jackson made his way to a workman who was stapling shingles around the area where water had been getting in and leaking into the upstairs bathroom with every rain. His father moved in that stooped half-crawl men employ when traversing the steep slopes of roofs, and James could not believe his limberness or the camaraderie he exhibited when he slapped the other man on the back. Soon, the two men were laughing like old friends. James hadn't heard his father laugh like that for years, and he smiled at the deep, hearty sound. Jackson spied his son on the ground below and, after waving, headed for the metal ladder propped against the side of the house.

He climbed down like a man half his age and beckoned for James to follow him into the kitchen.

"Lookin' good, ain't it?" Jackson asked, his cheeks rosy with exertion and his eyes sparkling with pride.

"Sure does, Pop. Have you been working up there the whole time?" James barely recognized the invigorated person standing before him.

His father turned, filled a glass with cold tap water, and then drank the liquid down in three gulps. Slamming the glass triumphantly on the counter, he puffed out his chest and exhaled happily. "Next, I'm gonna do somethin' about this kitchen. It's a disgrace. Your mama was all set to overhaul the whole room, but I kept frettin' about the cost." Jackson looked down at the stained and peeling linoleum flooring. "If I'd have known, I'd have given her the finest kitchen in all of Virginia." He looked up at James, his fuzzy eyebrows shooting high on his forehead. "But now it's you and me, boy. We gotta make this place the kind of home men would be proud to live in."

James didn't want to put a damper on his father's rare talkativeness or his enthusiasm for home improvement, but he had to be honest. "We just don't have the money for a new kitchen, Pop. I don't even know how we're going to pay for the roof. I had planned to talk to Hugh Carmichael over at Shenandoah Savings and Loan next week but—"

"We have the money, son," Jackson said with a gleeful cackle. "We just gotta decide on cabinets. I'm partial to oak or maple with a walnut stain. Nice and manly." Jackson spread out a few wood samples and then dumped out a bag of granite chips onto the countertop. "This granite stuff is what folks are doin' now, but it looks too shiny to me, like somethin' those fancy Hollywood types would pick. I'm thinkin' there's nothin' wrong with good old laminate."

James glanced at the array of materials. He then studied his father's face. Ten years seemed to have melted off the old man's visage in the single day he'd spent laying roof shingles in the temperate spring air. "I won't pry about the money, Pop. If you say we have it, I believe you. Even though it worries me a bit, I trust your judgment."

Jackson nodded in appreciation and James was relieved that he'd said the right thing. His father gestured at the samples. "Which one do you favor?"

"I prefer the laminate as well. Neither of us are gourmet chefs, so I don't think we need the granite, or fancy appliances, for that matter. If we can update the fridge and stove and replace the floor, that'll do."

"No, sir!" Jackson shook his head. "We're gonna get new cabinets, new appliances, new counters, and I'm puttin' in a dishwasher. You've got better things to do than wash up after every meal."

James was stunned. His father was being uncharacteristically thoughtful. "Oh, I don't mind washing up." This was the truth, for he actually enjoyed the quiet moments spent scrubbing up each evening. He mind contentedly wandered as his hands moved over the dishes and pans.

"Well, *I* don't have time for it, and once you get yourself a girl, you won't, either." Jackson eyed his son. "Weren't you sweet on someone from your Sunday night . . . uh . . . club?"

James felt himself reddening. "I don't know, Pop. I think I messed up with her. With Lucy, I mean."

"How's that?" his father asked as he refilled his water glass and took a seat at the kitchen table. James, half wondering if he was dreaming, sat down across from his father and explained how he felt about Lucy Hanover. Jackson listened carefully, staring at the strewn pile of samples and brochures, until James was done.

"So you've got another chance. When you see this girl tomorrow, you tell her you were a chicken before and now you're not. You gotta go after her, James, or someone else is gonna snap her up like a bass in the lake. You ain't too young, my boy. If you wanna start any kind of family with a good woman, then you'd better get in gear." Jackson paused. "Can she cook?"

James laughed. "She's not bad, I guess. She's kind of a slob, though."

"I don't know what the world's comin' to," Jackson grumbled with a trace of his usual gruffness. "There was a time when women cooked and cleaned and sewed and were damned proud of it. What's a man supposed to do these days?"

"Things are more equal now, Pop. Men and women share in the household stuff. Many women have careers outside of the home. They want to chase their own dreams and ambitions and don't have time to wait on others."

"What a bunch of crust." Jackson frowned. "Maybe you shouldn't show up for that coffee date after all."

James threw his head back and laughed.

• • •

"Hello, my friends!" Ronnie exclaimed that evening at the Witness to Fitness meeting. "I'm sorry I'm all sweaty, but Dylan was practicing his workout on me before you showed up." She dabbed the light sheen of perspiration on her brow with a purple monogrammed towel and took an infinitesimal sip from a water bottle. "But don't worry. He'll go much easier on you. You're going to have so much fun in there!"

James saw Lindy shoot Lucy a look of panic and his own stomach lurched at the thought of bouncing around in front of both friends and strangers.

"Let's get the tedious money part out of the way first, shall we?" Ronnie beamed at the group of nervous people waiting to enter the exercise room. "I have all of your entrées packed and ready to go home to your freezers at the end of class. Phoebe and I will accept cash or checks for this week's meals and for the three required exercise classes. But before we get started, why not give yourselves a hand just for being here tonight? Come on! Let's hear some noise for your courage and determination." She began clapping loudly and a few others tentatively joined in. "Good for you! Way to go, everyone!"

James reluctantly applauded when Ronnie turned a luminescent smile in his direction. Within moments, the twenty people gathered around the cubicles were rifling through purses and digging in wallets to cheerfully pay for their first week at Witness to Fitness. James blanched when he saw the actual total. Each meal cost nearly ten dollars and didn't include the salad or light dessert that was supposed to accompany a complete Witness to Fitness dinner. At almost five hundred dollars per month, James prayed that he would make amazing progress in the first six weeks or he wouldn't have a dime of spending money for the upcoming summer.

No one else seemed overly concerned with the cost, which was a surprise. With the exception of Gillian, who owned her own pet grooming business and was a partner in a second business involving the design and distribution of luxurious pet houses, the members of the Flab Five would struggle to pay the high cost of getting in shape.

When everyone had settled up, Ronnie ushered the group of participants into the exercise room. She closed the door behind them. As it clicked shut, the sound reinforced James's feeling that there was no turning back from this point.

"Are you ready for our star instructor? Are you ready for Dylan?" Ronnie cried. When she said Dylan's name, her eyes turned starry and James guessed that Ronnie was more than a little smitten with her employee. He wondered if Dylan was aware of his boss's infatuation and if it would make working with her uncomfortable.

Dylan came bounding in from the back room wearing only a pair of tight black track pants with silver stripes running up his muscular legs. "Howdy, folks! It's a great day to get in shape!" He beamed at the group. "You're probably all a little nervous, but there's nothing to be afraid of. I promise to take it slow until you get used to our routine. Help yourself to a mat and let's get moving!" He put his hands on his narrow hips and took several deep breaths while his new pupils grabbed the blue exercise mats stacked in the far corner of the room and hustled back to their places.

Dylan seemed pleased by their eagerness. "I like the energy I'm sensing. I think you guys and gals are going to go far. Let's begin with some simple stretches," he said. "First, let's reach down and touch our toes."

James made a pitiful attempt to reach his toes, but he couldn't get any lower than his kneecaps, no matter how much he strained. Casting a sideways glance at Lindy, he noticed that she was struggling to get past her shins.

"I haven't touched my toes since junior high," she whispered unhappily.

"I never could," James whispered back.

Next, Dylan leaned to the side to demonstrate how they'd stretch their oblique muscles.

"Okay, folks! Looking good." Dylan led them through a few more standing postures and then slapped a rubber mat on the floor and hopped onto it. "How about we go horizontal and stretch out those legs? Can you lean to one side and wrap your hand around the bottom of your foot? Like this?"

James struggled to touch his sneaker's laces, but he absolutely couldn't reach his shoe. Stretching to the point of pain, he brushed his fingers along the cuff of his white sock, sat up, shrugged, and looked over at Lindy. She was bending forward, her lips clamped together in a combination of misery and determination. In the mirror, James spied Gillian and Bennett, who had successfully managed to touch their shoes, and then caught sight of Lucy. Like him, she'd also settled for grasping her ankle and had sat back in frustration. Their eyes met in the mirror and she smiled.

Dylan shifted his position. He'd been practically folded in half on top of his left leg when he languidly raised his head, drew both feet fluidly toward his crotch, and exhaled loudly. "Okay, let's get our legs in the butterfly position and give a good stretch to those inner thighs."

Several men groaned as they attempted to replicate Dylan's position. James could barely fold his legs at all, let alone pull his feet that close to his protruding belly. As he stared at his dirt-splattered sneakers with their frayed laces, he began to wonder about his father's new carefree spending attitude. Where *was* the money coming from?

"Hey, Lindy," James whispered, trying to focus on anything other than the sharp pain that had begun to streak up his legs toward his groin.

"Yeah?"

"Do you remember when you told me your mother was going to contact my father about putting some of his paintings in her DC gallery?"

Lindy seemed startled by the question, but she gladly ignored the next stretch and inched closer to her friend. "I sure do. Your daddy's work is amazing. It's a lot like Audubon's. He's very talented." She hesitated. "Wait a minute. Do you mean that you don't know?"

When the woman to James's left tried to shush him, James ignored her. "Know what?"

Lindy's jaw dropped. "Oh, my stars, James! Every one of his paintings sold during my mother's winter show. He made a ton of money."

James couldn't believe his ears. "What's a ton, exactly?"

Lindy inched a little closer and whispered, "Over twenty thousand dollars. My mother sold a total of fifty paintings and at top dollar prices, especially for an unknown artist. Even after her commission, she was able to send your daddy a pretty nice check." Lindy stood as Dylan kindly commanded them all to rise. "I can't believe he didn't tell you. He should be so proud! Not only did he sell out, but there are at least a dozen standing orders for future works."

James began Dylan's exercise routine in a stupor. Twenty thousand dollars!

"We're going to burn some fat doing some leg lifts, folks!" Dylan turned up the volume on his CD player and loud techno music with a chaotic rhythm reverberated through the room. "This song ought to get you in the mood to *lift*, and *lift*, and *lift!*"

James felt like his thighs were on fire. How could his lower limbs be so heavy? After fifteen lifts per side, he didn't think he could raise even his foot off the floor. He could feel the extra flesh on his belly, thighs, arms, and chest shaking and flapping as if it were detaching from the bone. Glancing in the mirror, he saw that everyone else's bodies looked the same. Red faces were streaming with moisture, sweatshirts were stained with sweat, and people bent down to tie shoelaces every few minutes in an attempt to catch a prolonged breath.

"Stay hydrated, folks!" Dylan called in between jumping jacks. "Hang in there! We're halfway done!"

"Halfway?" James panted. He was miserable. His chest was tight and he had a sharp pain in his side. Sweat dripped into his eyes and his body felt as heavy as an anchor. He didn't think he could take another step, let alone raise his arms high above his head and wave them left and right.

"Trees in the wind!" Dylan shouted. "Wave those arms, folks!"

In the mirror, James saw Lucy behind him and off to his right. She was struggling but still managing to imitate Dylan's moves. She caught James watching her and gave him an exaggerated eye roll accompanied by a quick smile.

Wanting to appear as capable as Lucy of following through to the bitter end of Dylan's routine, James raised his elbows slightly above his waist and tried to follow the instructor's energetic side-stepping motions. As James held up his leaden arms and shuffled to the left like a zombie, the lights in the room seemed to gradually grow brighter. He gazed at the ceiling and the dozen tiny spotlights flared out like Christmas tree stars. The pounding beat of the music changed, too. Suddenly, James could barely hear it at all. His head filled with a pleasant feeling of emptiness and a curtain of darkness fell before his eyes.

The next thing he knew, he was lying down. Someone was saying his name.

"James! Can you hear me? James." It was Lucy.

James opened his eyes and stared up at her. Lucy knelt beside him, her chest quickly rising and falling. She was still short of breath from their routine and her cheeks were flushed. Her eyes were wide with concern.

"Are you okay?" Gillian's face appeared among the ring of people looking down upon his sweat-slicked body. "I think you need some water."

"I agree. Let's give him some room, folks." Dylan waved the small group back and squatted next to James. "Everyone grab a mat and we'll do some cool-down stretches in a second. Our friend will be just fine. He just overdid it today, that's all. He was putting forth one hundred and ten percent!"

The members of the class hesitated before laying out their mats and flopping down on them. No one even pretended to stretch. A few people just lay prone on the mats and groaned.

Lucy was the last to sit down, and even as she did so, she continued to stare in James's direction. She never turned her flushed face away and she kept smiling at James in encouragement.

"Did I faint?" James asked Dylan in a horrified whisper.

Dylan nodded. "Yes, but don't be embarrassed. You were working really hard and you didn't hydrate enough. Here, take some slow slips of this."

James refused to allow Dylan to hold on to his head as he propped himself up on his right elbow and drank some tepid water.

"Better now?" Dylan asked kindly and helped James to a sitting position.

"I'm all right. A little embarrassed. And I'm sorry to have interrupted the class." James slunk over to where the blue floor mats were kept and pulled one to the very back of the room by the door.

As Dylan led them through their final stretches, he reiterated the importance of drinking water throughout his classes. James was completely mortified that he'd fainted and avoided meeting his friends' eyes in the mirror. He knew they meant well, but he was too humiliated to accept their sympathy at the moment.

The second the class was over; James hustled out of the room as fast as his numb legs would carry him. He didn't even bother to clean off his exercise mat and return it to the stack. As he grabbed his bag of entrées, he felt like slugging Ronnie for encouraging him to join her program in the first place.

He was just about to escape when she clapped him on his sweat-soaked back. "Don't you have a healthy glow? It's *very* attractive." She winked at him and exclaimed, "Why, Mr. Henry, I swear you look thinner already. See you Wednesday!"

Chapter Seven

Almond Biscotti

James was settled in a booth at Dolly's Diner fifteen minutes before his scheduled meeting time with Lucy. This booth had become a favorite because the paneled walls above it were decorated with coconut shells, grass skirts, colorful leis, two small tiki torches, and a large poster of an azure sea bordering a strip of gleaming sand with a tag line reading *Need a break? Paradise is waiting for you!*

James always pretended that he'd been transported to an exotic locale when he ate beneath the tropical souvenirs. It was as if he only needed to step into the poster to escape the long winter days that make living in a small town enclosed by mountains dull and dreary. Now that spring had come to Quincy's Gap, James sat in the booth and dreamed of taking Lucy on vacation to a tropical paradise. They could stroll hand in hand on stretches of pristine sand just like the beach in the poster.

"Coffee, hon?" Dolly asked, jiggling a chewed pencil between her thumb and index finger. She always carried the pencil but never used it to write down orders because she had a photographic memory when it came to food.

"Please." James smiled at the busty middle-aged proprietor before issuing a quick wave to her husband, Clint, who'd just emerged from his domain in the kitchen to refill his soda glass. Dolly placed a tiny creamer filled with half-and-half in front of James. While he stirred a packet of artificial sweetener into his coffee, she scrutinized him closely.

"You do something different with your hair, Professor?" she asked, clearly in no hurry to check on her other customers.

James absently touched a nutmeg-colored strand and then shook his head. "No, ma'am. Do you have skim milk, Dolly? I've joined that new Witness to Fitness program and I don't think I can afford to waste any food points using half-and-half in my coffee."

"Sure do, hon. I'll back in a flash." Dolly hustled to the kitchen and returned with another metal creamer. Putting a hand on her hip as if to signal the beginning of a lengthy chat, she asked, "So what do you think of that Ronnie Levitt girl? She's a cute little thing if you like your women with no meat on their bones. That girl's a walking celery stick. But you men see things differently, don't you?" She raised her brows as if daring James to argue. Her blue-tinted lids shimmered beneath the overhead lights.

James shrugged. He didn't dare tell Dolly how he truly felt about Ronnie, or what he said would be spread around town faster than the winter flu. "She's a bit too perky for me," was all he could manage without fully revealing how irritating he found Ronnie Levitt.

Dolly frowned. She disliked terse answers. She lived and breathed for two things: gossip and the opportunity to play matchmaker among the singles of Quincy's Gap. James routinely disappointed her on both fronts. He'd had many a meal interrupted so that Dolly could introduce him to one unattached female after another. Most of the time, the women were mortified to have been led over to his table like mares to a stud farm, but on occasion, they tried to flirt with James.

Dolly was about to ask him another question when she spied a customer approaching the front door. "Oh! Here comes Lucy Hanover. Well, I'll be plucked and strung up like a chicken! She's all gussied up! I wonder who she's taken so much trouble over?" Her large head pivoted back and forth as she examined the customers seated in her dining room. "Hmm. Maybe it's . . ." she mumbled to herself and rushed off to take up her favorite viewing position behind the counter.

James was relieved that he'd chosen to sit with his back to the entrance. He was nervous enough as it was and didn't need to compound his anxiety by watching Lucy's arrival. He had no idea how he was going to tell her how he felt. The brightness of the diner seemed to induce loud conversation—not the whispered endearments he had in mind. And when Lucy slid into the opposite side of his booth, James regretted his choice of seating. He wished he'd been prepared for her dramatic change in appearance from a long way off because he barely recognized the woman before him.

Lucy must have come fresh from the hair salon because her thick caramel locks were neatly sheared and angled into an attractive bob. She wore pale red lipstick and a kind of dusk-colored frosted shadow that made her cornflower-blue eyes look larger and more luminous than ever. Her indigo blouse had a deep neckline and she wore a silver cross on a long chain that dangled playfully above her generous cleavage. A tendril of floral perfume wafted across the table, and James caught a pleasant hint of honeysuckle and jasmine.

Before he had the chance to compliment Lucy on her appearance, Dolly hurried over to the booth as fast as her two rubber-shoed feet would allow, the ends of her apron strings trailing out behind her like a kite's tail. "Lucy, darling! Don't you just look a picture! Isn't she stunning, Professor?"

James nodded in amazement. He cast a shy grin in Lucy's direction and then studied the contents of his coffee cup as if he were an augur.

Dolly's eyes shifted eagerly from Lucy to James as she took Lucy's order. "I'll just leave you two alone," she then whispered conspiratorially and promised to return as quickly as she could with another cup of coffee.

Lucy waited for her to leave and then giggled. "Dolly is something else, isn't she? She probably has every booth bugged so she can catch up on all the latest news."

James laughed. He immediately felt his tension dissipate. "But she's right about one thing. You do look terrific. *Really* terrific."

"Thanks. The sheriff sent me to Waynesboro this morning to pick up the specialist's report on the Polar Pagoda fire. I had to drive because our fax machine is busted again, so I decided to visit a friend of mine who just opened a salon there. Of course, none of the deputies noticed anything different about me." She frowned. "I could have come back with a purple Mohawk and the guys wouldn't even blink. They're all completely obsessed with the upcoming Law Enforcement Bowling Tournament."

"What kind of specialist?"

"A fire investigator hired by the company insuring Willy's business. Chief Lawrence met him at the scene after we had gone. I guess the two of them have been collaborating to figure out what happened."

James was unable to keep his curiosity from distracting him from the real reason he'd asked Lucy to meet him. "A fire investigator? Whoa. Did you get to read his report?"

"Of course! I read the whole thing while Cindi was working on my hair." Lucy gave James an affectionate look. "I can't resist knowing as much as the chauvinistic deputies I have to work with every day."

"Oh, it won't be long before you're working right alongside them, Lucy. As an equal. Or, as their superior," James said.

Lucy's smile lit up her whole face. "It's nice to know you have such confidence in me, James. You're so sweet." She reached across and brushed his hand with her fingertips, and James felt his heart quicken. "Anyway, the investigator and Chief Lawrence have ruled that the fire at the Polar Pagoda was the result of negligence."

James took a sip of coffee and grimaced at the foreign taste of the skim milk. He missed the rich creaminess of his half-and-half. "Was it Pete's fault? Can you tell me? I wouldn't want you to get in trouble."

"Don't worry about it. The details will end up in the paper soon enough," Lucy said. "They found traces of whiskey all over the back of the shop, especially around the cardboard boxes where the T-shirts were stored. Somehow, the fire specialist could follow the trail of flames and discover its source. Pretty cool, right? There were also several cigarette butts—Pall Mall Lights, I think—recovered from the same area. So I guess Pete was just hanging out, drinking and smoking throughout his whole shift. I guess he didn't serve too many customers that night or someone would have noticed he was drunk."

"Almost everyone in town was at the Brunswick stew dinner. That's why Pete had so little business." James paused and frowned. "But I always remember Pete as someone who chewed tobacco. Have you ever seen him smoke?"

"No, but who knows what the man did in private?" Lucy shrugged. "What seems strange to me is the amount of whiskey that was spilled. I can't see Pete accidentally knocking over a perfectly good bottle of booze, can you? Anyway, we'll know more soon. A medical examiner who specializes in burned cadavers is coming from Richmond to examine the body."

"You kids need a refill?" Dolly asked, appearing in front of James and Lucy like a magician. Startled, they both knocked their cups, sloshing coffee into their saucers. "I've also got some low-fat almond cookies for you to nibble on. Got some Italian name. Clint's been experimenting with low-sugar desserts to add to our menu. Let me know what you think." She set a plate of cookies on the table, poured more steaming coffee into their cups, checked the level of milk in the creamer, and hovered over them for a good five seconds.

James picked up a biscotti and took a bite, figuring that Dolly was going to stand there until he did. The crunchy almond flavor was a pleasant accompaniment to the coffee. "These are good, Dolly. Clint's got a winner. He can serve them to all the folks on our diet."

"Well, I hope we don't have to change our whole menu on account of this Ronnie gal. There's nothing wrong with some good old Southern cooking for at least one meal. My Grammy lived to be over a hundred and she ate fried chicken with biscuits and gravy every single day of her life!"

"No one could run you out of business, Dolly," Lucy assured her. "There isn't a diet in this world that could keep me from your meat loaf or blackberry pie. The whole town has favorites here. This diner is the heart of Quincy's Gap."

Pacified, Dolly smiled and went to check on her other customers.

"Speaking of our diet," Lucy said, turning her attention back to James. "We're all saving our baked ziti to eat at Gillian's house this Sunday. We figured we'd make a salad and a dessert and eat together even though we're just heating up a frozen dinner."

"I'm glad." James dusted biscotti crumbs from the table and onto the floor. "I'd hate our dinners to end just because we joined Witness to Fitness." After a moment's hesitation, he decided that there had been enough small talk and it was now time to come to the point with Lucy. "Besides, I especially look forward to seeing you—"

"Professor Henry! How lucky to have run into you!" Murphy Alistair cried and dropped a notebook onto the table with a decisive thwack. "I called the library, but you'd already left. I'm dying to get the scoop on your first Witness to Fitness class. You agreed to give me details, remember?" She looked expectantly from James to Lucy. "Oh. Am I interrupting? I can sit at another booth until you're ready to talk, James."

Since she made no move to collect her notebook, it was clear that she didn't want to wait in the next booth.

"That's okay," Lucy said with what James recognized as false sweetness. She eyed Murphy's form-fitting blouse and skinny jeans with ill-concealed envy. "I see Carter Peabody's just come in. I'll go say hello while you two talk." She gathered her purse and left money for the coffee while James struggled to find the words to keep her from leaving. "See you," she said to James, her face reflecting hurt and disappointment as she scooted out of the booth.

James opened and closed his mouth like a frog searching for flies. He knew he should send Murphy away and tell Lucy what he wanted to say to her, but the sudden presence of another woman, especially one with such a forceful personality as Murphy, had thrown him completely off balance. Before he could even say goodbye, Murphy had taken Lucy's place. Across the diner, Lucy greeted Carter as if they were long-lost friends and joined him at the counter. Carter looked slightly taken aback by Lucy's effusiveness, but his surprise quickly morphed into a smile. Lucy gazed at his handsome face with undisguised interest and James scowled.

"So." Murphy uncapped a ballpoint pen and turned to a fresh sheet of paper in her notebook. "How was your first class?"

James answered Murphy's questions as succinctly as possible, hoping to give her the information she needed and then reclaim his alone time with Lucy. He praised Dylan's teaching abilities and described some of the more difficult portions of the workout without mentioning his own collapse. Murphy scribbled away and encouraged James to share even the most mundane details, like the music used and what types of clothing the other dieters wore to class. As James spoke, he cast sidelong looks in Lucy's direction, where, to his dismay, he saw her order a fresh cup of coffee. She and Carter were having an animated conversation and were both laughing noisily. James couldn't help but wonder if Lucy was putting on a show to get his attention. If so, she was succeeding.

"Professor? Woo-hoo!" Murphy waved a hand in front of his face. "I was asking how your first meal tasted."

"Not great," James said without really thinking about the fact that hundreds of locals would soon read about his opinion of Witness to Fitness. "It was a rubbery chicken with sautéed vege- tables and tasteless noodles."

"You don't have to hold back," Murphy said with an encouraging grin. "You're paying good money for this stuff. How much did you say it cost?" She consulted her notes. "Around ten bucks a pop for these dinners? You should be dining on small portions of filet mignon and lobster tail for those prices. Don't you think the cost of this program is a bit steep?"

James nodded. "I do. That's why I really hope it works. Once the money is gone, it's gone. There are no guarantees with Witness to Fitness."

Looking triumphant, Murphy wrote down his last sentence verbatim. She then closed her notebook with a satisfying thud and said, "We'll do a follow-up after your first weigh-in. How about we meet here again next week?"

James glanced over at Lucy once more. Having just said goodbye to Carter, she walked out of the diner without looking back. James was debating whether or not to follow her out when Murphy signaled to Dolly.

"You ready to order?" Dolly was obviously put out because Murphy hadn't asked for anything to eat or drink when she first arrived.

"I'm in the mood for a bacon cheeseburger, fries, and a chocolate shake." Murphy patted her flat stomach. "I had a turkey sandwich for lunch and it didn't do the trick. Not like your Clint's food, Dolly. You two know how to send people home with full stomachs and a smile."

Dolly beamed. "Aren't you sweet? I'll be right back, sugar. I'm going to make your shake extra thick, so you won't faint dead away before that burger comes."

"You knew just what to say to Dolly," James said, trying not to focus on her food order. "Look, I'd better be going."

"Sure you don't want to join me for a meal?" Murphy asked, giving James that same flirtatious grin she'd employed at Chilly Willy's grand opening. "I'm sure Dolly could fix you an egg-white omelet or something."

James couldn't tell whether she was teasing him or not. Her presence had him flustered. "I have a ten-dollar frozen dinner waiting for me at home, remember?"

Murphy laughed. "Well, maybe after your first six weeks have gone by and you've slimmed down, you can take me out for a celebratory meal. What do you say to that, Professor?"

James stood just as Dolly arrived with an enormous malt glass filled with a thick and creamy chocolate shake. James stared at the miniature mountain of whipped cream and the plump maraschino cherry sitting on top. He almost groaned watching Dolly slide the glass, napkin, and a long straw in front of Murphy. Instead, he suppressed the animalistic noise, waved at both women, and fled the diner. He drove home to a frozen meal of Salisbury steak in mushroom sauce and an evening of watching game shows with his father. Neither his food nor his entertainment succeeded in driving away his misery over failing to connect with Lucy. Not only that, but he couldn't stop thinking about Murphy's chocolate shake and wondering when he would be able to order one again.

• • •

Having attended two more exercise classes, the members of the Flab Five spent a great deal of time complaining about their various bodily pains when they got together Sunday night at Gillian's.

Gillian lived in a large and beautiful Victorian filled with a mixture of antique and contemporary furniture. James was admiring the patina on the sideboard in Gillian's dining room when her cat, Dalai Lama, entwined himself around his legs and howled. James bent over and scratched the tabby behind the ears. Dalai Lama cocked his head for more until James's hand was covered in brownish fur.

James walked stiffly into the kitchen, wincing as his sore muscles ached afresh. His friends were gathered around the counter, helping themselves to glasses of diet iced tea. Thin slices of lemon were perched around the rim of each glass.

"Your legs hurting, man?" Bennett asked, noticing how James was nearly limping.

"Killing me. It even hurts to drive." James accepted a glass of tea from Lindy.

"At least you two don't have to worry about bras." She mimed cupping her large breasts with her hands. "I'll have to buy something made out of steel if I'm going to survive the next few weeks of that class."

Everyone laughed. "I feel like I'm exorcizing negative toxins by sweating so much." Gillian turned on the oven. "I really think the positive energy of Dylan and Ronnie is starting to have a powerful effect on me. I'm actually looking forward to our weigh-in on Monday."

"I like Dylan much, much better once class is over," Lucy said. "He's a hottie, that's for sure, but he makes us work so hard that I find myself hating him somewhere between our leg lifts and tummy crunches."

James smiled at her, relieved that she didn't have a genuine crush on their instructor. Since Tuesday, he'd been so busy making arrangements for the upcoming Spring Fling that he hadn't set aside time to call Lucy following their brief meeting at the diner.

He longed to just drop by her house and profess his feelings to her, but somehow he'd never made it there. And at home, he and Jackson had spent every evening making plans for a new kitchen. James was so thrilled by his father's exuberance that he didn't want to do anything that might cause him to revert to his former state of gruff detachment. Even when James cautiously inquired about his artistic success, Jackson mumbled something about the private nature of his work, but not in the same snappish manner that he would have used a few weeks ago. He simply made it clear that his paintings were not a subject open for discussion.

However, Lindy was more than happy to tell the supper club members about Jackson's astounding sales.

"And you didn't know any of this? How did you think the old man was going to pay for that new roof?" Bennett asked as he dribbled a light Italian dressing onto his salad.

James shrugged and smiled. He didn't mind admitting that he'd been clueless. "I was pretty stressed about the expense. With the cost of Witness to Fitness, I don't have much extra cash on hand."

"Speaking of extra cash," Gillian said, waving a forkful of salad in the air. "I talked Willy into working with me and Beau Livingstone selling Pet Palaces. Beau has had so many custom orders since Christmas that he hasn't been able to focus on sales or balancing the books. Normally, I do the accounting, but with two major horse shows this spring, I've gotten behind at the Yuppie Puppy."

Lucy cocked her head. "Willy's handling your bookkeeping?"

"Yes," Gillian said. "Not only is Willy good with numbers, but he's also an expert carpenter and has a whole garage full of tools. He's been helping Beau put the finishing touches on our orders. There is truly a higher power orchestrating our destinies so that we can all benefit from one another's gifts and talents."

"That's terrific news!" Lindy clapped. "I'm so glad to hear that Willy has a source of income. I can totally see him designing a Pooch Pagoda! Gillian, you are truly a generous person."

"There's a Chinese proverb that says *A bit of fragrance always clings to the hand that gives roses.* I guess I like to smell as sweet as I can."

"You smell better than this ziti." Bennett frowned over the large aluminum tray he'd just removed from the oven. "I think it's a bit burned around the edges, but that might actually give it some flavor."

"So this is going to taste as bad as all the other meals?" James groaned. "I've practically used up all the salt in my house trying to add a little flavor to this stuff."

"It's not that bad," Lucy snapped. "You men are just too fickle."

Bennett looked surprised by the hostility in her voice and Lindy, ever the diplomat, quickly changed the subject. Gillian helped Bennett pass out plates of ziti.

"So are there any updates on the fire investigation?" she asked Lucy while sprinkling heavy amounts of salt and pepper on her entrée.

"I was going to save all that juicy stuff for dessert," Lucy said, sounding like her old self again. "The liquor bottles were analyzed at the state lab. Huckabee sent them both off for further testing because he saw some strange-looking residue in one of them. Must be a slow time for the crime lab because normally we'd have to wait weeks for the results. Instead, we got them very quickly." She paused dramatically. "It turns out that one of the bottles was coated on the inside with something that had no place being there."

Lindy gazed at Lucy in confusion. "Do you mean that it was a defective batch or a bad bottle?"

"No." Lucy took a drink of iced tea and James sensed she was enjoying stringing this out. "The bottle had traces of a drug called diazepam. That's the generic name for Valium."

"What on earth?" Bennett said. "Was old Pete trying to kill himself?"

"I don't think he'd empty Valium capsules into his whiskey if he wanted to commit suicide. He'd just swallow the pills first and then take a drink," James said. "Why go through the extra trouble?"

"The man drank, smoked, *and* abused drugs. The poor soul is probably better off in whatever plane of existence he's gone on to." Gillian sighed mournfully.

James frowned. "But he *didn't* smoke. He used chewing tobacco. I rarely saw the man without a plug. He even had one that day we all officially joined Witness to Fitness. I bet those cigarette butts belonged to someone else."

"I didn't realize you knew Pete so intimately, James," Lucy said testily before turning back to the rest of the group. "In any case, office gossip is that the blame is being laid on Pete's door, and because the insurance company isn't interested in rebuilding, they're putting all the onus on Willy for hiring Pete as an employee."

"That's a load of bull." Bennett stabbed a noodle angrily. "Willy didn't know all the details of Pete's past. The man worked at the high school for over twenty years, so he had an employment record. I'm sure Willy hired him based on that record."

"Who can say how clean that record was?" Lucy said. "If James and I knew he was a drunk back in high school, everyone else must have known it too."

"This whole thing feels real odd to me." Bennett stroked his toothbrush mustache thoughtfully. "Maybe someone *gave* that tainted bottle of whiskey to Pete. You know, with the drugs already in it."

"But that would mean . . . You think someone tried to murder Pete?" Lindy was astonished.

"Or ruin Willy," Gillian suggested. "Maybe someone else started the fire and Pete was just too out of it to escape. Remember how angry Savannah Lowndes was over the whole architecture issue?"

"Or Mrs. Emerson and her youth group over those T-shirts?" Lucy said.

Bennett uttered an exasperated moan. "Come *on*, folks. You don't think a group of God-fearing middle-aged women slipped Pete some drugged liquor and then burned down Willy's store, now do you?"

"No," Lucy said, looking slightly chastised. "That does sound far-fetched. It must have been Pete. Just Pete."

While the group cleared their dishes and loaded Gillian's dishwasher, James debated over whether or not to tell his friends about the altercation he'd witnessed between Pete Vandercamp and Ronnie Levitt outside of Witness to Fitness. As Lindy passed out chilled cups of fat-free strawberry mousse, James decided to say something.

"I saw a bizarre interaction between Pete and Ronnie," he said. "I don't know that it's relevant, but let me tell you about it." He then quickly explained what he'd seen and heard.

"So you didn't actually hear anything that was said between them once they were outside?" Lindy asked skeptically.

James loaded his spoon with mousse. "Pete was sure that he'd seen Ronnie on TV. That seemed to bother her and then, when they went outside, I could tell that she was really upset. She threatened him. It was all in her body language."

"I don't know, friend." Bennett shook his head. "You're a smart man and I'm not doubting your powers of observation, but she seemed like her spunky little self when she came back inside."

"Plus, why would Ronnie do either Pete or Willy harm?" Lindy asked. "She's just as sweet as can be and really, if you think about it, the Polar Pagoda wasn't genuine competition for her. If it did well, Ronnie would just gain more customers!"

"I think her sweetness is fake," James insisted. "I saw her mask slip a little that day, and I just do not trust that woman."

"James, darling." Gillian reached over and patted him on the back. "I think our little adventure in helping solve a murder last fall has gotten your imagination all fired up. It's possible that you're unconsciously stressed, and the tension is affecting your judgment. I have a wonderful antioxidant red tea that could restore your balance and give you clearer vision."

James clenched his fists underneath the table but kept his voice calm. "Thank you, Gillian. I don't think I need tea. I was just sharing my experience from that day. I'm sure you're right and there was nothing to it."

Lucy had remained silent during the entire exchange. James

could feel her carefully studying him, but he couldn't tell what she was thinking because her face was a blank mask. Suddenly, she shifted her gaze to Bennett and propped her elbows on the table. "It seems like Carter has settled into Quincy's Gap quite nicely."

"Yep. I think he likes the quiet life we offer here. What with all the murders and arson, who wouldn't?" Bennett snorted in amusement at his own joke.

"What I want to know is much more personal," Lucy began, her eyes sliding away from Bennett's to rest on James. She gave him a brief but challenging look and then turned back to Bennett again. "I want to know if your hunky new coworker is single."

Chapter Eight

Butter Rum Life Savers

"You've lost four pounds!" Ronnie squealed, jumping up and down on the balls of her feet. "I am so proud of you, James! Aren't you thrilled beyond belief?"

James stared at the glowing red digits of the scale and for once, didn't find them a source of anger and disappointment. In fact, they shone with triumph—his triumph—and James decided that he'd never liked the color red so much as he did at that moment. He smiled, his eyes fixed on the digits, picturing bunches of red balloons or bags of atomic fireballs. He saw the kickball they'd used on the playground at school and felt a surge of that same youthful optimism he'd felt every time he stepped up to the plate to receive his pitch. He glanced at Ronnie, who was gazing at him expectantly, and couldn't help but grin. Perhaps he'd been wrong about her. Perhaps she was completely sincere and only wanted the best for him.

"This is a good start," he said. "I'm happy to be four pounds lighter." He stepped off the scale and reluctantly watched the lit numbers disappear. "Has everyone else done well?"

Making clicking noises with her tongue, Ronnie nudged James in his doughy side with a sharp elbow. "Your only competition is with yourself, mister. Don't be concerned about anyone else's progress. Why don't you pop by Phoebe's desk and check out the menu of this week's meals? After that, you can get a head start on your stretches before your cardio class starts."

She prodded him in Phoebe's direction and beckoned for Bennett to approach the scale. Bennett looked like he was being escorted to an execution chamber. He shot James a fearful glance before reluctantly stepping on the scale.

"I hear Dylan added a few more maneuvers to tonight's routine," Phoebe teased as she accepted payment from James and another dieter. "He told me that he doesn't want you folks to get bored."

"Bored?" The woman next to James was stunned. "I'm too busy trying to stay alive to worry about being bored. I'm surprised that

I'm still breathing after his class. I hope you plan on investing in a defibrillator."

James nodded in agreement. "Personally, I'd rather have more variety with these Witness to Fitness meals than variety in my exercise class." He frowned as he looked over the menu for the upcoming week. "This isn't much different from last week's menu. I'm worried that we'll get burned out eating the same things over and over."

Phoebe held up her own copy of the menu. "I noticed that, too." Though her manner was kind, she seemed rather distracted. Her eyes never settled on anyone or anything for long and she was constantly running her fingers through her blue-black hair and tugging at its ends. James wondered if she was stressed or if her hair pulling was just a nervous habit. "I'll talk to Miss Levitt about spicing things up a bit," she promised. "But I'm glad to see that both of you made progress this week. Congratulations."

James and the woman smiled shyly at one another as they shared a moment of dieting kinship. The woman then joined the weigh-on line while James entered the exercise room to catch up with the other members of the Flab Five before their class started. The supper club ladies, having already been weighed in by Dylan, were now stretching on their blue plastic floor mats.

"Did you lose anything, James?" Lindy called out as she reached her hands out over her knees and attempted to grab the shoelaces of her left sneaker.

"Yes, I did. How about you?"

"Everyone lost!" Gillian announced happily. "Our whole supper club has experienced remarkable success. The stars must have been perfectly aligned the day you and Lindy ran into wonderful Ronnie at that superstore. I believe we were destined to be placed on the path to good health by Ronnie, Dylan, and Phoebe." Gillian clasped her hands together and sighed loudly with contentment. She then began to twist her body sideways with her arms held aloft over her head as if she were exhibiting some kind of ballet move.

Lucy cast James a look that said *I told you so* and again, he questioned whether he had completely misjudged the spunky fitness guru. But before he could dwell on the unpleasant possibility that he'd totally lost his ability to read people, Dylan bounded into the room, turned on music with a frenetic beat, and started moving from side to side. For the next forty-five minutes, all James could think about was trying to get breath into his lungs and how to put a stop to the splintering cramp running the length of his left flank.

Throughout the routine, Ronnie leapt around in the back row, encouraging those who tried to slow down or give up by letting out energetic whoops whenever Dylan asked the class to pick up the pace. She continuously winked and smiled at Dylan when she wasn't motivating her clients. He acted like he didn't notice her flirtatious expressions, but everyone else did. After twenty minutes of Ronnie's clapping, whooping, and backslapping, James's initial feelings of dislike returned. He was more than ready to smother Ronnie with one of the blue exercise mats.

Once class was over, James joined his friends outside and they limped, lurched, or staggered to Gillian's compact hybrid. She wanted to show them her newly printed catalogue featuring photos of the complete Pet Palace line.

The foursome praised the brochure, but Gillian waved off their compliments with a flick of her hand. "We would never have had such a professional layout without Willy's help. He really has an eye for graphic design. He's a man with many gifts, indeed."

"I'm glad to hear he's doing well," Lucy said. "And speaking of Willy, I can fill you in on what the deputies found when they searched Pete's house this morning. They went in looking for evidence of his drug use."

Lindy's eyes flew open. "That's right—the Valium. Oh, do tell! What did they find?"

"That's the strange thing," Lucy frowned. "The search team found nothing suspicious at his place. Nothing at all. Donovan even went to speak with Mr. Goodbee afterward. Mr. Goodbee looked up Pete's prescription history. The man never ordered any medications other than a high-powered hydrocortisone cream. Apparently, he had eczema. In short, he had no recorded history of drug use."

"So he never ordered Valium from the pharmacy?" Gillian asked.

"No. However, he could have gotten it from another pharmacy." Lucy said.

A thought suddenly occurred to James. "Lucy, did the report

mention whether or not the deputies found evidence of cigarette smoking at Pete's place—ashtrays, empty cigarette packs, burn holes in the furniture, or butts in the trash?"

Lucy stared at James in confusion. "I don't think so. They were looking for drugs and for the brand of booze he drank."

"Was it Wild Turkey?" Lindy asked. "You and James said that was his brand of choice."

"Yes, they found two bottles of his favorite whiskey. There was a bottle in the living room and one in the bedroom."

Bennett raised his brows. "But no Jack Daniel's?"

Lucy shrugged. "No, just the Wild Turkey."

"That makes two things that were out of place at the fire scene," James insisted. "Pete didn't smoke, and he probably didn't buy that bottle of Jack Daniel's."

"I have to admit that this sounds a little weird to me too." Gillian looked at her friends. "It just doesn't add up."

"Let's not get bent into pretzels over small details," Bennett said. "The man could have bought the drugs elsewhere and he might have gotten some Jack Daniel's just for the heck of it. What do we know about Pete Vandercamp and his habits? Not a thing, that's what."

The five friends grew silent. A hesitant breeze tickled the tree-tops lining the parking lot and a dog barked from one of the houses in the development behind the strip mall. Low stars gathered on the lip of the darkening horizon and a pale moon, blurred by ribbons of gossamer cloud, hung low in the sky like a pendulum.

"Despite these new findings," Lucy said, breaking the silence, "I think something is amiss with the line of reasoning. I agree with you, Gillian. Something feels wrong about the fire. If it was just a feeling, I might be able to let it pass, but the sheriff himself said something that told me that, in *his* mind, this case is far from being closed."

"Did he say something to you or to the deputies that you over-heard?" James asked, seeking clarification.

Lucy scowled at him. "Directly to me. He was leaving for lunch and he seemed really distracted. And unusually agitated. He twists the ends of his mustache all the time, but he's been twisting it so much lately that I'm afraid he's going to pull it right off. Anyway, I asked him if everything was all right and he barely heard me." Lucy stared into the middle distance, lost in the memory. "Then, he perched on the corner of my desk and told me that he couldn't believe Pete would have elected to kill himself. He said that if Pete had ever planned to do that, he would have done it years ago. And he would have used a gun. Apparently, he and Sheriff Huckabee grew up on the same street in Lacey Spring. Huckabee said that Pete was an easygoing, fun-loving guy when they were young. He married right out of high school to a girl he'd been in love with since pre-school. Sadly, his wife died before they made it to their first anniversary."

Lindy gasped. "How awful! What happened?"

"Some kind of boating accident in the Rappahannock River. She was with a bunch of friends and their boat collided with another boat. I think the girl who was driving their boat was pretty sloshed at the time. When Pete drove out to the coroner's office to identify her body, the coroner informed him that his wife had been pregnant. According to Huckabee, she was going to surprise him with the news the very next day. She'd made dinner reservations at a place they couldn't really afford and had a pair of knit booties in her purse."

"Pete had a wife." James was stunned by the revelation. He'd never viewed the alcoholic janitor as a man with a past. As someone who'd once loved a woman and had dreamed of starting a family with her. Feeling remorseful, James said, "I never thought of him in that light. He was so hostile. He muttered angrily to himself while he cleaned and shot nasty glances at all the kids. No wonder he was so miserable. No one should have to endure such a tragedy. The poor man."

"I guess some folks have the right to be angry. Pete was certainly mad at the world and everyone in it for a long time," Lucy whispered as she looked up at the rising moon. "The thing is, Huckabee believes that if Pete didn't kill himself the day he identified his wife's body, then he would survive the pain. With each day that passed, he showed that he was a survivor. Therefore, it makes no sense that he'd decide to end it all now."

"And he'd just gotten a new job. He could have made a fresh start," Bennett added.

Lucy nodded. "Huckabee actually asked me to keep my ears open. He wants me to report any whispers or shreds of gossip about Pete or Willy directly to him. He never asked for my help before, and I feel like this is my chance to prove to him that I can be a more valuable part of the department than I am now."

"We'll help too!" Gillian laid a hand on Lucy's arm. "We know you have so much to offer and that the rooster house where you work doesn't always recognize your talent and integrity. But we believe in you. Not only that, but we don't want folks believing that Pete killed himself if he didn't. The man deserves a truthful obituary."

"If he didn't commit suicide, then someone else killed him," Bennett pointed out. "But who would do that?"

"Someone who recently bought a pack of Pall Mall cigarettes," James said.

Bennett nodded. "As well as a bottle of Jack Daniel's."

"And there's still the matter of motive," Lucy said. "Sure, he was a grumpy old man, but we'd have a pile of bodies as high as the Blue Ridge Mountains if all the town's cranky geezers were suddenly murdered."

"We'll just have to dig deeper into Pete's past. There has to be some clue there that could lead us to a motive," Lindy said. "And I'd say we should pay special attention to his recent past. No one paid him an ounce of attention until he started working for Willy."

At the sound of clicking heels, they fell silent and turned to see Phoebe heading their way. She took out her car keys and unlocked the creaking door of an old and heavily battered Chevy Malibu. The driver's-side door was light blue while the rest of the car was a shade of lackluster silver, and there were deep dents and large patches of rust on all the body panels.

"Parking lot powwow?" she asked, smiling at them.

"We're drinking bottled water around the car instead of having glasses of margaritas at Nacho House," Lindy said breezily. "Plus, Gillian's new Pet Palace brochure is hot off the presses. Check out her gorgeous products."

Accepting the invitation to join them, Phoebe peered at the open brochure. "Those are the coolest doghouses I've ever seen." She flipped to the back page, where the price list was printed. "I could never afford one of these for my pooch, however." She indicated her car door. "As soon as I can save a little money, I'm going to have two silver doors on my car again. Still, good luck with these, Gillian. Good night, everyone!"

"Good night!" the five friends echoed in return.

As Phoebe drove off, the supper club members promised to delve into Pete's past and to investigate events around town for several weeks leading up to the night of the fire. Lucy declared that she would find a way to obtain copies of the sheriff's reports on both the fire and the search of Pete's house and that she'd share their contents at the next supper club meeting.

"I'm starting the detective work right now," James announced.

"By doing what?" Bennett asked as they all turned toward their own vehicles.

"I'm heading to the liquor store. It's the only one within twenty-five miles. And the manager, Danny, has a memory like a minnow trap. Once he sees your face, it goes in his mental file and never leaves again." James opened the Bronco's door and called out, "Besides, my father is out of Cutty Sark and he likes to sip it while watching *Jeopardy!*"

As James stood beside the open door, he felt that he had forgotten something. His friends waved, loaded their food into their cars, and drove off. That's when James realized what he'd left behind.

"My meals!" he yelped and jogged back inside Witness to Fitness, his legs screaming in protest. The cubicle area was still lit but the exercise room was dark and empty. James didn't see his bag of packaged food anywhere, so he called out, "It's just me, James Henry! I forgot my meals for the week. Hello?"

No one answered, so James flicked on the lights. He spied his shopping bag of entrées sitting close to Phoebe's desk and, sighing in relief, grabbed it by the handles. As he turned to leave, Ronnie came out of the kitchen area, a fuchsia towel draped around her neck. She put her hands over her heart as if startled and then broke out into a giggle.

"Oh, my! You made me jump!"

James tried to look abashed, even though he didn't believe that she'd been the slightest bit frightened. "I'm sorry to scare you. I forgot my food and I just ran back in to get it."

"Well, you can make it up to me. My silly little car won't start. I'm sure it's the battery acting up again. I made an appointment to get it fixed on Friday, but I could certainly use a sweet hero to get me home tonight."

"Sure. I can give you a lift," James replied without a trace of chivalric enthusiasm. "Where do you live?"

"In that group of town houses behind the post office. You know, those charming yellow ones with the green shutters and the pretty flower boxes?"

James nodded. The quaint block of town homes had caused quite a stir during the town planning meetings. The builder of the three-story town homes had promised to paint them a delicate shade of butter yellow. Instead, he had gotten a deal on a different hue and the group of buildings had been covered in three thick coats of an orange-yellow so blindingly bright that hordes of bees and other flower-friendly insects constantly swarmed the homes. The poor bugs apparently thought that the wooden structures were oversized marigolds bursting with nectar. The fact that all the residents overloaded their window boxes with every variety of flowers during the growing season didn't help matters, either. James had heard Bennett complain more than once about having to douse himself with bug repellent before delivering mail to the Cozy Valley Town Homes.

"I need to swing by the liquor store on the way if that's all right with you," James said, holding the front door open for Ronnie.

A cloud passed over her face as she locked the door to her business. "Alcohol is just empty calories, James."

Her patronizing tone instantly grated on him. "It's for my father. He doesn't need to diet."

Ronnie smiled her false smile, clearly doubting James at his word. "Yes, I'm sure you're just trying to be a dutiful son."

James gritted his teeth and jerked open the Bronco's passenger door. He had never been fond of sarcasm.

As he parked in front of the town's only liquor store, Ronnie pulled a fitness magazine out of her cavernous gym bag. "I'll just sit tight. This is not a business I'd ever frequent."

A bell tinkled out a greeting as James entered the store. Danny Leary looked up from a book of word puzzles and dipped his chin in a friendly nod. James located a bottle of Cutty Sark and placed it on the counter.

"You any good at word scrambles, Professor?" Danny asked, pointing at a line of letters. "I can't figure this one out to save my life. The clue is that all the words are capitals of foreign countries." He shrugged, looking embarrassed. "I never traveled farther than Kentucky, so it's not like I recognize too many of these. Still, I've got them all except for one. Can you help? I've been staring at this clue for almost an hour."

James turned the book so that it was facing him and examined the letters.

lhieniks

Danny rang up the Cutty Sark, set the brown bag to the side of the word puzzle book, and waited. James got the answer right away, but he pretended to be concentrating as hard as he could so as not to hurt Danny's feelings.

"This is a tough one, Danny. Give me a minute to stare at it."

Obviously pleased that James was stumped as well, Danny settled back on the stool he'd sat in for over twenty years. He had long white hair pulled back into a neat ponytail and he tended to chew on toothpicks, especially when working one of his puzzles. His steel-rimmed reading glasses perched low on his nose, and with his earnest face and fleshy cheeks, he often reminded people of Ben Franklin.

"Nasty business about that ice cream store," James said, hoping to introduce the topic as casually as possible.

"Sure was." Danny unwrapped a piece of gum and popped it into his mouth.

"I heard a rumor that Pete Vandercamp was found inside with a bottle of Wild Turkey and a bottle of Jack Daniel's," James said. "It doesn't sound like the Pete I used to know."

Danny shook his head. "Not a chance. Old Pete has been a Wild Turkey man all of his life. He wouldn't touch another brand. Once, he told me that Wild Turkey was his daddy's drink of choice, and Pete admired that man to no end. Too bad the guy got cancer at such a young age. Pete could have used a friend back when everything fell apart."

"When his wife was killed, you mean?" James asked, not daring to look up from the puzzle book.

"Just a year after he lost his wife, yeah. Without his daddy, Pete was alone in this world. And from that time on, he never drank another whiskey—not in all the years I've known him. I suspect I talked to him more than most folks too." Danny swallowed hard and James could see that he was upset by Pete's death. "Pete had plenty of faults, but he'd never be disloyal to his daddy's memory."

James nodded. "My father's like that with his Cutty Sark." He pivoted, examining the rows of liquor bottles behind him. "I guess someone gave Pete that bottle of Jack Daniel's."

Danny seemed interested in bringing the conversation to a close. "I reckon so. We sell quite a bit of Gentleman Jack in here, so there's no telling. But I never sold a bottle to Pete, and that's all I've got to say about that. How's your daddy doing these days?"

"Oh, he's just fine, thanks for asking. I think the answer to this clue is Helsinki, but you'd better double-check."

Danny squinted at the clue and then smiled happily. "Darned if you're not right. Thanks, Professor." Danny looked past James to the parking lot. "You got a lady friend with you?"

James controlled his feeling of revulsion so that it wasn't reflected on his face. "That's Ronnie. She owns Witness to Fitness. It's a new weight-loss program. Her car battery is dead so I'm giving her a lift home. Trust me, that's the extent of our involve- ment."

Danny removed his glasses and gave the woman in the Bronco a good look, but Ronnie had her nose buried in her magazine. Another car pulled alongside James's truck on the driver's side and a group of young men jumped out of each of the four doors. Hearing the noise, Ronnie glanced up from her magazine. Danny's eyes narrowed as he looked at Ronnie. Then, he nodded.

"I recognize her now," he said. "She's a pretty lady, if you like them skinny. I like a lady who'll eat steak and potatoes with me. Shoot, if I could find a nice woman to share a meal with, I'd be happy to do the cooking and the cleaning every night. Anyway, It's nice of you to run her home."

"I'm surprised you recognize Ronnie. She told me that she's never been in this store," James said. "Have you seen her around town?"

Danny looked offended. "She most certainly has been in my

store. It was just one time and it was a few weeks back, but it was Ronnie. I don't remember what she bought, but I remember her. You know I never forget a face, and hers is a new one in these parts. Makes her stand out."

"I guess she was making excuses so she could be alone with her magazine," James said hurriedly.

"Well, shoot. Tell the gal I don't bite," Danny said a little huffily before turning his attention to his other customers.

James cast a glance back outside to see that Ronnie was again absorbed with her reading. "So she was in here at least once," he mumbled to himself.

On the way to her town house, Ronnie chattered on about how much she adored Quincy's Gap. James grunted every now and then, but he was too preoccupied with his discovery at the liquor store to reply in full sentences.

Before he knew it, he'd turned onto the road leading to Ronnie's town house. Beneath the Victorian lampposts, a man walked a dog on what appeared to be a very long leash. He wore a hooded sweatshirt, dark pants, and a baseball cap. He seemed to be the only person outdoors and seemed to be moving at a sluggish pace. The dog pulled at the leash, eager to increase their pace, but the man refused to walk faster.

"Him again," Ronnie said in a low voice, sinking down in her seat as they passed the man.

"Do you know him?" James asked, his curiosity alerted by Ronnie's derogatory tone. He wasn't used to hearing her utter a single sentence that didn't culminate in an exclamation mark.

Ronnie stuffed her magazine back into her gym bag. "He's my creepy mailman."

"Really? Why is he creepy?"

Ronnie gestured to the town house unit on the right. "The next one's mine. And I don't know why he bothers me. I guess it's because whenever he has to deliver a package that's too big for the mail slot, he knocks on the door over and over again until I open it. And when I do, he stares at me." She laughed lightly. "I'm used to men looking at me, so it's not that. It's the *way* he looks at me. It's not flirty. It's like he's trying to see through me. I can't really explain it, but I'm sure it's nothing." She glanced out of the side mirror. "Still, it's strange to see him here. He doesn't live in one of these town houses, so why is he walking his dog on my street?"

James couldn't think of an answer to Ronnie's rhetorical question and was relieved when she gathered her belongings, jogged into her town house, and shut the door. He wanted nothing more than to take this quiet time alone to think about every detail of the Polar Pagoda fire.

Reaching into his center compartment in the hopes of finding a stick of gum, James felt his hand close on a hard roll that felt like a sleeve of nickels. When he drew the package into the light of the interior lamp, he realized he was holding a Life Savers candy roll. A roll of Butter Rum candies, to be exact. His favorite flavor.

James examined the nutritional information while backing out of Ronnie's driveway at a snail's pace. Figuring that a few candies wouldn't disrupt his weight-loss progress, he eased the Bronco onto the road and popped two Life Savers into his mouth. Sucking contentedly on the candy, James drove by the man walking his dog just as the pair moved directly beneath a pool of lamplight.

The mailman who gave Ronnie the creeps was none other than Carter Peabody.

Chapter Nine

Chocolate Croissant

James was on his way to work the next day when he remembered that it was time for the monthly staff meeting. Even Mrs. Waxman, the retired schoolteacher who helped out on evenings and weekends, showed up early for her shift in order to attend.

It had become a habit on meeting days for James to stop by the Sweet Tooth and pick out an array of homemade treats for his employees to enjoy while they slogged through library budget issues and other challenging topics. Because the staff never knew which fresh baked goodies to expect, they looked forward to the meetings with anticipation each month.

Today, James was nervous about being inside the wonderful bakery. The owner, Megan Flowers, had decorated the window with whimsical, construction paper kites and giant tissue-paper flowers in primary colors. In the center of each flower, round baskets of cinnamon buns and apple streusel muffins bloomed. Trays lined with fudge and butterscotch brownies covered a red-and-white-checked cloth and a picnic basket overflowed with French baguettes and crusty Italian semolina bread. Chocolate- dipped sugar cookies shaped like ants marched around the base of the basket. James paused to take in every detail of the tempting sight before opening the door to the cozy warmth and heavenly smell of melted butter and baked dough that was the Sweet Tooth's ever-present perfume.

"Good morning, Professor!" Megan greeted James affably while dusting flour from her hands. "I was just whipping up some raisin bread. How are you?"

James inhaled the tantalizing aroma of sugary raisins mixed with cinnamon and felt his mouth grow moist with desire. Trying to focus on anything other than the tantalizing scent, James noticed that Megan's shelves were unusually full for this time of the morning. At this time in the morning, her supply of breakfast Danishes, coffee cakes, and muffins were typically depleted. James noticed, too, that Megan seemed especially thin. Her attractive face looked pinched around the mouth and she put her flour-and- butter-encrusted hands through her brunette hair without even realizing she was coating herself as if she were readying a pan for the oven.

"Everything all right, Megan?" James asked, genuinely concerned. "How's Amelia doing in school?"

Megan smiled wearily. "She's really excelling. I am so proud of her, Professor. After all that nonsense last fall, I wasn't sure what her future would be, but she's really come around. She works super hard here and works just as hard at school." Megan held out her hands in a gesture of helplessness and laughed. "I guess it takes a murder to straighten out some teenagers!"

"That's terrific news." James grinned, remembering how surly Amelia used to be. "We've got our staff meeting today, so I thought I'd load up on some peanut butter cookies and a few white chocolate macadamia nut bars as well." James paused, his eyes feasting on the rows of delectable items encased in glass. "And I think I'll bring Pop a loaf of rye for his sandwiches and one of those raisin breads you just finished baking. He loves a slice of raisin bread with cream cheese as an afternoon snack."

Megan seemed strangely eager to fill his order. "I have to tell you, Professor," she began as she stacked the cookies and bars into a white box and then tied the box with striped string, "Amelia might be doing well in school, but I'm not sure how much longer I can afford to send her." She sighed as she wrapped and bagged the two loaves of bread. "All of a sudden, my customers are on this crazy health kick. It's like the opening of Witness to Fitness has scared them away from my business completely. Sure, some of them come in for wheat bread, and I've started making light bran muffins, but those two items are my big sellers these days. And let me tell you, it's not much fun baking bran muffins all the time."

"Hold on a minute. Even folks who haven't joined the weight-loss center are cutting back on baked goods?" James was surprised. "Surely, you have plenty of regular customers who don't need to diet."

"I do!" Megan exclaimed. "Women thin as fence rails are telling me how they now feel guilty about eating a donut once a week. They feel just as bad buying cookies for their kids. I wouldn't normally resent another woman for trying to run a successful business. But I tell you what—I resent the hell out of that Ronnie Levitt because she is killing mine!"

James looked at Megan's haggard face and offered her a sympathetic smile. "Well, I know of an upcoming event where your business will shine. I can also guarantee that no one will be thinking of Ronnie Levitt or of dieting on this particular occasion." James proceeded to discuss how he'd like the Sweet Tooth to serve as one of the major food vendors at the library's upcoming Spring Fling.

Megan was delighted. "That's just what I need, Professor! We ought to have great sales that day, and then hopefully my regulars will start coming back into the store. How can I ever thank you? Here, take a chocolate croissant on the house. I know they're a favorite of yours."

James knew that he should refuse the treat before Megan had the opportunity to put it in a bag, but he held his tongue. Watching her gather his purchases together, James's thoughts were already fast-forwarding to the moment when he could sink his teeth into the flaky layers of croissant crust and hit the soft chocolate cache hidden in its center.

The moment he was safely out of sight in his truck, he retrieved the pastry from the white paper bag and took a generous bite from one of the ends, which was baked to an appealing bronze. The rich, buttery dough caused him to moan with pleasure and sink back into his seat. He took another bite, savoring the rich chocolate filling as it coated his tongue and sank into the grooves between his teeth. Within ten seconds, the entire croissant was gone, and James was plucking crumbs off of his shirt and popping them greedily into his mouth.

"Oh, man," he whispered, simultaneously thinking of the number of calories and fat the pastry must have contained and whether or not he should buy another one. Luckily, the possibility of being late for work spurred him into putting his car into gear. Licking his lips, he eased down Main Street and began to hum along with the radio. He couldn't help but note that nothing on the torturous Witness to Fitness menu had ever given him the urge to hum.

"Life is so unfair," he muttered, switching off the radio.

The first thing James did upon arriving at work was to send the members of the Flab Five an email about his conversation with Danny Leary the night before. He also asked Lucy to make sure that the deputies had thought to collect Danny's receipts for all of his store's March credit card sales. James believed there was a slim chance that a suspect—and in his mind the primary suspect was Ronnie Levitt, though he still had no inkling what her motive was—might have charged a bottle of Jack Daniel's to his or her credit card. Lucy immediately wrote back that the receipts had been brought in and sorted as soon as Sheriff Huckabee had learned of the Valium contained in the Jack Daniel's bottle. She promised to examine them when the other deputies were out to lunch.

Satisfied, James turned his attention to library business. The afternoon staff meeting was extremely productive and James was pleased to note that all of their plans for the Spring Fling were falling into place. As he deliberated over whether to have another of Megan's sumptuous peanut butter cookies, the bell at the checkout desk rang. It was a vintage brass bell of the type once used to summon bellhops in the finer hotels, and James had purchased it from the local antique store for the infrequent times when he and his staff were tied up in their monthly meeting and patrons needed help. Their meeting was rarely interrupted for more than a few minutes at a time, but when James approached the checkout desk to the sound of arguing and the pungent scent of manure, he knew he would be tied up for much longer.

"We're here to register our pigs for the big race," the first man said, hooking his thumbs on his overall straps as he rocked on the heels of his dirt-encrusted boots.

The second man adjusted the straw cowboy hat on his head so that James could view a pair of deep-set eyes surrounded by weathered skin. "Don't know why you're bothering, Jake. No one can beat my Truffles, except maybe her sister, Jiffy Pop."

"Ha!" the other farmer bellowed, and James strongly suspected that it was the first time either man had stepped foot inside the Shenandoah County Library. "Your fat sow's got nothing on my Blossom. Why, she's as streamlined as a speeding arrow. And I've got Rutabaga fit to run, too. There's no telling how that pig's will tear up that race course." He took off an ancient John Deere baseball hat and shook it at his fellow farmer. Then, he turned to James. "Shoot, son, you may as well hand over that fifteen hundred-dollar prize right now."

James shushed both men even though he didn't see other library patrons nearby. "Gentlemen, I'm sure you both own fine animals that have excellent chances of winning." He smiled. "But you should also know that there are forty other pigs entered in this race."

The farmer named Jake scowled. "Well, in that case, sonny, I'll enter both my swine. What about you, Lenny?"

"Count me in for two pigs as well," Lenny declared boisterously, slapping three fifty-dollar bills on the counter. "At the very least, you and me should beat the tar off of old Billy Ostler."

Jake gave an irritated snap to his suspenders and harrumphed. "That rat bastard will probably juice his pigs up on some kind of special slop before the race. Remember how he fixed that Cow Pull a few years back?"

"Do I?" Lenny roared. "He didn't need the prize money anyhow! His daddy's as rich as that fellow on TV—the one who's always worried about how his hair looks."

James hurriedly handed both the farmers receipts for their entries and wished them a good day, hoping they would leave quietly. Neither man paid him any attention as they continued to reminisce about the wrongs done to them by Billy Ostler.

After they'd finally exited, James noted the muddy tracks left on the library carpet and clucked his tongue. Scott or Francis would soon be playing rock, paper, scissors to see who'd be using the carpet cleaner before the library opened tomorrow morning. James could only hope the smell of manure would dissipate over- night.

When he returned to the break room to deliver the bad news, the twins were so elated about the entry of four more pigs that they both offered to do the carpet cleaning.

Scott whipped a tiny spiral notebook out of his front shirt pocket and eagerly turned a few pages. "Four more . . . why, that makes fifty pigs in all!"

"At a cost of seventy-five bucks per entry," Francis said, sitting taller in his chair, his eyes aglow behind the thick frames of his glasses.

James wondered, for the umpteenth time, why the brothers refused to invest in contacts. They were both handsome young men, but seemed to prefer to hide behind black or tortoiseshell frames similar to those seen in films of the early fifties.

"Even after we've handed over the fifteen-hundred-dollar prize purse," Scott said, performing a little drumroll on the table, "we've already cleared more than two grand to go toward our new Tech Corner!"

Mrs. Waxman clapped gleefully. "I've collected entry fees from forty women for the Ladies' Hat Contest as well. We'll have five hundred dollars to add to that kitty after we've paid out the cash prize to the winner." She smoothed her hairsprayed coif of gray hair. "Not only that, but Shenandoah Savings and Loan agreed to donate two bonds for us to use as runner-up prizes. One is for fifty dollars and the second is for one hundred dollars!" Mrs. Waxman giggled. "Little Hugh Carmichael might be president of that bank, but whenever I approach his desk, I swear he turns back into that boy I knew in English class. The one who trembled every time I returned a graded spelling test. I think he'd hand out bonds to me just to make me go away."

James and the twins joined in her laughter. Their dream of bringing the library into the twenty-first century was looking more and more like a reality.

• • •

As the week went by, James felt buoyed by the realization that having cheated on his diet on Tuesday didn't prevent him from losing weight. Once again, he and his friends got on the scale and were pleased to see lower numbers. Their weight had decreased by four or five pounds for a second week in a row. Though the exercise classes weren't becoming any easier, James felt that he could breathe during the workouts without his lungs turning to liquid fire.

By Friday, James was feeling less elated. He barely had the energy to make it to the end of Dylan's latest routine and he was thoroughly sick of eating the bland Witness to Fitness entrées. The other supper club members who gathered around his Bronco after their exercise class that night agreed.

"I could really go for a pizza right about now," Bennett groaned. "The thought of eating that stir-fry mixture of rubber bands and cardboard vegetables does *not* make me want to rush on home."

"Forget pizza. How about a spicy cheese and chicken enchilada?" Lindy sighed. "The Witness to Fitness Mexican Marvel dinner tasted like tree bark in red sauce. I don't think Ronnie's ever had real Mexican food."

"There are a few of those dinners that I just can't swallow," Lucy said. "I actually had a Happy Meal yesterday for dinner instead of that package of fettuccine and broccoli. I took one whiff of that as it came out of the oven and got right in my Jeep." She laughed. "I don't like broccoli as it is, but boy, that stuff smelled awful, like a chemistry experiment gone bad."

"I've been adding organic sea salt to all of my meals," Gillian confessed. "I don't think they're bad, they just lack a sense of complexity." She looked at her friends. "Let's not talk about food anymore. Does anyone have a report on Pete or the fire?"

"I do!" Lindy exclaimed. "Not a breakthrough on the case per se, but I did find out that Pete was kind of chummy with one of the history teachers from school. Mr. Wimple has long since retired, but, according to a teacher who's been at Blue Ridge High forever, this man was the only person Pete ever talked to. As you and Lucy might remember, Pete muttered to himself and grumbled in the general direction of students. He wasn't exactly friendly with the other teachers or staff members either. He didn't socialize with any of them. Only Mr. Wimple."

"Where's Mr. Wimple now?" James asked.

"Wandering Springs. It's a nursing home." Lindy pulled a piece of paper from her purse. "It's over in Harrisonburg. I have the directions here, along with Saturday's visiting hours, but I can't check the place out because I'm going to visit my parents in DC this weekend. Can anyone else go? Mr. Wimple might know something about Pete that we won't be able to discover on our own."

"Count me out," Bennett said. "I have to cover for Carter. He says he has something important planned for Saturday, so I'm taking his shift."

Gillian shook her head forcefully. "Sorry, but I have two horse shows. It'll be by the grace of Buddha that I'll even have the strength to make it to our Sunday dinner."

"James? Lucy? What about you two?" Lindy asked.

"I can go," James answered quickly.

Lucy hesitated before saying. "I'm free, too."

"Great!" Lindy smiled. "Lucy, did you have any inside news from the sheriff's department?"

Lucy shook her head. "I looked through the credit card receipts from the liquor store, but none of the customers have any connection to Pete. There weren't too many of them, either. You know most folks around here still like to pay for things with cash."

"So we're at a dead end." Bennett kicked at a stone with his shoe.

"I hope you and James can learn something from Mr. Wimple," Gillian said and slung her gym bag over her shoulder. James grinned at the sight of her orange hair, neon yellow bag, and shimmering purple tracksuit.

"We'll do our best," James promised. Suddenly, an image of Lucy's filthy Jeep surfaced in his mind. "Oh, and Lucy, I'll drive. Pick you up at ten?"

• • •

James couldn't believe his eyes when he and Lucy pulled up to Wandering Springs. The building, which resembled a miniature Monticello, had a manicured lawn and a sweeping gravel drive flanked by azalea bushes in an array of magnificent hues, from delicate pinks to fiery crimsons and oranges. Stately magnolias and tall pines studded the tidy grass and rows of dogwood trees flanked the road leading to the visitor parking area. Off to the side, beyond the front lawn, James noticed that the walking paths were congested with groups of elderly residents. A woman dressed in a kimono was singing from the center of a wooden bridge in the middle of a Japanese garden. Hummingbirds and bumblebees filled the air with industrious buzzing and a variety of bird feeders attracted groups of goldfinches, cardinals, and bluebirds.

"If this is what old age has in store, bring it on," James said, glancing around in admiration.

Lucy inhaled deeply. "Count me in, too. Even the air is restful here."

James glanced over at Lucy and smiled. She'd seemed tense and unusually taciturn during the forty-minute ride from Quincy's Gap to Harrisonburg. James had tried to coax a smile from her by recounting the tale of the two pig farmers, and she managed a tight grin when he listed the names of some of the cloven-hoofed racers, but she didn't seem very interested. After trying to coax her into conversation, James gave up. After all, every time she did speak, Lucy went out of her way to mention Carter. She talked about how much she liked him for being a dog lover and kept wondering what was so special about this Saturday for the hottest new mail carrier in town.

"It must have been important, or he wouldn't have asked Bennett to cover his postal route," she'd said, continuing her conjecture.

It was all James could do not to tell Lucy that Carter was undoubtedly smitten with Ronnie Levitt. Why else would the man walk his dog in a different neighborhood if not to catch a glimpse of the woman he admired? But James had kept silent. The last thing he'd wanted to do was draw Lucy into an argument.

Finally, James had resorted to rehashing details of the Polar Pagoda fire. Happy to find common ground, they'd discussed the investigation until arriving at the nursing home.

Despite the choppy beginning to their day of investigation, James felt a renewed sense of hope as they mounted the sweeping stairs leading to the brick mansion's elegant front doors. Inside, a willowy blonde seated at an ornately carved oak reception desk greeted them warmly when they asked if they might pay a visit to Fred Wimple.

"Oh, he'll get a kick out of talking about his days as a teacher," the blonde assured them. She directed them along a plush carpeted hall that led to the back of the building. "Mr. Wimple likes to read al fresco from midmorning tea until lunch, so I'm certain we'll find him on the sunporch, his nose buried in a book."

Lucy was craning her neck as they passed large oil paintings in gilt frames and magnificent pieces of antique furniture. "How many residents do you have?" she asked.

"About sixty. We keep it cozy so that it feels more like a home filled with extended family rather than a second-rate hotel or, heaven forbid, a hospital." They reached an intersection with another hallway and the blonde gestured gracefully to each side. "Our dining room and kitchen are to the left and we have exercise facilities, a music room, and a media center to the right. All of our residents live on the second floor. Every room has a private bath."

"This place must cost a fortune!" James blurted.

The blonde slowed her pace. "It's not inexpensive, that's true, but the people who live here are genuinely happy. They don't feel like they've been left to rot. Instead, they feel like they've been given a special place where they can live out their golden days in peace and comfort." She held open a heavy door leading out to a wide sunlit porch. Several men and women were reading in wicker rocking chairs with plump cushions, and a foursome were playing hearts as they sipped on glasses of cool tea. The sound of soft jazz floated through speakers tucked beneath the eaves, and a gardener was carefully pruning the hedge growing alongside the porch.

"This is heavenly," Lucy said.

The blonde smiled. "That's Mr. Wimple in the corner. He's wearing a gray vest. Oh, and I'm Trish. Come find me at my desk if you need anything. Someone will be popping by shortly to see if any of the residents are thirsty. Feel free to have a glass of our homemade limeade. It's on us. Enjoy your visit!"

Lucy moved forward in order to introduce herself to Mr. Wimple. He was a slim and dignified-looking octogenarian with thick wavy white hair and a large forehead. In addition to his vest, he wore a pair of comfortable chinos and leather house slippers. His hands shook slightly as he turned the pages of his book.

"Mr. Wimple?" Lucy interrupted him using a soft voice. "We came to talk to you about someone we believe you knew fairly well." She introduced both herself and James. "We heard you were a friend of Pete Vandercamp's."

"Yes, I was," said Mr. Wimple sadly. "And I must tell you that I was truly shocked to read about his death in the paper. Did you say that you work for the sheriff's department?" he asked Lucy.

"That's right," Lucy replied without batting an eye. "You see, a friend of ours teaches at Blue Ridge High, and she thought you might be able to shed some light on Pete's past. That's why we came, Mr. Wimple. We aren't convinced that Pete Vandercamp's death was a suicide, but we really don't want to disturb you if it's too upsetting to talk about."

Mr. Wimple slowly closed his book and removed his reading glasses. He studied Lucy and James for a few moments with a pair of shrewd, intelligent eyes and seemed to come to a decision. "Call me Fred. My days of being the teacher known as Mr. Wimple are long over. Young lady, do you really think I could be of assistance? Because I'd like to help if I'm able."

James spread his hands. "No one really knew Pete. We might have thought we did, but we only knew glimpses—small parts that he showed the outside world. I believe there was far more to him than what we saw."

Fred Wimple appeared to consider James's words very carefully. He turned and stared out across the wide expanse of lawn and didn't speak for a long moment. Finally, he laced his fingers together and looked at James. "Tell me everything you know about the fire. If we work backward from Pete's death, we might be able to fill in the blanks."

Lucy told Fred everything she'd witnessed the night the Polar Pagoda burned. She then went on to share the contents of the fire investigator's report, the sheriff's department file, and the conclusions drawn by Willy's insurance company. As she talked, James let his gaze travel over the lush and verdant greenery beyond the porch. A muscular young man wearing athletic shorts and a tight T-shirt wheeled an elderly man down one of the garden paths. James recognized the young man immediately as Dylan Shane. He decided not to hail him or wave hello because he didn't want to distract Fred Wimple.

When Lucy was done, Fred flagged down a woman taking orders for refreshments. He asked for three limeades and something to nibble on. When the woman moved off, he cleared his throat and said, "Peter didn't smoke cigarettes and he didn't use prescription drugs. I may not have seen him every day of his life, but I knew his habits—both the good and the bad." Fred's voice turned wobbly. "The whiskey was his biggest demon, followed by the desire to stuff his cheek with chewing tobacco. Believe me, those two did enough damage to my friend."

Lucy made a sympathetic noise.

"I don't know whether you remember Danny Leary, the owner of the only liquor store in Quincy's Gap, but Danny doesn't believe that Peter would ever have purchased a bottle of Jack Daniel's. Would you agree?" James asked.

"Yes. Mr. Leary had the right of it in telling you Peter would only buy one brand of whiskey. My young friends, someone else dropped those cigarette butts at the scene of the fire and someone else brought our Peter that bottle of Jack Daniel's."

James and Lucy nodded. They'd already come to these conclusions. "Do you have any idea who his enemies might have been?" Lucy asked.

Fred shrugged. "In all honesty, Peter was Peter's worst enemy. He punished himself day after day for not being with Ginny, his wife, the day she was killed. The whole world knows it wasn't his fault. Shoot, he wasn't even invited because it was an outing just for womenfolk, but that didn't stop him from blaming himself."

Fred smiled as he accepted a cold glass of limeade from the woman in a yellow uniform. She served each of them a tall glass of limeade and placed a bowl of pretzels in the middle of the table.

"Thank you, Mabel," Fred said.

The woman moved off to serve the other residents. After taking a sip of his limeade, Fred continued. "Peter and I shared a bond of loss, so to speak. My twin brother was killed in the Korean War. He actually died trying to protect me. Because of that, I understood the kind of guilt and grief that ate Peter up inside. Neither of us were men with many friends, but we spent time together. I don't partake of alcohol and I tried to be a positive influence on Peter. I don't know that I did him much good. Peter wasn't a popular man, that's for certain, but he never wronged anyone. He wasn't kind, he didn't smile, but the man Ginny fell in love with was still in there, deep down. And he was a decent man."

James reached for his own limeade. He could practically feel the sugar slide down his eager throat. Lucy finished her drink in four thirsty swallows and delicately dabbed her lips with a paper cocktail napkin. "Anyone could see that Pete was unhappy. That's why the authorities, with the exception of my boss, accept the ruling of suicide."

"Yes, Peter was unhappy." Fred nodded in reluctant agreement. "But he was trying to turn things around. I saw him just a few days before the fire. He was really looking forward to working with Willy. Peter saw him as a fellow survivor and genuinely admired the fellow. There was a connection between the two men, and I saw it as Peter turning over a new leaf." Fred leaned over and clutched Lucy's forearm. "If Peter was killed, then his enemy is someone I don't know. Peter associated with very few people. He was a true loner."

Lucy shot a quick glance at James as it to say that it was time for them to go. She clearly had no more questions to ask, so she put her hand over Fred's and said, "Thank you for your help. I'm more convinced than ever that Pete was murdered. We just have no idea why."

Fred leaned back in his chair, looking suddenly weary. When he spoke, however, his voice was strong and determined. "Peter was gruff. I know what he was like. He must have said something that made his killer very angry. Enraged. Find out who he talked to and I bet you'll find your man." He gripped Lucy's forearm. "And please let me know what you discover. I'd like to know the truth. I may be an old man, but my mind's still sharp as a razor blade."

James shook Fred's hand and thanked him for his time. He and Lucy promised to keep him informed and to return to Wandering Springs if they had any significant information to share. On the way out, James led Lucy around the outside of the house toward the walking paths curving through the back gardens.

"Why are we going this way, James?" Lucy asked curiously.

"I think I saw Dylan earlier. This must be the nursing home where he volunteers."

Lucy immediately brightened. "Wouldn't that be a coincidence? You're right! There he is, reading the paper to that man dozing in the wheelchair."

Lucy and James approached Dylan and called out a greeting. At first, Dylan seemed stunned to see them at Wandering Springs, but after they explained that they had come to visit Mr. Wimple, he smiled. "Fred doesn't get many visitors. His folks were really well off, but money doesn't do you much good if there's no one to spend it on. It was nice of you both to hang out with him."

"Well, we wanted to question him about—" Lucy began.

"Local Quincy's Gap history stuff," James quickly interrupted. Lucy gave him a look of annoyance, but before she could say anything, the man in the wheelchair suddenly woke from his snooze.

"Hello, kids," he croaked sleepily. "You all heading to the ball game with my son?" He gazed up at Dylan with pride.

"No, Randolph." Dylan patted the older man tenderly on the shoulder. "These folks are here to see another friend."

"Well, stop on over to our house afterward and we'll fix you some supper. My Louise just loves to cook for you kids after one of our boy's big games. Best point guard in the whole of Miami-Dade County, yes, indeed!"

"Thank you, sir. We'd be delighted to come," Lucy said, and Dylan gave her a grateful wink.

Dylan then leaned forward and whispered, "He's got Alzheimer's, poor man. He thinks I'm his son." He began pushing the wheelchair forward toward the Japanese garden James had seen from the parking lot. "Phoebe is here today, too. She's been singing Chinese folk songs for the residents. They think she's Japanese because she's wearing a kimono. She rented it from a party store and is going to host an Asian tea ceremony later this afternoon. The residents are really excited. Would you like to stay?"

"We'd love to," James said. "Unfortunately, I still have tons of work ahead of me if I'm going to be ready for the library's Spring Fling."

"Okay, then. You two have a nice day and I'll see you in class on Monday." Dylan smiled warmly before continuing on his way. As he pushed Randolph slowly down the path, he hummed a song to the older gentleman.

"Why did you lie to him?" Lucy asked angrily once they were back in the Bronco.

"Dylan's a stranger, Lucy. As much as I like him, we can't trust anyone we don't know. Not until we find out what happened to Pete."

"Oh, please." Lucy sighed in disgust. "I suppose Carter and Phoebe are suspects, too?"

"As a matter of fact, they are!" James snapped. "Any stranger is suspect. No one was interested in Pete's existence until this group of newcomers came to Quincy's Gap."

"Come on, James!" Lucy scoffed. "Next you'll be adding Willy to that list."

James scowled. "Willy was at the Brunswick stew supper, as was Savannah Lowndes, Mrs. Emerson, and the rest of us. He could hardly have burned down his own building from the firehouse."

"Well, neither could Ronnie. She was at the dinner too," Lucy said triumphantly. "Not only does Ronnie have an iron-clad alibi, but so does Carter."

"Good for him," James mumbled miserably.

The rest of the drive home was marked by a sulky silence.

Chapter Ten

Corn Dog

Over the next two weeks, the members of the Flab Five thought of every excuse they could to bring up Pete's name to the individuals who'd recently moved to Quincy's Gap. Bennett talked to Carter at work and Gillian questioned Willy as he was painting a pink San Francisco Doggie Town House on the front lawn of his rental house. Lucy and Lindy divided the task of grilling Phoebe, Ronnie, and Dylan during one of their weigh-in sessions, and James even talked to Savannah Lowndes and Mrs. Emerson after church. None of the supper club members discovered anything useful.

"All I learned is that my man Carter seems to have it bad for Ronnie," Bennett said at tonight's meeting. He shook his head, perplexed. "She's not the kind of woman I favor, but Carter likes everything about her."

"How do you know he's interested in Ronnie?" Lucy asked while violently stabbing a piece of chicken with her fork.

"Oh, he's always pestering me for little details about her. Where'd she come from? What did she do before Witness to Fitness? As if *I* knew or cared to know." Bennett smoothed his mustache, a sympathetic look in his eye. "That boy can barely concentrate on delivering the mail. Sometimes, I see him just staring off into space when he's supposed to be sorting letters. Shoot, I haven't seen a man moon over a woman this badly since the hound dog I had as a kid fell for the beagle next door. Too bad they were both males." Bennett chuckled.

Noting Lucy's stormy expression, Lindy said, "Ronnie's too old for Carter."

"She most definitely is not!" Gillian bristled. "Men can date women ten years younger and no one blinks an eye, so why can't women do the same? True, Ronnie might be closer to her fortieth birthday than her thirtieth, but she has a young and energetic spirit. Not only that, but *women* get better and better with age."

"Kind of like wine?" James teased.

"More like a priceless antique," Gillian continued. "All of that life experience only increases one's beauty and appeal."

Lindy tossed a lock of hair behind her shoulder. "Well, if I can look as good as Ronnie by this time next year, I'll be very happy."

"Please don't strive for that." James sighed. "Lose some weight if you want, Lindy, but don't end up resembling a praying mantis. All three of you ladies look like real women, which is pretty attractive in my book."

"Why, James Henry!" Lindy smiled, placing her hand above her heart. "Don't you just say the sweetest things?"

• • •

Later that week, James reluctantly agreed to grant Murphy Alistair an interview concerning his current weight-loss progress in exchange for some front-page publicity for the upcoming Spring Fling.

"This sounds like a fund-raiser to beat all fund-raisers," Murphy said as she took notes on the details of the festival. "Pig races? This is surely going to be a Saturday to remember. Sometimes, all it takes is a little competition and presto! you've got a crowd. I've been working on my hat entry for the last two nights." She winked at him coyly. "I don't suppose I have an 'in' with one of the judges, now do I?"

James felt his neck growing warm. "Mrs. Waxman and two of the library volunteers are judging the hat contest. I'm going to help the twins manage the pig races. Though the closer we get to Saturday, the more I wonder what we've gotten ourselves into."

Murphy swatted the air in dismissal. "Come on, what's the worst that can happen? Even if one of those pink speed demons races right off the track, we can just grab the little oinker and enjoy fresh ham and bacon for dinner!" Murphy gave James a playful nudge. "I'm just kidding. I think pigs make great pets and I'd never hurt one. Anyway, how are you planning to contain the thoroughbred swine?"

"With hay bales," James said with a frown. "I'm wondering if I ordered enough. Can pigs jump?"

Murphy laughed. "Most people wonder if they can fly, but jump? Oh, I am *so* bringing an extra memory card for my camera." She flipped open a notebook and uncapped a pen. "By the way," she said without looking up, "your weight loss is really beginning to show. I guess all the pain has been worth it. The question is, how long do you plan to stick with it?"

James had asked himself the same thing and told Murphy as much. "I just can't stomach the idea of eating those entrées much longer. If I could make my own food, I could hang on for months. In fact, I might be able to make permanent changes in how I shop and cook food." He opened the top drawer of his desk, where a package of Twinkies nestled among loose rubber bands and paper clips. "Can you see the evidence of my dissatisfaction? I'm starting to buy junk food again merely to inject some taste into my mouth during the course of the day."

Murphy scribbled on her pad. "What if you could make your own meals using a cookbook filled with healthy recipes? Is that realistic? Lots of professionals don't have time to cook every night."

"I could buy some light frozen entrées if I were too busy," James said. "But I honestly don't mind cooking. I like the way the kitchen fills with aromas. The whole experience reminds me of my mother. I cook for my father most nights anyway. He doesn't know how to boil an egg and I can whip up a decent omelet and much more besides that."

"A sensitive man with a multitude of talents." Murphy nibbled on the end of her pen and stared intently at James. "I can't believe Dolly hasn't gotten you married off yet."

James noted the glint in Murphy's eyes, which shifted from gray to green depending on the light, and hastily changed the subject. Leaning closer, he whispered conspiratorially, "Listen, Murphy. There's something really strange about the Witness to Fitness meals."

"Aside from their bad taste?" Murphy's eyebrows rose up her forehead.

"Yes." James hesitated and then decided to take the plunge. "I think they're the same as the other frozen entrées from the grocery store. You know, like Lean Cuisine and Smart Ones?"

"As in, they taste the same?"

"As in, they're identical. I think Ronnie is just repackaging the frozen meals in foil containers." He watched as Murphy absorbed what he was suggesting. "For example, she gave us this ziti entrée again this week. We have it every week. Well, I bought one of the ziti entrées from Food Lion's freezer section and put the two meals side by side, and I think they're the same product."

Murphy considered the implications of what he was saying. "We're talking about a possible case of fraud here. Especially with the amount you're being charged for meals." She slammed her notebook shut, jumped out of her chair, and pulled a large black satchel over her shoulder. "I'd better check this out right away. This could be a big story."

James also stood. He threw out his hands and said, "But what if I'm wrong? It's just a theory. I don't want to damage anyone's reputation."

Murphy smiled indulgently. "Don't worry, Professor. Nothing will be printed in black and white without solid research. I'm nothing if not thorough." She turned to leave. "I'll let you know what I discover before the story goes to press. If there is a story. Deal?"

"Okay," James agreed quietly.

"And don't worry about promotion for your event," Murphy threw back over her shoulder. "Your Spring Fling will be on the front page for the rest of this week. After all, you have an 'in' at the *Star*!"

• • •

James was almost afraid to open his eyes that Saturday morning. The local news had predicted a day of scattered storms, and the entire Spring Fling event was outdoors. Every event, from the pig races to the kids' games, was meant to take place beneath a cloudless blue sky.

Feeling groggy and slow, James got out of bed, stuffed his feet into an ancient pair of maroon slippers, and pried his bedroom curtains apart just enough to catch a glimpse outside.

"Eureka," he whispered in relief. Though overcast, the sun was elbowing its way through the dense knot of gray clouds, creating ribbons of peach and salmon near the horizon. In the east, light scored marks over the shadowy trees and gently eased the darkness from the woods.

James exhaled happily. Fully awake now, he felt a rush of inexplicable optimism and joy. It was going to be a glorious day. He could feel it in his bones.

Throwing on his favorite pair of jeans, which had become distinctly loose at the waist and baggy in the rear, James was pleased to note that he was pulling his brown leather belt a full two notches tighter than when he'd first begun the Witness to Fitness program.

Even though it was barely seven in the morning, Jackson was already on his second cup of coffee and was engaged in a lively debate with the plumber over which brand of toilet was superior to all others on the market. Their voices echoed around the gutted kitchen and carried noisily up the stairs.

"You going to stay and help us install the pipes, Professor?" the young man named P.J. asked with a sly grin.

"You know he's got to raise money for the library today," Jackson said. "It's men like you and me, the guys who can't get a single crossword clue right, that have to get down and dirty." He eyed James seriously. "Still, it's never too late to show a young dog a trick or two. Maybe tomorrow, you and I will have a little Carpentry 101." He chuckled. "Isn't that what they call them classes at college? 101 or 500 whatever?"

"Yes, Pop. That's what they're called." James filled his thermos from the coffeepot, which had been moved to the downstairs bathroom. "I'd really like to be handier. I know I'm not much good with tools, but I'd like to learn."

Jackson looked pleased. "Well, you'd best get a move on," he said. "You've been sleeping like Rapunzel and those computers you want are going to cost a pretty penny, so it's time to go get lots of pennies."

James almost corrected Jackson's choice of fairy-tale heroine. However, he considered the overall atmosphere of harmony in the house and decided to let it go.

"That's Sleeping Beauty, old-timer," P.J. said and threw Jackson a look of mock disdain. "Didn't you pay attention in school?"

"Listen here, you little whippersnapper. No school has ever seen a boy take to shop class like I did. Why, they had to come up with all new projects just to keep me busy. By the end of high school, I was teachin' the teacher!"

P.J. was clearly impressed. "So *you're* the one who came up with that tissue holder project. Thanks a lot, man." He clapped Jackson on the back.

Jackson grumbled something unintelligible and James left the two men alone to create an even bigger mess in the kitchen and to add to the growing tower of rubble in the backyard. Somehow, tearing their house apart had brought the Henry men together, so James didn't care how much clutter stacked up on the lawn. He hadn't felt this close to his father in years and it added another level of zip to his step.

• • •

At the field where the Spring Fling was being held, Scott and Francis were busy showing vendors where to set up their stalls. In addition to the two large food booths—Dolly's Diner and the Sweet Tooth—James had reached out to another pair of vendors. These were Doggone It! Hot Dogs and Italian Sausages from Culpeper, and The Way to San Jose, a Tex-Mex restaurant out of Blacksburg.

An area farmer had sold James a mountain of hay bales and several volunteers transformed them into a pig's racetrack. Other than a few extra hay bales behind the racetrack, there was no seating for spectators, but James knew that most people stood for the event anyway. How could one sit with five heats of pigs snorting and scrambling their way around a dusty circle while people wildly screamed out their names? James also lived in the kind of town where the hay seats would be reserved for the elderly, disabled, or pregnant women of the community. It was simply one of the many unspoken codes practiced by small towns all across the South. Another such code was to arrive at a fair in a state of near-starvation—breakfast skipped and stomachs churning—so that each and every type of food could be sampled before the day was over.

Megan Flowers came prepared for a ravenous crowd. James was amazed at the sheer number of sweets she had baked and at the amount she planned on making throughout the day.

"Like my deep fryer?" she asked James cheerily. "I'm going to fry Oreos and Twinkies and Rice Krispy bars. They were all the rage at the state fair this year. We're also serving homemade raspberry lemonade. I hope we have huge lines, Professor, because some of

Amelia's friends from school have volunteered to help out. We're crossing our fingers that today turns things around for the Sweet Tooth."

Amelia appeared next to her mother bearing a large tray piled high with layers of frosted sugar cookies.

"Look at these, Professor. Amelia came up with the design." Megan put a proud arm around her daughter's shoulders. "We call them our 'bestseller' cookies. Here, try one."

Megan placed a cookie on a paper napkin and handed it to James.

"It's almost too pretty to eat," James said. Each cookie was shaped like an open book. V Colored frosting formed the edges of the book covers and thin black lines of icing created the appearance of stacked pages. On one of the open pages, a single word had been written. James's cookie James said *Wisdom*. Wriggly stripes of chocolate, which were supposed to represent lines of text, covered the other open page.

"We put words on all the cookies to remind folks how much we cherish our library." Megan gestured at the cookie tray. James read the other terms aloud. "Community, Friendship, Fellowship, Knowledge, Exploration, Discovery, Love." He raised his eyebrows. "Love?"

"Hey, you have self-help books, don't you?" Amelia said. "Those kinds of books are all about loving yourself and others. Do I need to mention Dr. Phil?"

James bit into his cookie, chewed, and smiled. "Amelia, if the clothes you design are half as wonderful as these cookies, you will take the fashion world by storm. You are an extremely creative and talented young woman."

Amelia blushed prettily and moved away to unload more baked goods from her mother's van. James could see cardboard cartons mounded with chocolate brownies, butterscotch squares, éclairs, donuts on sticks, pretzels with dipping sauces, miniature Key lime tarts, bite-sized cheesecakes, and slices of pecan, chess, and Megan's mouthwatering caramel apple crumb streusel pie.

"You're going to make a killing," James said, tearing his eyes away from the hoard of tempting treats inside the van. "I'd better get out of here before I hijack that vehicle."

"Stop by later and we'll fix you a whole sampler plate. On the house, of course. If things go well today, you might just have saved our business, Professor." Megan tied an apron around her narrow waist and began taping price lists to the front of one of the many folding tables set up to display her wares. Beneath a second small tent, Amelia started assembling the largest deep fryer James had ever seen. As James walked off, he thought he heard both women humming softly as they worked.

After leaving the bakery stall, he stopped at the other food booths to welcome the vendors. He finished by checking on Dolly and Clint.

"You've got a winner with today's event, Professor," Dolly said, reaching out to hug him.

"Only because you're here." James tried to give her a brief hug, but once Dolly got her arms around someone, it was difficult to break free. Luckily, Clint called her name and she released James to help her husband arrange the chafing dishes.

After James took several sips of coffee from his thermos, he helped Scott and Francis test the security of the pigpen. The twins had used hay bales and chicken wire to contain the droves of pigs awaiting their chance to race. Both Jake and Lenny, the two farmers who'd muddied the library carpet, arrived shortly after eight to construct the starting gates and to make final adjustments to the racecourse.

"It was awfully kind of you to help us out with this, gentlemen," James said.

"Never mind that, sonny," Jake said, shifting a wad of bubble gum from one cheek to another. "We want to make sure we know the turf so when that rat bastard Billy Ostler tries to pull some of his shenanigans, we'll be ready for him."

"Yes, sir," Lenny added, shifting his straw hat back and forth on his head as if scratching an itch. "It's going to be a Shenandoah pig that wins this here race."

After spending an hour working on the racetrack, James pulled yet another piece of straw from the inside of his sock and decided to leave the swine containment in the capable hands of the farmers and the Fitzgerald twins. He was not surprised by the brothers' adeptness at construction and engineering. After all, they'd built the winning float for the town's Halloween parade and had claimed a handsome cash prize on the library's behalf. James watched them for a few minutes, his expression reflecting the affection he felt for the two younger men, and then marched off to visit Mrs. Waxman and her troop of volunteers.

Mrs. Waxman was calling out orders in the same voice she once employed to settle down a classroom full of rowdy students. Middle-aged women fluttered to and fro, placing trash cans around the field, decorating the table where the entrance tickets would be sold, and arranging the judging area for the Ladies' Hat Contest. They jumped to obey their supervisor like fresh army recruits, and James wouldn't have been surprised if Mrs. Waxman suddenly produced a whistle and commanded her troops to "fall in." Still, the bustling women seemed utterly content as they fretted over who should be in charge of the cash box and whether the portable toilets would arrive before the attendees.

The ride vendors had arrived the evening before, so the merry-go-round, Tilt-A-Whirl, spinning teacups, magic train ride, and Ferris wheel were all in place. The operators double-checked their machines, making sure they were set to receive scores of adventurous children and adults. James knew the air would soon be permeated with squeals and screams, and though he was not a fan of rides, he wouldn't mind a turn on the Ferris wheel, provided he had company. He decided to ask Lucy to accompany him and looked around to see if any of his supper club friends had arrived yet.

The next hour sped by as James ran around the makeshift fairground chatting with the vendors, ticket takers, volunteers, and delighted townsfolk.

At noon, he positioned himself at the racetrack to watch the five heats of pigs take two turns around the circle. The crowd laughed and cheered, and James felt like a five-year-old boy as he witnessed his first pig race. There was something extremely comical about the frantic movement of their rotund bodies and their stumpy pink legs, and James whistled and hooted along with the rest of the spectators.

He saw Farmer Jake celebrating after his Rutabaga won the first heat. A young couple in overalls won the second heat with a pig named Pork Chops. Jake's friend Lenny was the victor of the third heat. He scooped up Truffles and gave her a kiss on her snout. A young girl of about seven took the fourth heat, and a man dressed in a pale blue suit and a white cowboy hat decorated with a band of turquoise studs won the final heat. James noticed Jake and Lenny sneering at their finely attired competitor and James could only assume that he was looking at the notorious Billy Ostler.

When the final herd of pigs were shuttled into the starting gates to await the onset of the championship race, two things became clear to everyone in the audience. The first was that Billy Ostler's black pig named Stallion was twice the size of all the others and that Chester, the white pig with the black splotches on its flanks belonging to the little girl, was far smaller than its competitors.

As the announcers spoke the names of the pigs and their owners, the excitement of the crowd seemed to crescendo. When Chester's name was called, the townsfolk roared their support. The little girl, whose name was Becky Abram, beamed with pride. James noticed that her clothes were ill fitting and faded and that she held the hands of two smaller children, most likely siblings, who were dressed just as shabbily. Behind Becky, a weary-looking woman balanced an infant on one hip while a toddler tugged insistently at her worn shirt. Another small child was perched high on the shoulders of a lanky man. James assumed he must be the patriarch of the large clan. Like his wife, he wore patched jeans and a threadbare plaid shirt.

James looked back at Chester and thought about how much his family could use the prize money he might win. But Chester was so small—a veritable runt in a field of racing giants. Stallion looked like he would devour the little pig as soon as the race began. It must have been a fluke that Chester had won his qualifying heat in the first place. Glancing around, James saw that the other spectators seemed to be assessing Chester's chances with the same hopeless looks, but before anyone could ponder the dismal situation any further, a loud horn sounded, and the gates snapped open. The race was on!

James leaned forward so he wouldn't miss the pigs battling for an early lead. Stallion swung his massive head against Truffles's hip and the smaller pink pig stumbled and lost the advantage. From the corner of his eye, James saw Lenny shout in anger as Billy Ostler grinned wickedly and cheered on his pig. Stallion decided to bully Pork Chops next by pressing up against his rival until Pork Chops was forced to run smack into one of the hay bales. Squealing, he fell down with only one lap to go.

That's when Stallion made his fatal error. In the lead, Jake's pig, Rutabaga, grunted noisily along the course, dust flying from beneath his dirty hooves. Stallion was closing in on him rapidly, and with so few feet of track to go, it looked like the race would end in a draw, but at the last second, Stallion turned his head to the side, opened his hairy mouth, and tried to bite Rutabaga on the front leg. Distracted, both pigs slowed down enough for Chester to shoot by. The diminutive pig had run the entire two laps at the rear of the pack, successfully avoiding Stallion's bullying, and crossed the finish line a snout ahead of his competitors.

The crowd went wild. They tossed their baseball caps into the air and exchanged celebratory hugs. James hollered as loudly as his neighbors and returned a round of merry embraces and high fives. Taking the envelope containing the sizeable check for the first-place winner from his pants pocket, James threaded his way to Becky Abram and moved to the front of the assemblage gathered to congratulate Chester's family.

James shook hands with Becky's parents. He then knelt down to present Becky with the check.

"As they say in *Charlotte's Web*, that's some pig you have there, Becky."

Becky accepted the check, her face glowing with happiness. "I begged Mama to let me enter Chester in the race. He's a pig with the heart of a lion. I had to use my allowance and my Christmas money to enter, and Daddy was real mad when he found out, but I guess it's all right now, isn't it, Daddy?"

"Sure is, Pumpkin Pie. Your piggy bank just got a heck of a lot bigger." The man ruffled his daughter's hair. "She's a real devoted reader, sir. Saves all her nickels and dimes so she can buy books from the Goodwill store. Has one in her hand all the time. Most are awful old though. Seems like we just don't have the time to bring her to town just to go to the library, but I know she'd like to get her hands on the kind of books she hears about at school." He looked down guiltily. "There's always too much work to be done."

"Don't worry." James put a hand on Becky's shoulder. "You give me your address and I'll have the bookmobile swing by your place twice a month. That way you can check out new books all the time."

Becky threw her arms around James. "Oh, thank you! This is the *best* day of my whole life!"

"Your family also gets free lunch from Dolly's Diner today. And you can all pick out a cookie from the Sweet Tooth. Just tell the ladies working the booths that you won the pig races and that Professor Henry is treating you to Quincy's Gap's finest food."

The announcement earned him hugs from all the children, and by the time they were done, even a baffled Chester was brought over and shoved into James's arms. James left the triumphant family to their admirers and, smelling too much like pig for his liking, headed over to the food vendor area to grab some lunch.

After loading up on two corn dogs, small fries, and some raspberry lemonade, James made his way to the judges' table so he could deliver the check to the winner of the Ladies' Hat Contest. As the women paraded slowly in front of the judges, Mrs. Waxman made notes on a piece of paper and conferred importantly with her fellow judges.

More than fifty women had created hats with literary themes. James watched as each contestant paraded past the judging area and then returned to her place in back of a long line. He spotted Murphy right away. Her wide-brimmed hat sported a red wooden barn filled with crochet livestock and the title *Animal Farm*. Right behind Murphy was the organist from James's church. Her hat paid homage to Harper Lee's *To Kill a Mockingbird*. It was a simple straw affair featuring a mockingbird that had been stabbed through the side with a toy knife. Other hats that caught his eye included an *Of Mice and Men* bowler upon which the creator had sewn Ken dolls and plush mice and a *Lord of the Flies* crown featuring dozens of rubber flies hanging from invisible wires.

When the judges announced the winners, James was in complete agreement with their choices. A teenage girl who'd designed her own *A Tree Grows in Brooklyn* chapeau earned the second runner-up position. She had used Lego blocks to create a New York City skyline and made a beautiful tree out of papier-mâché and tissue paper. The first runner-up was Witness to Fitness's Phoebe Liu.

She'd constructed a boxing ring on an old cowboy hat, and, instead of two human pugilists, she fashioned a pair of battling grapes out of plastic fruit. She added to her *Grapes of Wrath* theme by periodically ringing a small bell, as if a new round of fighting was about to occur.

The grand prizewinner was Ms. Beasley, a middle-school science teacher. Her hat was a tribute to *Cat on a Hot Tin Roof* and showed a two-dimensional feline walking across a piece of metal sheeting with buildings in the background. The minute windows of the town's buildings lit up, and every now and then a hiss of steam would escape from beneath the piece of tin and the flat cat would literally jump up in the air. Children were mesmerized by Ms. Beasley's hat and clustered around her the moment James delivered the prize check. Seeing a chance to educate young minds, Ms. Beasley began to explain how she used dry ice, battery components, and other materials to create her hat. James listened for a spell but eventually his attention wandered.

He gazed contentedly around the field, watching families line up at the food booths or wait for a turn on one of the rides. Finally, he stole away from Ms. Beasley and strolled around the field, smiling as he walked by both children and adults trying to win plush toys in the games area. The sight of clusters of bright balloons, the scent of delicious food, and the sounds of bluegrass music broadcast by the town's only local radio station filled James with a sense of contentment that he hadn't experienced for a long time. In fact, he hadn't felt this way since he had kissed Lucy Hanover.

James stopped in his tracks and spent a long moment remembering that kiss. Without realizing it, he'd halted directly in front of a large group of teenage boys wearing baggy jeans and T-shirts exhibiting a variety of offensive expressions. Their forward momentum impeded, the boys veered toward the picnic tables, where a pod of teenage girls wearing heavy makeup and short skirts giggled and nibbled on bites of cotton candy.

As James turned to watch the two groups meet, he caught a glimpse of Lucy wandering toward the carnival rides. It was as if his thoughts of their kiss had conjured her. He knew that it was time for him to seize the moment.

Dropping his cup of soda into the trash, James hustled through the crowds, trying not to lose sight of the sunlit corona of Lucy's hair as she moved through the throng. He caught up with her at the entrance to the Ferris wheel.

"Care to share a cab?" he asked, taking her by the arm.

"I'd love to." Lucy gazed up at the multicolored wheel. "I like being as high off the ground as possible. How about you?"

James glanced upward. "Not particularly, but I'd love to see how our blue hills look from up there." He pointed at the car that had just reached the highest elevation. As they watched, the ride controller began the long process of releasing people from their cars and loading on a fresh round of riders.

"We're in violet—my favorite color," Lucy announced when she boarded their car. It rocked unsteadily for a moment as she sat down and then lurched violently when James stepped in. There was barely enough room for their two wide bodies and they found themselves pressed tightly together.

Lucy laughed. "Guess we need to lose more weight."

"Aw, it's cozy. I like it," James said and then fell silent until all of the riders had settled into cars and the wheel began to turn in its languid circle. As they rose above the field, a swollen sun was dipping toward the horizon and the sky was mottled with mango-hued clouds.

"It's so beautiful!" Lucy exclaimed as they reached the pinnacle.

James gazed at her and had just opened his mouth to speak when their car came to an abrupt halt. It swung wildly forward, and James felt his stomach flip-flop as he looked down to see his feet swaying to and fro over the small heads of oblivious townsfolk below.

Lucy looked at James with pity. "It's okay, James. This happens all the time on these things."

James cleared his throat and squared his shoulders. "Actually, I hope we're stuck up here for a long time."

"Really? Why?"

"Lucy." James cupped her soft cheek in his hand, turning her face toward his own. "I'm so sorry we were interrupted that day at Dolly's. I told you that I had important things to say to you and I allowed an unscheduled meeting to get in the way of what really mattered."

"I understand." Her voice was tender, and her blue eyes reflected the twinkling lights of the Ferris wheel. "And I'm still interested in what you wanted to tell me."

James exhaled nervously. "I'm never so happy as when I'm with you, Lucy. I know I acted strange and distant after that one time when we . . . well . . ."

"When we kissed?" Lucy offered helpfully.

"Yes! I was so afraid that you'd find me as dull as my ex-wife did and then I'd get hurt again, so I didn't pursue you." James forgot about their swinging car and the din of the crowd below. Only this moment with this woman existed for him. "Even though I tried to hide it, I feel something very strong for you and I'd like to try to make us work if you're still willing."

Lucy's smile was radiant. "I'm very willing, James."

"But what about Carter?" James asked. "I thought you were interested in him."

Lucy shook her head. "I just pretended to have a crush on him to get a reaction out of you."

"A reaction?" James faked a scowl. "How's this for a reaction?" He leaned in and pressed his lips against hers.

The pair never noticed that the ride had started up again until their car reached the bottom and the controller began coughing loudly to attract their attention.

"Folks!" he finally shouted at them. "Let some other people see the sunset now. Come on. Out with you!"

James and Lucy separated themselves, their faces flushed in embarrassment. "Sorry," James said, grabbing Lucy's hand. "That's a pretty romantic setting you've arranged for folks, though."

"I feel like celebrating," Lucy said as they drifted away from the ride. "What should we do?"

"Megan's probably got a fresh batch of fried Oreos waiting at her booth," James replied, only partially in jest.

Lucy raised herself up on her tiptoes and gave James a peck on the cheek. "Deep-fried cookies? That sounds absolutely perfect."

Chapter Eleven

Chicken Florentine Lasagna

James took a rare personal day from work the Monday following the Spring Fling. Even though he was exhausted, he woke in a state of dreamy happiness. Lying in bed, he replayed how Lucy's face had looked Saturday night. The winking multicolored lights of the Ferris wheel had shone in her eyes and made her more beautiful than ever. Thinking about their kiss gave him a feeling of invulnerability.

As he stretched his arms wide and yawned, he had an overwhelming sensation that anything was possible. His weight loss was progressing, he and his staff had thrown a successful fundraiser for the library, and he had taken the first step in winning the heart of a good woman. Even his home was becoming transformed. When he heard the whining buzz of an electric drill coming from downstairs, James smiled. He'd taken this unplanned holiday to spend time with his father.

After getting ready for the day, James called the Fitzgerald twins at home to tell them that he wouldn't be coming to work. He also suggested that they look over the schedule and each take a personal day later on that week.

"You've earned it," he said. "And you must be worn out from all the prep work."

"No, thanks, Professor," Francis cheerfully rejected the idea. "We love our job and we get plenty of time off as it is. Besides, we need to figure out how to rearrange the fiction section to accommodate our Technology Corner. College finals are coming up and those new computers will be in high demand."

James was unsurprised that the twins refused to take a vacation day. At the end of the Spring Fling, he and Mrs. Waxman had tried to heap praise on Francis and Scott for coming up with such a unique and profitable event, but they'd insisted that they'd done nothing special. It was the same reaction they'd had after winning the float contest in the fall. James didn't know what he'd do without these brilliant and humble young men and he knew that he was lucky to have them in his life.

"Those pig races were a hoot. You boys are too clever!" Mrs. Waxman had gushed Saturday evening. She'd then fluffed their unkempt mops of hair as if the twins were a pair of cute toddlers. "This might have been like any other country fair until you dreamed up that charming hat contest."

"If only you two could use those massive brains to find yourselves some girlfriends," Dolly had murmured while serving the library staff a supper of fried chicken, corn pudding, and green beans with bacon.

"We're waiting to meet a set of twins who love sci-fi and video games, Dolly," Scott had said, his mouth stuffed with one of Clint's fluffy buttermilk biscuits. "We have our priorities, you know."

"And it would be great if they liked pizza," Francis had added.

"And *Star Trek!*"

"And the Discovery Channel."

James had laughed at Dolly's reaction to this. She'd clucked her tongue, clearly struggling to come up with a way to find two young ladies in their early twenties who shared the Fitzgerald brothers' passions.

Thinking back on the conversation, James decided that the least he could do while he enjoying his day off was to surprise the twins by having a few pizzas delivered to the library a little before noon. Francis and Scott were always hungry, and James knew they didn't often splurge on takeout because they preferred to spend their hard-earned money on the latest technical gizmos featured in *Wired* magazine.

Dressed in a worn pair of sweatpants and an old William & Mary Athletic Department T-shirt, James arrived downstairs to find Jackson holding a cup of coffee as he surveyed the dust-covered room that once was their kitchen. His toolbox was propped open on the floor and each metal item glinted in the morning sunlight. James might only know how to use half of the gadgets in his father's red Craftsman box, but he knew he was seeing a set of tools that were lovingly cared for. His father's array of wrenches, pliers, screwdrivers, and other implements looked brand-new.

Jackson eyed his son's attire with curiosity. "You havin' casual Mondays at the library now?"

"No, Pop," James said, stirring a liberal amount of fat-free half-

and-half into his coffee. "I thought I'd take you up on your offer to teach me to be a bit handier. You're working on the floor today, right?"

Jackson took a moment to top off his coffee, as if he needed something to do while he mulled over his son's request. Finally, he nodded and said, "All right, let's start with a little demolition. There's nothin' like rippin' out old flooring to get your day goin' right." He paused and then patted his stomach. "You'd best get a real breakfast down your throat. Those bars you've been eatin' aren't workin' man's food." He pointed at the box of multigrain breakfast bars sitting on the dining room table. "Clusters of nuts and grams of fiber are meant for bushy-tailed rodents, not men."

"I'll fry us some eggs," James offered. "Since the stove is about all we have left hooked up in this kitchen."

"With sausage and cheese?" Jackson asked, a hungry gleam in his eye.

James hesitated, silently wondering how many Witness to Fitness points such a breakfast would cost him. Shutting off his mental calculator, he said "Sure, Pop" and went into the dining room to retrieve the frying pan from a haphazard pile of pots, pans, dishes, and cutlery.

Less than an hour later, James and Jackson worked side-by-side removing the yellowed linoleum Jackson had laid down with meticulous care almost thirty years ago. He showed James how to cut into the vinyl using a utility knife and how to slowly and painstakingly scrape up the glue residue left behind.

"You can't rush a job like this," Jackson warned as they plodded along. "We need to take off all the glue and paper sittin' on top of the subfloorin' just as careful as if we were wipin' a baby's bottom." Jackson set the radio to his favorite country and western station and began to hum along to a Toby Keith song.

"That boy knows how to make real American music." Jackson grunted as he pulled off a large segment of flooring and launched it out the back door where it settled with the rest of the kitchen debris.

James knew there was no way to avoid having the backyard look like a work site, but he wished it weren't the case. He wanted to host the next supper club meeting at his house and had even toyed with the idea of having an outdoor picnic. Now, without a working kitchen and a backyard that could have doubled as a set for *Extreme Home Makeover*, he didn't see how he could invite his friends over at all.

"What's eatin' you, boy?" Jackson asked. "You're burrowin' into that subfloor like you're a dog diggin' for a bone."

James explained his concerns and half expected Jackson to shrug off his problem without much interest, but to his surprise, his father got to his feet and reached for the phone book. "I was going to order a dumpster anyway. I'll just make sure they come this week and get all this crap out of here. Then you can have your friends over without bein' embarrassed."

"Thanks, Pop," James said gratefully. "Would you like to join us?"

Jackson paused in the middle of dialing. "I'm actin' a bit more lively these days, Lord knows, but there's no way in hell I'm ready for a whole night of chitchat and bad food. Count me out."

James laughed. "Fair enough. But once we get this kitchen finished, I would like you to have dinner with my special friend, Lucy."

His father left a mumbled message on someone's voice mail and replaced the receiver. He then gave James an appraising look. "So, you finally made a move. About damn time."

"You're right about that, Pop," James agreed, continuing the tedious scraping. "It was about damn time."

Over the course of the day, James and his father completely removed the linoleum and prepped the subfloor for the tile. Both the new cabinetry and the palettes of tile were being delivered that afternoon, and the mountain of construction materials in the backyard almost prevented the Henry men from exiting and entering their own house. However, Jackson promised James that both the dumpster and P.J. would be arriving the following day and that the kitchen would be complete by the end of the workweek.

Later, Jackson stood next to the oven as James heated up their dinners: a container of Chicken Florentine Lasagna (a Witness to Fitness entrée) for James and one of Dolly's succulent pot roasts for Jackson. James sprinkled a liberal amount of salt and pepper over his lasagna and began to eat. He tried his best to ignore the sight of the tender meat and plump potatoes that Jackson happily dunked into a pool of rich brown gravy.

"I'm tellin' you, boy. That's not man's food you're eatin'." Jackson took a pull from his bottle of Budweiser. "You worked with your hands all day. You deserve a meal like I'm havin'. Go on, taste some of this," he said.

"I can't, Pop. Besides, this lasagna's not that bad. It just needs some extra salt."

• • •

At that evening's Witness to Fitness meeting, James was already so sore from a day of squatting on the kitchen floor that he didn't think he could survive one of Dylan's high-energy workouts. Examining his calloused hands while waiting for his turn on the scale, he started to seriously worry about the amount of cheat foods he'd eaten over the past week. While he stood scowling at the thought of gaining weight instead of losing it, Lucy breezed into the cubicle area and greeted him with a radiant smile.

"Why the frown, James?" she asked.

James shared his fears and she nodded in understanding. "I think we're cheating because of the food we're required to eat on this diet. It's getting repetitive. We keep eating the same thing every week and it's not like we love the taste of these meals. There's simply not enough variety to hold our interest."

Several other people overheard Lucy's comment and began to exchange whispered complaints about the entrées. Eventually, a buzz of dissatisfaction permeated the space.

Phoebe listened to the gripes of one of the male clients as he stepped on the scale. After she finished recording his weight, she congratulated him for his work and then turned to face the disgruntled dieters. Raising her hands, she asked for quiet.

"Please, I'd rather not shout," she pleaded, and everyone fell silent. They all respected Phoebe. "I talked to Ronnie last week about the blandness of the food, and she assured me that she made a serious effort to spice up this week's meals. Give them a chance for a week, okay? We'll see how you all feel by next Monday. Does that sound fair?"

It was impossible not to respond to Phoebe's soft-spoken tone and sincere manner, and the dieters stopped grumbling and agreed to give the food one more shot.

"So Ronnie's not here tonight?" James asked, looking around.

"No, she said she came down with a bad cold," Phoebe said and beckoned James toward the scale. James thought he'd caught a hint of skepticism in Phoebe's voice.

"Maybe she has seasonal allergies," James said. "They seem to get to people more than the common cold once the weather turns warm."

"Maybe." Phoebe looked unconvinced. She fixed her attention on sliding the levels on the scale. "You've made more progress, James. Good work."

James discovered that despite his lack of faithfulness to the food program, he'd miraculously lost two more pounds. His feelings of invulnerability and good fortune surged even higher.

"I'm down another two pounds," he whispered in Lucy's ear as she waited in line for her turn. "It must be all the exercise because I ate plenty of illegal foods at the fair."

Lucy grinned and whispered back, "It bet it was that *special* exercise session on the Ferris wheel."

Unexpectedly embarrassed, James glanced around to see if the other members of the Flab Five were close enough to have overheard Lucy. It suddenly dawned on James that he wasn't prepared to express his feelings for her in front of his friends. After all, he and Lucy hadn't even been on an official date yet, so James could hardly tell their friends that they were a couple. The kiss had been a start, but it wasn't enough. James needed to ask Lucy out and continue to get to know her on an intimate level.

"You're next, Lucy," Phoebe said.

Lucy stepped on the scale with Lindy and Gillian close behind her.

I need to take her on a real date, James thought with conviction as he took up position outside of the exercise room before class. *Not coffee. Not me waiting to bump into her in a public place. A date for two people with feelings for each other.*

As soon as Lucy entered the exercise area, James pulled her aside and asked if she was free for dinner and a movie that Friday night.

"Sounds great," Lucy said while pushing her hair back into a headband in preparation for the upcoming workout. "What's playing?"

James shrugged. "I honestly have no idea. I haven't been to the movies in so long that I don't even read the film section in the newspaper anymore."

"I go all the time. Lindy and I saw a great period film two weeks ago. An Austin remake." She sighed. "There's something about those British men in breeches . . ."

"You can choose the movie, but I'd rather avoid films featuring men with silk cravats or ponytails tied with silk ribbons," James said playfully. Then, seeing Gillian and Lindy heading their way, he gathered his bag and his exercise mat and whispered, "Just call me at work tomorrow and we'll plan everything."

Lucy smiled. "Okay, but why are you whispering?"

Panicking at the sight of the other supper club women, James mumbled something about a dry mouth and darted over to the water fountain, his stomach fluttering with nerves as he watched Lucy in the wall-length mirror. She casually greeted Lindy and Gillian and the three women began chatting as they prepped for class.

"How's it going?" a voice asked from James's right, causing him to jump.

James looked at Dylan's toned, muscular figure in the mirror and was momentarily thrown off balance by the differences in their physiques.

"Sorry to hold you up." James leaned over to drink from the water fountain, but in his increased state of agitation he jammed the button with too much force and water shot directly into his face. Backing away, he used his forearm to catch the moisture running off his chin and onto his T-shirt.

"This fountain has a finicky release button," Dylan said, smiling. "Glad to see that you're hydrating, though. Once you're thirsty, you're already too late. I like that you're drinking water before class. Thumbs up, man."

James returned the gesture before slinking to his customary place in the back row.

Halfway through the exercise routine, in which Dylan had the group performing a series of nasty lunges, James noticed a familiar face peek around the door separating the exercise room from the office area out front. It took James a moment to recognize the woman because she wasn't enrolled in the Witness to Fitness program. The female visitor, who was clad in a powder blue pants suit, was easily half the size of the rest of the individuals in the exercise class. She seemed unnaturally delighted by what she was seeing, but when Murphy Alistair entered the room and started making her way toward James, he stopped mid-lunge, grabbed her by the elbow, and pushed her out of the room.

"What are you doing here?" he asked breathlessly. He was angry with Murphy for invading the exercise room. He didn't appreciate having an observer, and he doubted his classmates would either. "We were in the middle of a class!"

Murphy's eyes were lit with mischief. "I thought you'd be grateful to me for saving you from those lunges. They look like hell on the thighs."

"They are, but that's the point." James dabbed at his face with his towel and tried to calm down. He was afraid that if Lucy spotted them together again she would leap to the wrong conclusion. He'd already explained that Murphy was interviewing him on his weight-loss experience, but Lucy replied by saying that she believed Murphy had her cap set on James.

"There's a look she gives you, James," Lucy had said the night of the Spring Fling. "It's flirty, and frankly, a little predatory. Women recognize that kind of look much better than men do. Just don't be fooled. And you should know that I'm the jealous type. I'm sorry, but I just am."

Now, Murphy stood in the empty Witness to Fitness office area fixing James with a calculating gaze. Her stare was so intense that James felt like she was trying to read his mind.

"I wouldn't have showed up here if this wasn't urgent," she said. "I just wanted you to know that you were one hundred percent right about those entrées. They are all store-bought. Every single one of them." Squaring her narrow shoulders, Murphy took a deep breath and turned to leave. "But since I seem to be causing you distress by being here, I'll tell you about it tomorrow."

James danced in front of her, holding out his hands in surrender. "No, please don't. I'm sorry. It's just that none of us look too graceful bouncing around in there, so it's kind of unsettling to have someone who's not enrolled in the program suddenly appear in the doorway."

"Don't be ridiculous, James. Your group looks great. I was thrilled to see all the energy in there. And think of it this way: every man and woman in that room is working toward a positive change. You're all showing incredible willpower, you're staying focused, and you're becoming more empowered about your health every day. You're not sitting at home ordering products from infomercials because they offer magical promises to make you thin without diet or exercise. You're doing it the hard way." She moved closer to the exercise room. "It's an inspiring sight. It really is." She paused, looking confused. "By the way, where is your fearless leader tonight?"

James wanted to yank Murphy away from the doorway, but before he could make a move, she took a step away from him, her gaze still locked on the exercisers. "Are you referring to Ronnie?" James asked.

"Yes, Ronnie. The one who's selling you repackaged frozen food and pocketing the profit." Murphy turned back to James and put a hand on her hip. She seemed suddenly impatient to complete her investigation, and James realized that she probably intended to accuse Ronnie of fraud in front of her clients.

James shrugged. "We were told she was home with a cold. Dylan teaches all of the exercise classes, and Phoebe took over the weigh-ins and some of the counseling sessions. Frankly, it was a relief not to listen to another of Ronnie's pep talks. If I wanted any counseling, I'd talk to Phoebe anyway. She's much more sincere."

"Well, Ronnie may not be your counselor, but she's certainly *advised* you to spend money on her food," Murphy said sardonically, her gaze returning to the group of sweaty dieters jumping in time to the music.

To his horror, James noticed Lucy catch his eye in the mirror. She raised a suspicious brow and then faltered in the middle of a leg lift. James hurriedly strode to the front door, forcing Murphy to follow. "How were you able to confirm my theory about the food?" he asked.

"I have a food chemist friend who was willing to help. I simply brought one of Ronnie's meals and the comparable store-bought meal to my friend's lab and she ran an experiment. It was fascinating to observe." Murphy rifled through her bag and produced a notebook. "According to her findings, the only thing Ronnie did to doctor the store-bought product was to add a sprinkle of grated Parmesan cheese and fresh parsley. Somehow, I doubt her cost for those two garnishes merit the nearly seven-dollar difference between the store-bought meal and the one she sold you for ten dollars."

"Especially since that's seven dollars times seven days!" James was furious.

Murphy jabbed her notebook with her finger, expressing a shared indignation. "Exactly! That comes to just under forty-eight dollars per week, which really adds up over the course of the month. Even though Ronnie had to buy aluminum tins for all of the meals, they sell those in bulk at those discount warehouses."

James shook his head angrily. "That's where Lindy and I met her! She was probably stocking up in preparation to rip us all off!"

Murphy shut her notebook with a triumphant flourish. "We need to compare the rest of the week's meals to firm up our research. Can I follow you home and get whatever you have left from last week's entrées? I know you mentioned having skipped some of the required dinners last week. The paper will reimburse you for the cost, of course."

James hesitated. If he left now, Lucy would be convinced that something was going on between him and Murphy. And since he hadn't told anyone that Murphy was investigating the Witness to Fitness meals, it would look exceedingly odd if he were to simply disappear in the middle of class.

"Can I meet you at my place after class instead?" he asked. "I don't want to miss the rest. I need to be able to deduct these exercise points."

"Such dedication," Murphy said. James didn't know if she was teasing or if she was genuinely impressed. Taking one last glance around the exercise room, she said, "Fine, I'll see you at your place in about half an hour. And don't worry, I already know where you live."

James was about to caution Murphy about both his father and

the mess in the yard, but she slipped out the door and into the evening like a silent breeze. James hastened back inside the exercise room, only to find that the rest of the dieters had started their post-workout stretches. James grabbed a mat, sat down, and reached for his toes, feeling guilty that he was no longer breathing hard.

When the class was finished, and people were too focused on drinking from water bottles or wiping their sweat-soaked brows to ask James where he'd been, Bennett moved to James's side and clapped him on the back. "That's a fine-looking excuse for blowing off those miserable lunges, my man."

"What excuse?" James asked.

"That cute reporter." Bennett stroked his mustache and grinned. "She can ask me for my story any time."

James lowered his voice. "Actually, she may have discovered something pretty incriminating about Ronnie."

Bennett gazed at him with interest. "Go on, now. You can't mess with a man by dangling a carrot like that. What did our fine Ms. Alistair find out?"

"I'll tell everyone tomorrow, I promise." James shouldered his gym bag. "Murphy needs to do a bit more research first and I need to meet her at my place right now. I really don't want to be late."

"You're a lucky fellow!" Bennett winked before he was suddenly bumped from behind by a figure hustling toward the front door. "Hey! Where's the fire, woman?"

James sighed in exasperation as Lucy, her jaw clenched in anger, marched outside and got into her car without so much as a backward glance in his direction. She slammed the door to her Jeep and reversed so rapidly that her tires screeched in protest.

"Must be the moon," Gillian sympathized as she watched Lucy peel out of the parking lot. "I always feel especially sensitive during a full moon week. The ebbs and flows that make up the mystical tides of womanhood are surely connected to the celestial body."

"What are you going on about?" Bennett murmured, and after exchanging bewildered looks with James, walked off to where his car was parked.

James waved goodbye to Lindy and Gillian before trudging to his Bronco. This time, he couldn't blame the exercise class for wearing him down. After all, he hadn't participated in half of the routine. The elation he'd felt all day vanished like an extinguished candle. He wondered if he would ever say or do the right thing when Lucy Hanover was concerned.

Chapter Twelve

Pretzel Sticks

"We figured it all out, Professor," Francis said, leaning over the Information Desk. He brandished a piece of paper covered with his messy handwriting. "We can afford eight new computers—"

"As long as they come with only basic programs," Scott interrupted. "We can't get machines loaded with every bell and whistle."

"Right." Francis nodded. "Internet capabilities and Microsoft Word and such, but no fancy graphics programs. If we buy everything during the Memorial Sale at Wired City, we can pick up eight computers, two laser printers, one color printer, and a scanner."

"Of course, we'll have to charge our patrons more per page for the color printouts than for the black and whites." Scott pointed at a red-and-white sale circular on which he had drawn a dozen black stars. "But since we don't have a color copier yet, I don't think they'll mind. Francis and I have already done the cost-value comparisons on all the machines using our online subscription to *Consumer Reports*. I think we'd be getting a darn good buy if we go to Wired City."

James looked over the circular while chomping on a pretzel stick. "We're getting much more than I thought we could afford. What happens to our old machines? Can we still use them?"

"Our current computers are serious dinosaurs, Professor. They're old and really, really slow, but we've got a buddy who might be able to add some RAM for a reasonable cost and bring them up to a decent speed."

"That would give us ten computers!" James exclaimed. "That would be remarkable."

"True, but if we spend money on extra memory, we'll have nothing left over for the actual furniture to put all the computers on," Scott said.

"If only we knew someone who could custom-build what we need without gouging us." Francis looked at the sales circular with a wistful expression. "We're pretty handy, but we couldn't make anything that looks as sleek as this stuff. Or as tough."

James pulled the circular a little closer. "These prices are even higher for furniture than they are in our library supply catalogs. Truthfully, we don't really need workstations with bookshelf space. What we need is some sort of massive wooden island."

"Like an oversized dining room table?" Francis asked, trying to form a picture.

"Exactly, but with holes in the center for all of the wires and a wide shelf underneath to keep the hard drive off the ground." James paused to lick salt from his lips. "I might know just the person to build this for us. Let's determine measurements and do a rough drawing. We have enough money left in our quarterly budget to come up with the cost of labor and supplies for this kind of table. If I my friend agrees to make it, we'll be ready to open our Tech Corner in the beginning of June."

Buoyed by the improvements their patrons would soon enjoy, the three library employees went back to work. Scott returned to his station at the checkout desk where he assisted a young mother trailed by four children, all carrying a stack of picture books. Francis escorted a patron to the reference section while James studied the Wired City circular. He was reviewing their technology budget for a second time when a slender hand covered the photographs of computers, digital cameras, and plasma-screen televisions. James looked up to see Murphy Alistair grinning at him.

"I just sampled milk and honey hand cream down at the Food Lion," she said, thrusting her hand closer to him. "Isn't it nice?"

"Yes. Very nice." James stashed his snack-sized bag of pretzels under the desk.

"That's not forbidden fruit, is it?" Murphy pointed at the desk. "A jelly donut? A jumbo candy bar? A vial of cocaine?"

"Just your run-of-the-mill pretzel sticks. If I dipped them in chocolate and then dusted them with cocaine, I'd really be breaking the rules." James smiled. Suddenly, he realized that he was flirting with the attractive reporter. "Did you come to see me about the Witness to Fitness food?"

"I sure did. I was hoping to catch you before you left for home. Not that I'd mind seeing your house again, but I have a time crunch." She drummed her plum-colored nails on her messenger bag. "My chemist friend worked through her lunch hour and we now have our proof. Ronnie has been scamming all of her Witness to Fitness clients. I wanted you to know before the story appears on the front page of the *Star* tomorrow morning. I'm expecting our local businesswoman to feel some serious heat by the end of the day."

"She'll certainly be receiving plenty from me!" James whispered forcefully. "Ronnie had better start handing out refund checks like a volunteer distributing water to marathon runners or she's going to feel more than heat. Someone is bound to take legal action."

"Are you going to sue?" Murphy asked excitedly.

"No, not me. There are already too many civil suits clogging our court systems. But someone else may go after her. I mean, isn't this an open-and-shut case of fraud?"

"That's what my headline says!"

James felt his cheeks growing warm with fury. "I *knew* she was too good to be true. I told my friends that she was a phony, but they made me feel like I was totally off-base." He fought to get his emotions under control. "Thanks for looking into this, Murphy. I owe you one. I have to run right now, though. I want to contact my friends so they can decide what action to take." James checked his watch and wondered which supper club member to call first.

"Sure thing, Professor." Murphy smiled. "And if you're truly grateful, you can prove it by taking me out to dinner sometime this week."

Completely focused on the wrong done to him and his friends, James absently nodded before hurrying into his office to call the Flab Five. "Meet me at the library right after work. It's serious," he told each of them. Even when he spoke with Lucy, he refused to divulge specific information other than to urge her to come into his office as soon as she arrived at the library.

"Does this have something to do with that Murphy woman?" Lucy demanded tersely.

"Yes, but not in the way you think. Please, Lucy, just trust me. Can you do that?" James waited on pins and needles for her answer. After all, he'd asked her a loaded question.

Lucy hesitated. "I'm trying to, James. I really am. I guess I'll find out if that was a good decision soon enough. See you after work."

• • •

"What's going on, James?" Lindy asked when she arrived shortly after five. Her face was tight with concern.

Bennett and Gillian hustled into his office seconds later with the same question on their lips.

"Give Lucy a chance to get here and I'll tell you all at once. Can you browse some magazines or check out a few books in the meantime?"

Bennett shrugged. "All right, but my curiosity is as piqued as one of the Sweet Tooth's meringue kisses, so Lucy had better be breaking some speeding laws right now."

"Settle down, Bennett," Gillian admonished gently. "Take a few moments to center yourself. I've been dying to get a look at the new *Herbal Almanac.* Maybe I should research some relaxation herbs for you when I get my hands on that book."

"No, ma'am." Bennett pulled a face. "I still remember the taste of that blue lotus tea you made me drink after Virginia Tech lost their bowl game. Instead of cheering me up, it gave me the runs."

"That's because you added too much honey," Gillian said. "Now, help me find that book."

Lucy arrived shortly after the other three were already settled into reading chairs. Bennett and Lindy were flipping through magazines with the false concentration of patients in a physician's waiting room, but Gillian was genuinely absorbed in her almanac. Seeing Lucy, James shepherded his friends inside his small office and closed the door.

"Sorry to be so dramatic," he began, "but I have some shocking news and I wanted to tell you about it before you read it in tomorrow's paper."

"Is something wrong with you, James?" Gillian leaned forward, her hands clutching the arms of her chair.

"No, no. It's nothing like that. What's happened is that we've all been cheated. Ever since we joined Witness to Fitness, Ronnie Levitt has been selling us store-bought frozen entrées." He paused. "Basically, she's made a nice pile of money by tricking us, and she would have continued to do so had Murphy Alistair not taken the meals to a food chemist and had them analyzed."

Lindy laughed. "That's it? Lord have mercy, James! I thought you had some terminal illness or had accepted a job in Alaska and would be moving within a matter of days! So we're out a few pennies. Is that all?"

Lucy frowned. "Wait a minute. Just how many pennies are we talking about? None of us are exactly living high on the hog and I'm not one to throw my money away—especially for someone else's fraudulent gain." She looked at Lindy curiously. "Art teachers count their pennies too, don't they?"

"Of course." Lindy scowled. "Our salary is paltry at best. But how much could Ronnie have cheated me into spending? Is it enough to get steamed up over?"

James explained the total cost differences.

"Why, that stick-legged, ponytailed louse is going to pay us back!" Bennett exclaimed. "I put off getting a new satellite dish in order to buy those meals and now you're telling me I could have gotten them at Food Lion for three bucks apiece?"

"Hold on, everyone!" Gillian raised her hands. "We're all getting very emotional right now. Let's just take a deep breath." She inflated her chest with air and then let it escape through her lips with a faint whistle. "We have to remember that we *are* losing weight on this program. Witness to Fitness has not been a complete sham."

"That's true," James said, imitating Gillian's calm tone. "But I'd attribute most of that success to our exercise classes. We could have bought these meals ourselves and joined the YMCA for a fraction of what we've been paying Ronnie each week."

His friends grumbled in agreement.

"What do you think she'll do when the news hits?" Lucy looked at James for an answer. "You're the one who didn't trust her in the first place, so what does your gut tell you her next move will be?"

"Guys, I wish I had been wrong and that she was exactly what she seemed." James sighed. "Personally, I think Ronnie will deny the whole thing. Cut and run is the approach I see her taking."

"You mean she'll just close up shop?" Lindy was astonished by the idea. "But she's got equipment, employees, a rental agreement."

"What equipment? She owns a radio, two scales, two cubicles, and some floor mats!" Bennett spluttered. "She's leasing the space, so she could just load up her cute little car and start over in another town. Be gone before the *Star*'s ink is dry. What's to stop her from launching a new scam in a different state? You have to realize that she's making this profit from all her clients, not just us."

Lucy sprang out of her chair. "She's not going anywhere with my money! I'm going to confront her right now, *before* the article comes out."

"What? Like, at her house?" Lindy's mouth fell open in surprise.

"I'm with you, sister." Bennett stood and squared his shoulders as if he were about to sack an unsuspecting quarterback. "Let's drag her down to the nearest ATM and get our hard-earned cash back. She owes us at least a partial refund."

James hadn't expected such a strong reaction from his friends, but a large part of him relished the idea of seeing Ronnie squirm in the face of their accusations. For once, that superficial smile might disappear from her smug face.

Gillian was the only person who felt they should give Ronnie a chance to do the right thing. "Ronnie could refund our money to-morrow evening when we come in for class," she said quietly. "How can you all assume the worst of a fellow human being? She made a mistake. Let's give her the opportunity to correct it."

Gillian's pacifistic attitude gave the rest of them pause.

"You're right about giving her a chance, Gillian," Lindy said, smiling appreciatively at her friend. "However, I still think we should go over to Ronnie's house and talk to her. She should listen to how we all feel about being cheated, and I'd sleep much easier tonight knowing that she's going to rectify this situation as soon as possible."

"That sounds fair. And I would like to expresses how I feel be-trayed and confused by her actions. Perhaps she'll have something to share with us as well. Some reason to explain her behavior." Gillian got to her feet, plucking at the hem of her black and char-treuse polka-dot blouse. "But we're not a lynch mob. We need to approach her with kindness and respect."

"In that case, you'd better be our spokesperson. I don't feel like being kind to that swindling praying mantis." Bennett's voice was a low growl.

"I'll drive," James offered as he locked up his office. "I know where she lives because I had to give her a ride home a while back.

Plus, my Bronco can hold all of us."

Bennett made an hourglass figure in the air. "Good thinking. Witness to Fitness has slimmed us down, but not enough to get us all in my old mail truck. You drive, James, but let me ring Ronnie's doorbell. I'm going to shake the pom-poms right out of that cheerleader's hands."

• • •

Pulling into the Cozy Valley Town Homes, James tried to recall which unit belonged to Ronnie. Fortunately, her VW Bug was parked right in front of her home.

James left his truck at the curb and opened the back door for the ladies.

"This place is so cute!" Lindy said as she alighted. "I love the replica gaslights and how every unit has flower boxes."

"Ronnie's daisies are fake," Lucy scoffed, pointing at the window box perched next to Ronnie's gray front door. "How appropriate."

"Now, friends," Gillian said in a quiet, soothing voice. "Let's consider the tone we want to set. Think gentle. Imagine yourselves approaching a scared animal. We need to speak softly and —"

"Carry a big stick," Bennett muttered, pretending to look around for one.

James gazed up at the town house. "She may not even be home. Go ahead, Gillian. You're our voice of reason."

With a take-charge set to her shoulders, Gillian rearranged over her hips and rang the doorbell. A series of tinkling chimes could be heard from within.

They all waited.

James fiddled with a jagged fingernail and wished Ronnie would just come to the door. He disliked confrontation and wanted to get his money back and return home as soon as possible. He resented Ronnie's dawdling almost as much as he resented being swindled by her.

Gillian pressed the doorbell again.

"Figures," Bennett said after a full minute had passed. "She's probably out on a leisurely fifteen-mile run followed by a few thousand stomach crunches. Then, she'll eat a wheat germ and alfalfa sandwich while watching exercise videos. That's probably her idea of fun."

Gillian peered in the vertical rectangle of glass flanking the front door and said, "She has to be in there. I see a candle burning on the kitchen table."

"Can you see anything else?" Lindy asked.

"No. I'll try to get her attention once more and then we'll have to assume she's . . . indisposed." Gillian raised her fist and began to pound heavily on the door. She then uttered a startled "Oh!" as the door swung inward.

"Guess it wasn't closed all the way," Lucy whispered, and James felt an inexplicable chill tickle the length of his spine.

"Ronnie!" Gillian called out as if she and Ronnie were old friends. "Yoo hoo! Some of your clients have stopped by to see you." She paused, listening. "Ronnie?"

Joining Gillian on the stoop, James pulled at her sleeve. "Let's just go. She's obviously not coming out."

Gillian sniffed. "It smells like eucalyptus. What a nice fragrance. Let me just tiptoe in and blow out that candle. If Ronnie's gone out, I don't want her to return to a pile of ashes just because she was careless."

"Why not?" Bennett asked crossly. "Would serve her right."

Gillian cast a long look of reproach at Bennett before breezing inside the townhouse. The others watched her from the open doorway.

"Uh-oh," Gillian said sotto voce as she pointed at the table where the candle burned. "She must have company. There's an empty wine bottle and two glasses." She gestured wildly toward the stairs. "Who knows what's happening on the second floor?"

"Get out of there!" James whispered urgently, but Gillian was too busy examining something else on the dining room table.

"What are you looking at, woman?" Bennett craned his neck to see what their friend was doing

"There's a loaf of bread and a plate of cheese." Gillian wore an expression of bewilderment. "It's not fresh, though. These slices of Gouda and Jarlsberg are hard as rocks. I think Ronnie may not be here after all."

"Or she's passed out upstairs," Lucy said. "Remember, she was too *sick* to come to work yesterday."

"I'm going to run up and check on her," Gillian said. "There was a time, back in my wilder days, when I had a few too many wine coolers myself. I just want to make sure she doesn't need any help. I know some very effective natural cures for a hangover."

Before anyone could protest, Gillian began ascending the stairs. Pushed from behind by both Lucy and Lindy, James found himself inside the house, peering up at Gillian as she made her way to the top.

A door opened somewhere above their heads. "She's not in the bedroom!" Gillian called down. "But there are more candles up here, and they've all burned down dangerously low."

From his position on the first floor, James heard another door creak overhead.

This was followed by a heavy thump. James and his friends exchanged worried glances.

"Gillian?" Lindy shouted. "You okay?"

There was no answer.

"Gillian?" Lucy yelled and hit the stairs running. James, Lindy, and Bennett were right on her heels.

In the narrow upstairs hallway, they saw Gillian sitting on her bottom, her legs stretched out before her. Her mouth hung open and her eyes were glassy. Without turning to her friends or speaking a word, she lifted her right arm and pointed at the doorway across from her.

Following a hair's breadth behind Lucy, James entered a bathroom. It took his eyes a moment to adjust to the darkness because the only source of light came from half a dozen white tea candles. These had burned so low that the wicks were smoking. Shadows danced over the walls and there was an ominous silence in the closed space.

James swept his eyes over the countertop, taking in the bottle of Jack Daniel's among the candles. It was about a quarter full. Moving his eyes from left to right, he saw a pile of towels stacked neatly by the sink, a toilet at the far end of the room, and a large whirlpool tub to his right.

He and Lucy shouted at the same time, and suddenly Lucy was

grabbing his arm. She squeezed hard with trembling fingers.

"Lord help us," Lindy cried softly from behind them.

Ronnie was in the bathtub. Her naked body was completely submerged with the exception of the tip of her nose, her knuckles, and her toes. These poked above the waterline in small archipelagos of flesh. Her brown hair floated like the tendrils of an aquatic plant and her open eyes gazed up at them from beneath the stagnant water. Her small breasts were barely visible in the darkness and deeper shadows covered her midsection.

As James stared in disbelief, he couldn't help but notice the small tattoo of a chameleon inked into the skin above Ronnie's heart.

"She could be sleeping. She's so still. But her eyes are open . . ." Lucy whispered.

James couldn't tear his gaze from Ronnie's sunken face. He looked at her and saw a drowned Ophelia, lying peacefully in a watery grave. But the comparison made little sense. After all, Ronnie wasn't a young girl. Nor was she wreathed by flowers. Instead, dying candles and an empty bottle of booze surrounded her.

"We're too late!" Gillian wailed from the hallway. "She drank herself to death!"

It was then that James noticed the note taped to the bathroom mirror. It had been typed on a piece of white copier paper.

"What does that say?" Lindy asked in a hoarse, low voice.

James leaned closer to the paper and read it out loud.

> *To the Authorities,*
> *I am responsible for the Polar Pagoda fire. I started it using whiskey and matches. I wanted Willy's business to fail and I can't live with myself any longer because of the guilt. I am truly sorry.*

Lucy drew in a sharp breath before turning to the others. "Everyone needs to get out of the room. Be very careful not to touch anything. Let's go, Gillian. We need to retrace our steps."

Bennett and James helped Gillian to her feet because she was shaking too violently to stand on her own. Lucy put an arm around Lindy and ushered her downstairs. The friends sat around Ronnie's kitchen table in mute shock while Lucy called Sheriff Huckabee.

James locked his hands together and stared at the tableau. As Gillian had said earlier, there was a bottle of wine, two glasses, a plate of cheese, and a breadbasket filled with an untouched French baguette that could only have come from the Sweet Tooth. Lipstick marks stained the rim of a glass with less than a swallow of wine in its bowl. The second glass looked untouched. James squinted in the light to see if fingerprints marred the transparent surface, but the glass was unblemished.

Gillian, Lindy, and Bennett sat motionless and unspeaking, but Lucy inspected the area. She didn't touch anything. She simply eyed the contents on the table as closely as James had. After that, she walked around the kitchen, her arms crossed and her brow creased in thought, absorbing and memorizing every little detail.

As sirens screamed in the night air, James met Lucy's eyes. He saw a mixture of trepidation and excitement flickering there, and he knew that she would have to handle all of the difficult questions as to why the five of them were sitting in a dead woman's kitchen.

"You can do this," he whispered to Lucy, and she managed a small smile of gratitude.

Outside, the sound of multiple engines cut through the air and several car doors slammed.

"This will be a good test for me," she said in a hushed voice. "If I pass, I'll know that I'm ready to get out from behind my desk. One day, I'll be the one responding to calls for help." She gazed toward the front door. "And investigating suspicious deaths."

Chapter Thirteen

Kentucky Chocolate-Chip Pie

"I should have known you'd be here," Deputy Donovan said derisively to Lucy. He'd burst through the doorway seconds earlier—his gun drawn and his body poised in an aggressive stance—and was clearly bewildered to find Lucy standing calmly in the hallway. "You always have to be in the thick of things, don't you? Thick. That's you, Lucy Hanover."

"Holster your gun, Keith. There are no assailants present," Lucy said as if she were the sheriff. "That's not how you enter a civilian residence unless you've been presented with an imminent threat, though you look really fierce when you're on high alert. I saw a similar expression during the wildlife documentary I was watching the other night. This segment featured baboons." She took a step closer to the deputy. "And how they attract females by drawing attention to their bright red asses."

The freckles on Donovan's face merged into a crimson mass. Just as he was about to launch a full-fledged verbal assault on his coworker, Sheriff Huckabee and Deputy Truett marched across the threshold.

"Evening, Lucy," the sheriff said as he glanced around the entranceway and into the front room of Ronnie's home. "You always seem to be calling me away from a good meal. The missus made beef brisket tonight. It was as tender as a groom on his wedding night." He frowned. "It'll never taste the same after it's reheated. Never does. Ah well. Word is that you called in to report a dead lady upstairs in the tub?"

"Yes, sir." Lucy immediately turned on her professional demeanor.

Donovan rudely brushed by her and bounded up the stairs, but she ignored him. "It looks like she had a good deal to drink. It's possible that she drowned in the bathtub," she told Huckabee. "There's a suicide note as well. None of us have touched a thing."

"Except for the cheese!" Gillian piped up from the other room. "I squished a piece or two to see if it was fresh."

Huckabee moved deeper into the front room and took in the

foursome seated at Ronnie's table. "For the life of me, I can't imagine what kind of party you're throwing here, Lucy. Why don't you tell me the whole story while we take a look at the scene?"

"It would be my pleasure, sir." Lucy spoke in a calm and steady voice as she and the sheriff headed upstairs.

After what felt like an interminable amount of time to James, the two deputies returned to the kitchen and asked each of the supper club members to give a brief statement.

James was relieved to talk to Glenn Truett instead of Keith Donovan. Truett seemed like a straightforward soul whose main purpose was to get his job done so he could spend his time on other pursuits. Lucy had mentioned that he was an avid fisherman and a rabid NASCAR fan.

Truett jotted down a few notes while James was talking, and then asked him to swing by the station the next day to review and sign an official statement. When he was free to leave, James waited for Lucy and the others by his truck, but Lindy told him that Lucy was staying behind.

"As for me, I can't wait to go home." Lindy opened the Bronco's passenger door and practically collapsed into the front seat. Bennett and Gillian climbed in the back. James got in the car and, deciding that it felt stuffy in the cabin, put all the windows down.

"Here comes the coroner," Bennett said as a small man carrying a toolbox in one hand and an old-fashioned leather physician's bag in the other nodded politely in their direction.

Lindy watched him enter the town house. "He shouldn't have a hard time making a ruling in this case. Suicide. Plain and simple."

Gillian moaned. "I feel like my energy is tainted from having been in that house. I can't wait to put my feet up and sip some lemon myrtle leaf tea. You're all welcome to join me if you'd like. We need to recover from this shocking tragedy."

"Thanks for the offer," James said and pulled away from the curb. The unit was now ablaze with light as uniformed figures moved about inside. "But I think my recovery can only be helped along by raiding my father's supply of Cutty Sark."

. . .

Lucy was so involved with work the next day that James barely heard from her. She sent a brief email to the supper club members informing them that the cause of Ronnie's death was drowning. She also wrote that the coroner refused to rule the death a suicide. During his examination, the coroner had found suspicious bruises around Ronnie's ankles, implying that someone may have held her by the ankles so that her head was underwater. Her assailant kept holding her until the oxygen in her lungs ran out.

"Her blood alcohol levels were through the roof," Lucy told James during a short phone call. "She may have barely been conscious or completely unconscious when she was drowned."

"So it's a murder case?" James asked, both horrified and intrigued by the news.

"Yes, it is." Lucy couldn't hide her excitement. "Huckabee had a team searching for forensic evidence, but the whole town house was bleached and vacuumed and every surface was wiped clean of prints. Not only that, but the bottle of Jack Daniel's we saw in her bathroom had a familiar residue inside."

James gasped. "Like the bottle found at the Polar Pagoda fire?"

"Exactly! This one's been sent to the lab for analysis, but I'd bet my next paycheck that the residue came from pulverized Valium tablets."

Thoughts spun in James's head. "Does that mean Ronnie really set that fire, like her note says, or did her killer start it? I still don't think she had a reason to put Willy out of business. He wasn't a threat to her success."

"I know." Lucy sighed into the receiver. "Also, that note didn't sound like her. It was so flat."

"Completely without personality," James added.

"That's what I mean. If Ronnie were to leave a suicide note, I could see her writing it on custom stationery with a million exclamation marks, you know?" James heard a faint click and knew that Lucy was receiving an incoming call. "I'd better go, James. Can you fill in the others for me?"

James initiated the supper club phone tree by calling Lindy. She was stunned by the news of Ronnie's murder and began to weep. James felt a prick of guilt when he heard Lindy sniffle. A woman was dead. Ronnie may have wronged them, but she didn't deserve to be drugged and drowned. James said as much to Lindy.

"It's just terrible," she cried. "And what happens now? Are we supposed to show up for our exercise class like nothing's happened?"

On Wednesday night, James stopped by Witness to Fitness to see if Phoebe or Dylan were there, but the space was dark, and a sign taped to the front door announced that the business would be closed until further notice. James checked out a low-fat cookbook from the library and decided to create his own menus until Phoebe and Dylan were finished sorting out what would become of Ronnie's business.

"I can do this on my own," James said and made a shopping list. And although he bought the right food and cooked a healthy meal that night, he felt empty inside. Not hungry, but hollow. He realized that the news of Ronnie's murder had upset him more deeply than he'd expected. It was all he could think about. In fact, it was all anyone in Quincy's Gap could think about.

Clearly, Murphy's article focusing on the fraudulent Witness to Fitness meals had been forgotten. Instead, the *Star*'s headline the following day announced Ronnie's death in big, bold print. Murphy had left James several messages begging him to call her, but so far, he'd avoided talking to her about the case. He felt that if anyone should be the supper club's spokesperson on the incident, it should be Lucy.

In search of a distraction from the memory of Ronnie in the bathtub, James threw himself into planning the next supper club meeting. He left a message on Lindy's answering machine inviting her to his house Sunday night and briefly outlined his plan for their meal. He then asked Lindy to forward the information to Gillian. Just as he was settling in a recliner to finish the last chapter of a Michael Crichton novel, the phone rang. It was Bennett, and he sounded uncharacteristically flustered.

"Can you meet me? I'm at Woodrow Wilson Tavern."

"Now?" James frowned as he gazed first at his book and then at his feet, which were comfortably encased in his favorite slippers.

Over the din of background noise, Bennett said, "I could use your advice, man."

Hearing the need in his friend's voice, James kicked off his slippers. "I'll be right there."

• • •

No sooner had James sat on one of the tavern's red leather-covered bar stools than a mug of amber ale appeared in front of him.

"What are we drinking?" James asked, picking up the heavy mug and eyeing the generous head of foam appreciatively.

"Presidential Ale Light. Our faithful bartender Sammy bought it from a brewery in Staunton."

James caught the bartender's eye and raised his glass. "Here's to President Wilson."

"To Wilson." Sammy raised his own glass and took a sip. Froth dotted his gray mustache and he gave it a satisfied wipe with the hem of his apron. As always, Sammy wore a MADE IN THE USA baseball cap, and his sideburns were thick and unruly. Sammy fancied himself a dead ringer for the famous Southern Civil War general, Joseph Johnston, and styled his facial hair to mirror the black-and-white photographs of Johnston decorating the walls of the Wilson Tavern. Sammy was a Virginia history buff and knew more about the Old Dominion than anyone James had ever met. The tavern, the only bar in Quincy's Gap, was located on a side road off the highway. Its clientele was a mix of bikers, truckers seeking a respite from the road, professionals looking to relax after a trying workday, and a mishmash of local mend and women catching up with friends over a cold beer.

Bennett grabbed a handful of peanuts from a bowl on the bar and popped the nuts into his mouth. "I have an ethical dilemma, James. As one of the supervisors at the post office, it is my honor and privilege to handle customer complaints." He chewed for a moment before sipping his ale. "Usually, the gripes are about nothing. Mail got delivered to the wrong address, the protective wrapper on some guy's nudie magazine is missing, a mail carrier scared a lady's prize poodle—those kinds of things."

Bennett paused for another sip and James followed suit. The ale was rich and honey-smooth on his tongue. As a refreshing stream ran down his throat, he was able to ignore the tension in Bennett's hands as his friend crushed a peanut between his thumb and index finger.

James gave him an encouraging nod. "Go on."

"Well, I got a complaint on Monday that I normally wouldn't give a flying fiddle about, but ever since Gillian called to tell me that Ronnie's death wasn't a suicide . . ." Bennett suddenly stopped talking. He filled his cheeks with peanuts and stared at the counter with a tormented gaze.

"You think this complaint might be tied to the murder. And you're wondering how to bring it to light while still protecting a coworker?" James guessed.

Bennett sighed. "That sums it up nicely, my man. You see, the complaint's about Carter—about how he's been hanging around Ronnie's place like a tomcat on the prowl. She is . . . or was, on his route, but the boy rearranged his delivery times so he could see her when she came home for lunch every day. I hear from the gossips in the mailroom that the foolish kid even followed her around town. But that was off the clock and therefore, none of my damned business."

"Who called with the grievance?"

"That's the thing." Bennett tugged on his mustache. "Ronnie did. On Monday, right after lunch."

"Did you talk to her?" Unable to restrain himself, James gripped Bennett's shoulder with a firm hand. "That might be the last time anyone heard from her."

"Don't I know it? But I didn't talk to her. She left a message on the branch voice mail, and I didn't listen to it until yesterday. I was real busy because one of the sorters called in sick and I had to lend a hand." Bennett gently shrugged off James's hand. "But look, there's no way Carter is some crazed killer. He just had it bad for that woman. If I tell the sheriff, Lord knows what will happen to that boy."

James took a silent pull of beer as Bennett finished his mug in three swallows and signaled Sammy for a refill. "You have to share that information, Bennett. I know you're worried about Carter. I'd feel the same way if it was the Fitzgerald twins, but if Carter's innocent, then it'll all come out just fine. In the end, he'll understand why you had to report Ronnie's call. It's better for the authorities to find out now, from you. If they discover Carter had been stalking a murder victim on their own, it'll look much worse for both of you."

"This is exactly what I was afraid of!" Bennett shouted. "You're already throwing words like 'stalk' and 'murder victim' around. And that's just you! What chance does Carter stand against that redheaded pig, Donovan?"

"I'm sorry. I didn't mean to imply anything," James was quick to say. "But you have to wonder about why Carter didn't just talk to Ronnie. Why not ask her out on a date like an ordinary guy approaching an ordinary girl?"

Bennett spluttered in his beer. "I don't know how things were for you back in Williamsburg, but it's not exactly easy! I can't even remember the last time I had the nerve to ask out a pretty lady. Shoot, Ditka was probably still coaching the Bears. It's hard, man. Carter's real shy to boot."

Thinking of all his missteps with Lucy, James nodded in understanding. "If that's the case, the sheriff will come to the same conclusion. Huckabee's a good man, Bennett. You and Carter should take a copy of Ronnie's voice mail to the sheriff together. Carter's cooperation would make a strong statement about his innocence."

For the first time since James had entered the tavern, Bennett looked marginally less worried. "Hey, that is a good plan. I'll tell Carter about the call first thing in the morning. At lunchtime, we'll head over to the sheriff's department and get this whole mess straightened out. Thanks, man." He managed a slight smile. "I knew you could help."

"Don't worry about it. I'm glad you called me and I have no doubt that you guys will be back delivering mail before your lunch break is over," James said cheerfully, raising his newly filled glass and saluting his friend.

He was dead wrong.

• • •

"I'm not going to make the movie," Lucy said, sounding crestfallen.

James had been preparing to leave the library that Friday afternoon when she called. Now, he sank back into his chair with a frown. "Why not?"

"Bennett and Carter came in at noon today with new infor- mation about Ronnie, and I can't leave until I find out what's going on."

"They're still at the station?" James was stunned.

"Just Carter. Bennett was told to leave. He looked terrible, James. He wouldn't even stop to talk to me. I've never seen him so shaken." She paused. "Wait a minute. Do *you* know what this is about?"

James quickly recapped his conversation with Bennett at the Wilson Tavern. "I feel horrible, Lucy. This is totally my fault. I told Bennett that it would be a walk in the park as long as he and Carter were forthcoming about Ronnie's complaint. Do you think Carter's been charged with a crime?" He heard his voice rising along with his stress level.

"No, not yet, but he's been questioned all afternoon. Donovan's having the time of his life. I can hear him shouting all the way down the hall."

James moaned.

"Maybe Carter *is* a reasonable suspect, James. The guy was obviously fixated on Ronnie. They say it doesn't take much for a romantic obsession to turn into something darker. Something violent. What if Carter didn't want to give Ronnie the chance to reject him? Either that, or he didn't want anyone else to be with her."

"No one wants to be rejected, Lucy, but that doesn't mean we go around drugging and drowning the object of our desire!" He heard the shrillness in his tone and immediately calmed down. "Sorry, I didn't mean to yell. I just feel terrible for Bennett. He did exactly as I suggested and he's probably sorry he ever called me last night."

"I understand." Lucy's voice was soft and tender. "I'm not saying Carter is guilty either, but I want to stick around to see what develops. I feel like I owe it to Bennett to keep an eye on Carter. Can we meet at Dolly's later for dinner?"

James thought back to his last meeting with Lucy at Dolly's. "Dinner, yes, but not at Dolly's. Let's go to that restaurant just off the interstate instead. It's about twenty minutes away and the architecture reminds me of a farm. I can't remember the name."

"The Red Barn? The place with the buffet loaded with homemade Southern dishes? You're on. I love that place." James heard men's voices in the background. "Oh, here they come with Carter. I'll catch you later," Lucy said hurriedly and was gone.

• • •

By the time they reached the Red Barn, dinner service was long over, and a few night owls were having cups of coffee as the wait-staff wiped tables and disassembled the buffet. James and Lucy also ordered coffee and were given a piece of Kentucky chocolate-chip pie on the house.

"Y'all are here at the right time," their waitress said. "We bake fresh desserts every mornin', which means we give away all the leftovers right about now. Thing is, we've been selling out of this pie ever since the Derby. I can't believe there's any left. Guess folks are finally sick of it." She lowered her voice. "It's a damn fine pie, but I'm lookin' forward to servin' our regular chocolate chess again."

James and Lucy savored their pie. Each bite was a heavenly blend of crunchy walnut pieces, soft semisweet morsels, and creamy chocolate. The homemade crust had been baked a buttery golden brown and tasted like a shortbread cookie.

"It's almost good enough to make me forget about today," Lucy said, licking whipped cream from her fork tines.

James pushed his plate away a few inches in an attempt to leave his dessert unfinished. "Was Carter released?"

"Eventually, yes. The coroner's report stated that Ronnie's death occurred sometime between six and eleven p.m. on Monday night. Carter had a pretty firm alibi. After dinner at Dolly's Diner, he went back to Clint's house while Dolly closed up. Carter and Clint have become good friends. They both have this thing for *America's Most Wanted* and Court TV. The two of them split a six-pack and hung out until almost midnight. Carter was able to provide plenty of detail about the shows they watched, as well as a catalogue of highlights from the Orioles game."

"There was a game that night?"

Lucy also pushed her plate away after dabbing at the last crumb with her index finger. "Apparently, it was a make-up game after

Sunday night's rainout. Clint was switching to the game during commercials and Carter could practically give a play-by-play of the parts they watched. Huckabee seemed convinced, though he gave Carter the don't-leave-town speech before letting him go."

"Thank goodness." James sighed in relief. "I hope that means Bennett will speak to me again."

"You gave him good advice, James." Lucy put her hand over his. "Your heart is always in the right place." She smiled and then tried to cover her mouth as the smile merged into an enormous yawn. "I have to be back at work early tomorrow. The sheriff asked me to go through the personal items from Ronnie's town house. It's a great chance for me to shine." She yawned again. "If I can find a decent clue about the identity of her killer, that is."

"I'd better get you home," James said and paid their bill. He drove a weary Lucy to her front door and kissed her chastely on the cheek. "Get some sleep. I'll see you Sunday."

• • •

The weekend flew by. On Saturday, James called Willy to ask if he'd be willing to build a custom computer table for the library.

"I'm right busy with Pet Palace projects, Professor," Willy said. "But I'd be happy to build your library the finest computer table anyone has ever seen as soon as I'm caught up on pet house orders. After all, you and your friends welcomed me to this town straight off. Without Ms. Gillian, I'd be on the unemployment line by now."

"You're a true Renaissance man, Willy. You can run a business, keep the books, and you're a skilled carpenter. Gillian says you could assemble Noah's ark out of a pile of toothpicks."

Willy laughed. "She's too much!" He quickly sobered. "I am a grateful man, that's for sure, but I do miss dishing out my custard. I love the look of delight on people's faces when they're eating my sweets. You can watch folks letting all their cares drift away like feathers in the breeze. Not much company out here in this garage. I'm a bit of a social butterfly and there isn't much chitchat between me, myself, and I."

James felt a rush of guilt. It had been weeks since the fire and he hadn't taken the time to check on Willy. "How would you like to join our supper club for dinner tomorrow night?" he asked, confident the others would approve.

"It'd be my pleasure." Willy sounded grateful. "I'll stop by the library later today to take some measurements for that table. You say you have some drawings for me, too?"

James told him that a rough sketch was behind the checkout counter and that Mrs. Waxman would be glad to assist him.

"See you Sunday," Willy said cheerfully and rang off.

After leafing through the pages of several cookbooks, James decided to make lemon chicken with lima beans for Sunday's dinner. He jotted down a grocery list and headed out to the Sweet Tooth in hopes of avoiding the early lunch crowd and scoring one of the prized parking spaces along Main Street.

James spent a few moments admiring Megan's new window display, which featured oversized butter cookies shaped and decorated to form an enormous bouquet of flowers. There were pink and purple tulips, white and yellow daisies, blue iris, red poppies, and orange tiger lilies. Inside, the bakery was busy, especially for in between mealtimes. Megan and Amelia were both working, and James recognized several of his fellow dieters from Witness to Fitness waiting to be served. As he listened to their orders, he noted that only some were sticking to bran muffins and loaves of multigrain bread. The others opted for more decadent selections like tiramisu or butterscotch brownies.

"Professor!" Megan greeted him warmly when he reached the front of the line. "What can I do for you today?"

James chose a loaf of Italian bread for Sunday's dinner as well as raisin bread for his father. As he examined the bread, he noticed the French baguettes on display in a wire basket and remembered the last time he'd seen such a baguette. It had been sitting, untouched, on Ronnie's kitchen table.

"Are you the only local baker to sell that kind of bread, Megan?"

"I sure am. The closest our grocery stores have are those thick loaves in the freezer section. That's too much bread unless someone's hosting the whole family for Sunday supper. And even so, their dough is bland and the crust is limp. My crust is crisp and flaky because I bake the bread fresh every day."

"Did Ronnie Levitt buy a French baguette from you on Monday?" James asked in a soft murmur.

Megan frowned. "We're closed Mondays, and Amelia worked the Sunday afternoon shift, so you'll have to ask her." Studying James for a moment Megan began to look worried. "Wait a minute. Does my bread have something to do with . . . with what happened to Ronnie?"

"No, it's nothing like that," James hastily assured her. "But if Ronnie didn't buy it, then whoever came to her house for wine and cheese did. I just thought I'd find out who paid for the bread. I guess I'm chasing down a lead." He lowered his voice even more. "As a favor to Lucy."

Megan nodded. The whole town knew about Lucy's aspirations to become a deputy. After filling James's order, Megan approached her daughter and whispered in her ear. Amelia paused in the act of packing frosted carrot cake muffins into a cardboard box and mumbled something inaudible to her mother.

"It was Ronnie," Megan told James sotto voce. "She bought the bread at about three o'clock on Sunday. Sorry we couldn't help you more than that. After all, your Spring Fling, combined with the horrible truth about those fake diet meals, has saved our business." She put her hand to her mouth. "Oh, that came out wrong. I mean, I feel terrible about what happened to Ronnie and I wish I hadn't said anything negative about her. I'm just grateful to have customers lining up in front of my counter again."

"You don't need to feel ashamed, Megan," James said. "You were just worried about your business and your daughter's welfare. We all say things we regret from time to time, but everyone in this town knows you're as sweet as the name above your door."

Megan smiled and handed James his bag. "I snuck a treat in there for you—one of our raspberry cheese Danishes. Have a nice day!"

• • •

On Sunday afternoon, after church service followed by a light lunch of tuna salad, some crackers, and a juicy peach, James tidied the backyard. He mowed the lawn, pulled weeds, and drove a dozen tiki torches into the ground around the picnic table in hopes of creating a festive atmosphere. Jackson was decked out in his painting overalls, but instead of holing up in his shed to work on a still life of birds and foliage, he was painting the kitchen walls a soft blue.

"I love this shade, Pop. What gave you the idea to paint the kitchen this color?"

Jackson jerked his thumb at an old *Southern Living* magazine. "Your mama had a page turned down in there. Told me it was her dream kitchen. I've tried to match everything I saw in those pictures."

James picked up the dog-eared magazine and immediately found the page showing his mother's fantasy kitchen. Jackson had done his best to reproduce it. He'd copied the stainless steel appliances, the terra-cotta tile flooring, and the vintage-style light fixtures. Now, he was completing the final touches by painting the room the exact color as the kitchen in the glossy photographs. James stared at the magazine and tried to hold back tears. He hadn't realized how much his father had loved his mother, or how much he still missed her. Their new kitchen was a masterpiece, created in memory of a woman who derived such pleasure from cooking for the two men she loved.

"Don't you have something to do with your time?" Jackson growled, sensing the mood that had overtaken his son.

James put the magazine aside. Avoiding his father's sharp gaze, he said, "I'm going to the garden center to buy petunias and a few pots of geraniums. Be back soon."

Because it was a mild, sunny afternoon, the garden center was crowded, and it took James over an hour to make his selections and maneuver his loaded cart around throngs of industrious homeowners to stand in the back of the long checkout line. By the time he finally loaded his plants into the Bronco and returned home, he had to work furiously to get ready for his guests.

He'd just finished setting the geranium pots by the kitchen door and planting the violet and fuchsia petunias in the raised bed around the cracked concrete patio when Lucy's Jeep appeared in the driveway.

"I have been working like crazy," she began breathlessly. "Sheriff Huckabee brought me a bunch of boxes with Ronnie's personal effects to sift through. There wasn't much that seemed personal about her life, though. No diplomas, letters, yearbooks, scrapbooks—just financial records and receipts and stuff like that. I brought two photographs with me. I'm hoping that one of us can identify where they were taken." She paused, catching sight of the picnic table and its checkered cloth, the lit tiki torches, and the vibrant flowers. "This is lovely, James."

"Hello!" Gillian waved the tail of a long, gauzy orange scarf in greeting as she and Lindy walked up the driveway. "We rang the front bell, but no one answered. Oh! We're dining outdoors! How marvelous! We can break bread under a canvas of star light."

Lindy peered up into the thick canopy of trees and smiled. "I don't know. We all eat so fast that it might not get dark enough to see the stars. Hello, Willy! I didn't hear you walking behind us. You're as quiet as a cat."

"Howdy, all." Willy hugged the three women and handed James a bottle of sparkling cider. "You've got a mighty fine place here."

"Renovations still going on?" Bennett called out, appearing around the corner of the house. "Is that why we're roughing it tonight?"

James grinned. "Actually, the kitchen is so incredible that I'm almost afraid to use it. It looks like a celebrity chef should be at the stove instead of me. Make yourselves comfortable. I'll show you how the kitchen turned out after dinner."

As James stepped inside to collect a pitcher of sun tea, he stuck his head into the den where his father was chewing on a bologna and cheese sandwich while watching the evening news. "You sure you won't come out and join us, Pop?"

Jackson eyed the doorway suspiciously. "Nah. I need to keep up on current affairs. Go on and visit with your friends. And shut the den door before you go."

Gathering a wooden tray, the tea pitcher, and a set of glass tumblers covered with faded lemons and limes that the Henrys had used for decades, James rejoined his friends. Sipping the refreshing sun tea, The members Flab Five took turns studied the two photographs Lucy had laid out on the picnic table.

"Is that Ronnie?" James asked, pointing at a woman with an

athletic build. A fringe of thick bangs hung over a pair of round glasses. She wore a Red Cross vest over a dirty white T-shirt and a pair of loose-fitting walking shorts. She carried what appeared to be a Red Cross donation box and her mouth was curved into a triumphant smile.

"This woman doesn't look like the Ronnie we knew," Lucy said. "She's not as bony here, and there's this pageboy hairstyle, but it's her. I found the vest and glasses in with her personal effects, and if you look at her face using this, you'll recognize that smile." She handed Bennett a magnifying glass. "The question is *where* was this taken?"

"That's easy." Bennett pointed at the building in the background. "That's the Astrodome in Houston. Though out of focus, those red, yellow, and orange seats in the background are the upper tiers of the ballpark."

Lucy squinted at the photo. "I'm glad we have a sports nut in the mix. Thanks, Bennett."

"And I can tell you where that second picture is taken." Lindy held her hand over her ample bosom. "My family would be sorely disappointed if I couldn't, considering I have about twenty cousins living there. See that art deco building off to the left? That's a hotel in South Beach. Some of my mother's family live in an apartment across the street."

"Miami?" Lucy asked.

Gillian took hold of the photograph. "My, my. Ronnie is so young in this shot. She looks like an all-American girl."

James leaned over Gillian's shoulder and examined the image of Ronnie in her early twenties. She was lounging on a low wall next to a red hibiscus bush and was soaking up the sun like a lizard. Her light brown hair was streaked with blond and fell over her shoulders in soft waves. A pair of glasses with cat's-eye frames and tinted lenses was pushed up over her forehead and she wore a blue sundress, a pair of white Keds, and very little makeup. Her eyes were shining with a mixture of hopefulness and delight and her smile seemed self-conscious.

"She looks like a completely different person in each photo," James said.

"And totally different from the Ronnie we knew," Lindy added.

"May I?" Willy held out his hand. He was sitting quietly at the end of the picnic table and had yet to examine the images of Ronnie.

"Of course." Lucy slid the photos in front of him. "I've been dying to figure out where these were taken in hopes of shedding some light on Ronnie's past. But even now that I know the settings, no bells are going off."

Willy examined the shot of young Ronnie and pushed it aside. When he picked up the photo of her posing at the Astrodome, he drew in a sharp breath.

"Well, I'll be damned," he muttered darkly.

"What is it, Willy?"

"I've seen this woman. On TV." Willy stroked his chin.

James felt a prickle on the back of his neck. "That's what Pete said that night at Witness to Fitness. He told Ronnie that he remembered her from TV."

"In what context?" Lucy looked at Willy intently. "Does it have anything to do with this photo?"

"Yes, it does." Willy exhaled heavily. "This picture was taken when all the folks beaten up by Katrina were refugees in the Astrodome. Ronnie, or whatever her name was then, pretended to collect money on behalf of the Red Cross."

Gillian was horrified. "Pretended?"

Willy nodded sorrowfully. "So many folks showed such generosity of spirit during that awful time. They wanted to help people like me get back on our feet, and they wanted to help right away. The churches, the Red Cross, and all kinds of groups were collecting money to get us out of our ruined neighborhoods and put food in our bellies." He sighed lugubriously. "Sadly, the snakes came out of the grass too. Ronnie was one of the vilest snakes. She collected money for days from volunteers that had come from across the nation to help, from the fine people of Houston, and from any giving soul who'd drop a dollar in her box. Then, she ran off with every dime."

"What a terrible creature!" Gillian exclaimed.

"Well, she was caught." Willy's eyes gleamed. "Not all of the scoundrels were, but she was. She got jail time for it, too. Her story was all over the news for nights on end. I think the media used her to show other thieves and sneaks that people had grown wise to their kind."

The group was silent for a few minutes and then Lucy passed her hands over her face in exasperation. "The list of suspects who must want her dead must be as long as a country mile. People would take a number to get revenge on such a piece of scum. To profit from another person's tragedy . . ."

Involuntarily, James stared at Willy. The rest of his friends did the same.

"Don't look at me!" Willy threw his hands into the air. "I haven't got a violent bone in my body. Besides, I didn't even recognize that wretched woman until I saw this picture."

"We know you're no killer, Willy." A deflated Lucy reclaimed the two photos. "But Pete was able to identify her. That means someone else from her past could too. But how am I going to discover that person's identity?"

"It might help if you knew her real name," Willy suggested. "When she got arrested she wasn't Veronica Levitt. I'm sorry that I can't remember what she went by then."

"No problem, Willy. She's a bona fide criminal, and that means I know exactly who'll know her name, place of birth, and complete wrap sheet," Bennett declared.

"Who?" they all asked in unison.

"Carter Peabody," Bennett said, and when his friends gazed at him blankly, he added, "Also known as Mr. Court TV."

Chapter Fourteen

Strawberry Banana Smoothie

Lucy told James all about her conversation with Carter over smoothies late Wednesday afternoon. The pair sat at a large plastic table in front of a gas station. Though lacking in ambiance, the convenience store served the best grilled cheese sandwiches and fruit smoothies within hundreds of miles, and it was nearly impos- sible to secure a table during the summer months as both teenagers and families with young kids liked to socialize on the patio.

"You talk, I'll drink and listen," James had said when they first sat down. It was easy to wait for Lucy to summarize her meeting with Carter when he had a delicious smoothie to occupy him.

"This morning, I waited for Carter outside the post office holding the photograph of Ronnie from when she was in Houston," Lucy began. "Bennett had called Carter the night before to tell him that a member of the sheriff's department wanted to speak to him before his shift."

Carter appeared to be unfazed by his afternoon of intense questioning the previous Friday and cheerfully told Lucy he'd spent the weekend creating an outline for a screenplay he planned to write. He explained that the story was about a postal worker turned bank robber and that he was actually grateful to have gained firsthand knowledge about the interviewing process. Not only that, but he'd love to be included in any investigation being conducted by her department whenever possible.

With a smile, Lucy told James that it had taken a great deal of restraint not to tell Carter that he had a screw loose. She showed him the photograph instead. He'd squinted at it for a few moments before snapping his fingers in recognition. Finally, he'd jabbed his index finger at the image of Red Cross Ronnie.

"He remembered hearing about her from a member of a chat group he's in," Lucy said. "The group is for people who share a common interest in America's most notorious criminals. Carter went on to say that he suspected Ronnie was a woman with a crim- inal past all along. He claims that he has a knack for sniffing out felons."

James grunted in disbelief at this.

"I know, it's ridiculous, but I had to humor him to get what I wanted." Lucy shrugged. "Anyway, Carter said that her name at the time this photo was taken was Martha Hari. He thinks Ronnie picked it because it sounded like Mata Hari, the infamous spy."

"What did he mean by 'picked it?'"

"Carter was certain that it was another alias—that no one's given a name like that at birth. Because we have Ronnie's prints and she already has a criminal record as Martha Hari, we might be able to discover her true identity using the National Crime Information Center database. I explained this to Carter."

Grinning, James said, "If he spends his free time reading about criminals, that news must have had him drooling."

Lucy laughed. "It sure did! He actually asked if he could be there to witness the process." Her smile vanished. "But I don't have much more pull than Carter. I'll probably need to *borrow* one of the deputy's passwords just to access the database. In some ways, Carter and I are both amateurs looking for a taste of what it's like to be a member of a law enforcement team."

"You'll get there," James assured her. "What did you say to Carter next?"

"Just that I knew exactly how he felt. I confessed that I was trying to solve Ronnie's murder in order to prove to myself, and to Huckabee, that I'm ready to take the written test and become a deputy." Her eyes grew glassy. "I might even be ready to take the physical this summer."

"You can do anything you set your mind to." James squeezed her hand. "Did you learn anything useful about Ronnie's past?"

Lucy stirred her orange cream smoothie and looked dejected. "Not much. She served less than a year of a three-year sentence for her Katrina scam. She was another case of overcrowding in our country's correctional facilities. She was also brought up on charges of fraud in the state of Florida when she was only eighteen, but her case was dismissed due to lack of evidence."

"Was her name Martha then?"

"No. Trudy Axelrod. Which is her real name. Her birth certificate and social security number are tucked away in a safe-deposit box at the bank along with a slew of fake driver's licenses and other falsified documents, but it looks like she was actually born in Coral Springs, Florida."

James thought of the photograph of a much younger Ronnie in South Beach. "What was she accused of doing in Florida?"

"Creating a telemarketing fraud that tried to part people from their money for a bogus investment. Trudy claimed to be raising capital to build a new senior center and casino south of Fort Lauderdale. The case fell apart because no one could link her to the phone calls or to the post office box where the checks were mailed."

James angled his straw to capture the last drop of red liquid in his cup. "She probably used a pay phone. Research shows that many senior citizens are too polite to hang up on telemarketers. They're more susceptible to scams than the rest of the population." He laughed. "The experts should do a study on my father! He loves giving those telemarketers what-for. They never call back a second time. Never."

Lucy's smile was distracted. "At least the sheriff was impressed that I was able to discover more facts about our victim, and I was only successful because of our supper club meeting. However, we're still miles away from solving this mystery. Despite our combined efforts, Ronnie's killer has outsmarted everyone."

"Why don't we go out and visit Mr. Wimple on Saturday?" James suggested, hoping to keep Lucy from becoming morose. "Someone donated the two latest David McCullough books in pristine condition and I thought, as a former history teacher, he'd enjoy reading them. If nothing else, the visit would take your mind off the case for a bit."

"That's a great idea, James. I'm sure he'd love the company. Besides, he might have remembered something else that could tie Ronnie and Pete together. Have you called him yet?"

"No. Those McCullough books just came in this morning."

"Well, let me do that much." When she next spoke, her smile was as bright as a star. "After we visit Fred, we could go out for that movie I owe you."

James squeezed her hand again and said, "Sounds like a date."

• • •

It was difficult to ignore Lucy's nervous energy on the drive to Harrisonburg. She drummed her fingernails against the passenger window, crossed and uncrossed her legs, and continuously changed the radio station.

"You seem a bit edgy," James said, casting her a sideways glance. "Is something on your mind?"

Lucy's lips curved in an enigmatic grin. "You'll find out soon enough. But while I have the chance, I just want to tell you how glad I am that you're with me today."

A rush of warmth filled James.

After another mile of silence, he nudged Lucy playfully in the arm. "Come on, aren't you going to give me a hint?"

Lucy refused to elaborate. Instead, she began to sing along to a Carrie Underwood song. When she was finished crooning, she asked James questions about his life in Williamsburg. They talked about his past until he pulled his truck into the visitor lot of Wandering Springs.

Fred Wimple was waiting for them in the same sun porch chair he'd been in on their previous visit. This time, he rose to his feet and greeted them eagerly. After thanking James profusely for the books, he turned to Lucy, his eyes gleaming with animation and intelligence.

"I took a look at your requests, and you were correct on both counts, young lady," he said as they all settled into their chairs. Fred showed Lucy the cell phone in his left hand. "I borrowed this from one of my friends, and though I'm not a big fan of these smart phones, I can press certain numbers if need be. You just give me a signal and help will be on its way."

Lucy nodded in approval. "That's an excellent idea, Fred, thank you. Shall we have some of that famous limeade while we're waiting?"

"Absolutely." Fred winked at his guests and raised a hand into the air. As if by magic, a young woman appeared and took their order. "I'll bring y'all some Thin Mints, too. We had to buy so many Girl Scout cookies this year that we'll never get rid of them if we don't offer them at every opportunity. Be right back."

"Would someone care to tell me what is going on?" James asked in what he believed was a very calm, patient tone.

Lucy cast her eyes around the sunporch and lowered her voice so that the pair of elderly women who sat in matching rockers on the opposite end of the veranda couldn't listen in. James doubted they could hear anything above the sound of their own voices and the steady clicking of their knitting needles, but he leaned closer to Lucy anyway.

"After you mentioned coming to see our friend Fred, I started thinking about our last visit to Wandering Springs. At first, I was just fantasizing about that delicious limeade." She stopped talking to thank the waitress, who set a pitcher of limeade and a plate loaded with cookies in the center of the table. After distributing tall glasses filled with ice, the waitress disappeared inside, and Lucy continued her narrative. "But the more I rehashed the details of our last visit, the more I began to suspect that the answers to our riddles lay within these walls. With a little help from Fred and your friend Murphy, I was able to confirm my suspicions."

"What suspicions? Can you *please* stop being so vague?" James grabbed a Thin Mint and snapped it in half in frustration.

"Sorry, I'm just having a good time now that I finally have the answers." Lucy helped herself to a cookie. "Do you remember the older gentleman Dylan was with when we were here before?"

"The man in the wheelchair? The one who seemed to be suffering from Alzheimer's?" James asked.

"Yes. That man is Dylan's father," Fred said in a soft, sad voice.

James sat back in his chair and tried to work out how that fact connected to either murder case. "I don't get it. What does that information tell you?"

Lucy grabbed James's hand. "Mr. Shane told us that Dylan was the best point guard in all of Miami. Remember? Who else spent time in Miami, James?"

"Ronnie. When she was in her twenties. So?" James absently rubbed Lucy's palm. "I need a few more hints."

"This is where Murphy helped me out." Lucy took a long swallow of limeade. "She researched any archived news stories relating to the Shanes of Miami. In doing so, she discovered two terrible things. The first was that Mrs. Shane, Dylan's mama, died of uterine cancer when he was in high school. The second is that the nurse hired to provide Mrs. Shane with in-home health care successfully ran off with the family savings immediately after Mrs. Shane's death. The nurse was never seen or heard from again."

James felt the pieces of the puzzle come together. "Was the nurse's name Trudy Axelrod?"

"Actually, no. It was Stacy Leach." Lucy shrugged. "And neither I nor Murphy could find a single piece of information on this woman. According to databases on Floridian residents, Stacy she never existed."

"But if we're assuming Ronnie, or whoever she was back then, was Stacy The Stealing Nurse, then Dylan would have only been a boy when she was around. I'd guess she was in her early to mid-twenties when that photo was taken."

Lucy popped half a cookie in her mouth. "That's true. Dylan would have been a junior in high school. However, I have more proof to tie him to the murders."

Fred cleared his throat and looked around. "Which is where I came in. Miss Hanover phoned me and filled me in on the latest murder. She asked me to find out all I could about Mr. Shane. Once I'd confirmed his identity, this astute young lady requested that I do something highly irregular. Basically, she asked me to snoop where I'm not permitted to snoop."

Fred stopped speaking as another elderly gentleman wearing a white and green argyle sweater vest over a pink golf shirt settled into a nearby chair. Within seconds, two rambunctious boys joined him and began to set up a portable Chinese checkers board on the glass-topped table. As the trio started playing, the noise of their chatter and game play swept over the entire porch, allowing Fred to continue without fear of being overheard.

"Miss Hanover asked me to discover whether sleeping aids were on Mr. Shane's list of medications. To accomplish this, I had to access the confidential records. These are kept in a staff office. Residents are not allowed to enter this office." He grinned mischievously. "Suffice it to say, I was able to access the office after midnight. After picking the file cabinet lock with a paper clip—a skill I picked up because I used to lose my file cabinet keys on a regular basis—I discovered that Mr. Shane had a prescription for Valium. It was meant to relieve anxiety. However, he was only given the pills on Saturdays, and only when a visiting family member was present."

"Saturday. The day of the week Dylan regularly volunteers." James shook his head in disbelief. "But he's such a kind and caring person. I can't see him poisoning two people, let alone drowning one of them and setting fire to Willy's building with an innocent man left inside. That sounds like the work of someone who's come completely unhinged!" He released Lucy's hand and rubbed furiously at his temple. "Can a person really lead an exercise class, compliment all of us on a job well done, and then go out and kill someone within the hour?"

"We'll see what caused him to act like a madman when we confront him." Lucy pointed off in the distance and James saw a figure pushing a wheelchair. The two men were heading toward the mansion.

Looking at James, Lucy's said in a soft, sorrowful voice. "I wanted to give him a few more moments with his daddy before his life changes forever. That old man may never see his son again."

James gaped at her. "But we don't have any hard evidence, do we? What's the motive? Why would Dylan hurt Pete? Or burn Willy's shop? Did Dylan have any reason for committing those crimes? They have nothing to do with Ronnie."

"I need him to explain that to us. Nothing we've discovered will hold up in court without Dylan's confession. That's why we have to corner him and pretend to know the whole truth."

"I still believe this is a foolhardy endeavor, Miss Hanover," Fred said.

"And I firmly believe that Dylan Shane was seeking revenge," Lucy calmly replied. "I don't think he'll become violent with us. We never did him any harm."

Fred lifted a pair of binoculars from the empty seat next to him. "I'm going to call the authorities if I see the slightest indication that your reckless plan has gone amiss."

"Thank you, Fred." Lucy stood up, dusted crumbs from her lap, and planted a kiss on the Fred's forehead. "Coming, James?"

Determined to support Lucy's convictions, James followed her up the garden path. It seemed surreal that a murderer could be lingering in such a tranquil setting. Monarch butterflies hovered above clusters of bachelor's buttons and fat bumblebees settled on the feathery heads of golden yarrow. The gravel of the garden path crunched pleasantly underfoot and the twitter of wrens and finches darting about feeders and birdbaths filled the air with an orchestrated harmony. Turning back to the house, James saw Fred Wimple raise his binoculars and point them in their direction.

Something in Lucy's bearing must have alerted Dylan that she wasn't approaching him for an idle chat. He slowed his pace until he and his father came to rest next to one of the wooden park benches bordering the path. He raised his hand in greeting, a forced smile on his face, and before taking a seat on the bench.

"Hello, Dylan," Lucy said. There was a hint of sadness in her voice.

"Hi, there. Back to pay another visit to Mr. Wimple?" Dylan managed an airy tone, but his eyes betrayed his wariness.

Lucy sat down at the opposite end of the bench and James stood behind her, his bearing as stiff as a soldier's. "How's your daddy doing today, Dylan?"

Dylan's eyes narrowed for a split second, but he quickly recovered and flashed Lucy a puzzled smile. "Who?"

Lucy turned to Mr. Shane, who was gazing happily out across the sweeping expanse of green lawn. "Good afternoon, Mr. Shane."

"He's not my father," Dylan said, putting his hand out as if to protect the old man in the wheelchair. "I told you before, he gets confused. And I shouldn't have to say this to you, but it's not nice to mess with folks with memory issues."

"When did his memory loss first occur?" Lucy asked gently.

"Randolph's?" Dylan darted a covert look of tenderness at the man Lucy believed was his father. "From what I've heard, he was quite young. Still in his forties. His was a case of early onset dementia. It's pretty rare and pretty debilitating. Folks afflicted with his condition at that age deteriorate faster than older people. They forget stuff at home, at work. They end up losing their jobs. Their homes. Everything." He swallowed hard. "Take Randolph here. He couldn't even remember how to make simple meals for u—" He checked himself and then continued, "For his two kids."

"You were going to say 'us,' weren't you? You are one of his two kids." Lucy spoke rapidly, giving Dylan no chance to interrupt or offer another denial. "I can't begin to imagine what that was like for you. It must have been really hard, Dylan. You already had to deal with the passing of your mama and the betrayal of having Stacy Leach run off with your family's savings. You were just a kid. That's too much for any child to bear." James was surprised to see tears in Lucy's eyes. "That's too much for any person to bear."

Dylan stared at his hands and said nothing. The seconds dragged by. The inner turmoil expressing itself on Dylan's face seemed so incongruent with the lush and peaceful garden. The sun was shining directly down on them and James wiped off the perspiration gathering at the nape of his neck with the back of his hand.

"What do you want?" Dylan finally asked. His shoulders were slumped, and he sounded defeated.

"I know that Ronnie and Stacy are the same woman. How did she succeed in swindling your family, Dylan? How did she get away with such treachery?"

Still focused on the lines etched into his palms, Dylan said, "My father started to show symptoms of his illness even before my mom died. He was an electrician, and he began making the kind of mistakes you can't make doing that job. He almost fried himself and his coworkers more than once before he was finally fired. Stacy knew right away what was wrong with him. She said she saw the signs when she came to live with us. She told my mom and gave her advice on how to handle it."

Dylan touched his father's shoulder before continuing. "Stacy volunteered to stay and help after mom died. She said she felt like part of the family and would be with us until she could arrange for the insurance to pay for a substitute—someone from her nursing school program who could live with us and keep an eye on Dad while my sister and I went to school."

"I'm assuming she never contacted the insurance company," Lucy said.

Dylan shook his head. "Of course not. She was too busy figuring out how to get certain legal documents signed by my clueless father so that she could get her hands on his retirement funds and the money in his savings account. Both accounts were at the same bank. Stacy showed up at the branch with power of attorney and other official papers, withdrew every cent, had the money wired to a different account, and BAM! She was gone." Dylan balled his hands together and James watched nervously as the fists trembled violently.

Lucy gave Dylan a moment to get his voice and hands under control. "How old were you when she betrayed your family?"

"I was a senior in high school. Had a full ride to U of Miami come the next fall, but there would be no college for me. That was the end of school and basketball forever. I went straight to work. I've been a garbage collector, a shirt presser, a short-order cook— you name it. I kept moving around like *I* was the one on the run. I couldn't settle down for long in any place or at any job. Then I started managing a gym in a little town in Tennessee. That's when I saw Stacy again. It was total coincidence."

"In Tennessee?" Lucy was surprised by this revelation.

"Yeah, except her name was Kelly Davies and she ran a business called A Leaner You. It was just like Witness to Fitness. Same food scam. She made a tidy profit for about six months before splitting. I'd only lived there a few weeks, but I was pretty sure Kelly and Stacy were the same person, so I followed her. I kept following her —all the way to Quincy's Gap. I guess someone was getting wise to her scam in Tennessee, and because of that Stacy decided to set up shop in a new place as Ronnie Levitt. Since I wasn't worried about her recognizing me, I applied for the exercise coach job so I could get close to her."

"You mean, so you could get even with her," Lucy corrected.

Dylan turned to her, his eyes blazing. "There was no getting *even*. She destroyed the lives of *three people*. Me, my father, and my kid sister. She took everything from us—weeks after we lost my mom!" He slammed the bench with his open hand. "We couldn't even mourn her, my sister and me. We were too busy figuring out how to pay bills, or make macaroni and cheese, or keep my father from wandering out of the neighborhood! We never got to grieve!"

Seeing that Dylan was getting worked up, Lucy quietly asked, "Where's your sister now? Is she doing okay?"

Dylan released a long breath. "Julie's still in Florida. As soon as she turned eighteen, she married an old rich guy. She's had three husbands and never loved a single one. After her second divorce, she admitted to me that she never wanted to feel as insecure as she did after our mom died. So she marries for money. Never love." He gestured toward the mansion. "She pays for this place."

At that moment, Dylan's father pointed at a bird and smiled. "My wife would it here. She loved gardens. When is she coming to see me?" He looked at Dylan. "I'm sorry, I forgot your name, son."

Dylan put a hand on his father's shoulder. "Don't worry about it, Mr. Shane. Your wife is coming soon. Real soon." He turned back to Lucy. "Julie and I seem like lucky people on the outside. We're both good-looking. Athletic. Friendly. Julie's loaded, I'm popular with the ladies, but both of us are haunted. We can't get close to other people because we trust nobody. We've been drifting through life."

James and Lucy looked at Mr. Shane. He seemed content to follow the haphazard flight of a pair of bumblebees. James wished they could all sit and enjoy the beautiful spring day, but the sunshine and birdsong held no charm.

"So you know all about my motives now." Dylan was also watching his father. "You here to arrest me?"

Lucy handed Dylan her cell phone. "I'm going to let you turn yourself in. Things will go easier for you if you do that. Just press the Send key and your call will go right through to Sheriff Huckabee."

Dylan accepted the phone. His face was grim. "I want you to know that Pete's death was an accident. Ronnie was the one who started that fire, but it's my fault Pete couldn't get out of the building. The spiked whiskey was meant for Ronnie. I had no idea that she'd given it to Pete until I read about the presence of drugs in his body in the local paper." He absently rubbed the surface of the cell phone. "I'm glad this is all over. I searched for that demon of a woman for years. I've wasted my life and my potential seeking revenge. Now that I have it, I just want to sit in a quiet place and not feel anything." He leaned back against the bench and lifted his face to the sun. "At this point, I feel older than most of the residents here."

James and Lucy exchanged pained looks.

"I'm sorry about your daddy," Lucy said and took Mr. Shane's hand in her own. "Will it be hard for him to be without you?"

Dylan's eyes grew watery as he looked at his father. "He hasn't recognized me for weeks. He won't even know I'm gone. It's a small mercy, I suppose."

"We'll check up on him. So will our friend Mr. Wimple," James said, speaking for the first time.

"Thanks." Dylan glanced at his father for a long moment. Then, he pressed a button on Lucy's phone and waited for Huckabee to pick up. "Sheriff. I'm calling about the deaths of Pete Vandercamp and Ronnie Levitt." Dylan's gaze was fixed on his father's placid face. "Sir. I'd like to make a confession."

Chapter Fifteen

Sweet Lucy Light Frozen Custard

The first Friday evening in June was hot and humid, and the residents of Quincy's Gap knew to prepare for the sticky, sweltering summer Mother Nature had in store for them. James was too excited to notice the weather because Willy had asked the supper club members, along with Carter Peabody and Phoebe Liu, to attend a special "unveiling" ceremony that evening.

However, James had another engagement to attend first. Lucy had invited him to a casual dinner at her house prior to Willy's mysterious event, and by five in the afternoon, James had showered, put on a bit too much aftershave, dressed in his tidiest clothes, and driven to the florist. Now, he stood deliberating over bouquets wrapped in colorful tissue and buckets filled with single blooms. He'd already been in the shop for twenty minutes and was in danger of being late when the salesclerk approached him.

"Why not just get red roses?" she asked, growing frustrated with James's dillydallying. It was nearing on closing time and she clearly ready to lock up.

"Too cliché," James said, glancing around for the umpteenth time. "I want something vibrant. Something with blues and purples." He smiled happily. "My Lucy has the most beautiful eyes. They're like cornflowers. I'd like to find a bouquet to match her eyes."

The clerk frowned. "I'm afraid we don't carry cornflowers. They grow in fields all over Virginia, and in this shop, we tend to offer a more sophisticated selection of blooms."

Normally, James would have been put off by the woman's pretentiousness, but he was feeling too buoyant to allow her sourness to affect him. "In that case, I'd like a mixture of irises, purple carnations, white lilies, and those cream-colored roses." He paused and cast his eyes around the shop once more. "With some greens and Queen Anne's lace mixed in. And I'd like the bouquet tied with a lavender bow, please."

Although the woman grudgingly gathered the stems, James was pleased to see the care with which she assembled the bouquet. After he paid, he whistled his way to the front door. As he reached for the door handle, he stuck his nose into the bouquet to smell the lovely fragrance. However, having his face so close to the lilies made him sneeze. He sneezed three times consecutively while trying to open the door.

"I hope your girlfriend isn't allergic to lilies, too," the woman remarked as he made to leave.

"Or to Queen Anne's lace," he said, sniffling on the threshold. "After all, *it grows in fields all over Virginia*." Having fired his departing shot, James left the shop and resumed his whistling.

When he arrived at Lucy's house, James was relieved to see that her three enormous dogs were safely penned in the backyard. Lucy whipped open the front door before he had a chance to ring the bell. Seeing the flowers, she threw her arms around James so forcefully that he nearly fell backward down the steps. They held each other for a moment, laughing at their mutual awkwardness.

Once they were both inside, Lucy filled up half of the double kitchen sink, plopped the stem end of the bouquet into the water, and continued to show her appreciation to James. She put her arms around his neck and kissed him. He slid his arms around her waist and pulled her closer to him. They were both lost in their embrace until Bon Jovi, Lucy's largest male shepherd, began raking at the screen door dividing the kitchen from the back deck. He scratched and whined piteously, showing no sign of relenting. When Lucy continued to ignore him, Bon Jovi's whine turned into agitated barking. Finally, Lucy finally broke away from James to calm her frantic dog.

When she turned back to him, her cheeks flushed and her eyes shining, they both started laughing again.

"I guess we'll have to close all the blinds whenever you come over." She winked at James playfully. "My dogs might think you're attacking me instead of . . . making my heart sing."

"They'll have to get used to me, because I plan on spending plenty of time here making your heart sing," James said, taking Lucy in his arms again. Instead of kissing her, he tenderly stroked her beautiful, soft hair. "If that's okay with you, that is."

"It sounds perfect." Lucy gestured at the kitchen table. "Shall we eat? We need to be back in town by seven."

James put his finger under Lucy's chin and raised it until her mouth was inches from his. "We have a few minutes to spare," he whispered huskily. "After all, I'm a fast eater."

Outside the back door, Bon Jovi resumed his mournful howling.

• • •

Willy's unveiling ceremony was held in the parking lot next to the site where the Polar Pagoda once stood. Because it was seven o'clock, the other businesses had closed for the day and the only living creatures in sight were the clouds of gnats swarming the parking lot lights. Luckily, they dissipated when a rain-scented breeze swept down from the mountains, cooling the evening air and sweeping away the humidity.

Willy greeted his guests with hugs and handshakes. He was even more cheerful than usual, and James could sense a mounting excitement in the atmosphere. Willy was electric. His entire body seemed to hum and glow.

When everyone had arrived, Willy asked his friends to make themselves comfortable in the folding chairs Phoebe had let him borrow from the Witness to Fitness storeroom. Apparently, Phoebe was one of Willy's regular customers and had been sneaking over to the Polar Pagoda during her lunch hour ever since Witness to Fitness opened.

Facing his audience, Willy held out his arms and began by thanking Phoebe for the use of the chairs. "I'm going to miss seeing this pretty lady every day," Willy said, smiling at her. "Phoebe is moving on to greener pastures. There's a Weight Watchers center over in New Market and she's been hired as one of the counselors. I think she's going to be wonderful for the folks in New Market." Willy gestured for Phoebe to stand. "Tell these fine people all about it, my friend."

Phoebe smiled shyly and smoothed her crisp white cotton blouse. "I am moving, but I'm not abandoning my Witness to Fitness clients. All of you will be given a free month's membership at Weight Watchers so that you can continue the excellent work you've begun. I've also spoken with the Membership Director at the YMCA, and he's agreed to let you try out their exercise classes for the same period of time."

There were happy murmurs from the supper club members and someone shouted, "Thanks, Phoebe!"

Phoebe unfolded a copy of the *Star Ledger* and held it out to the crowd. "I've placed an ad in this weekend's paper explaining these offers for the benefit of all the Witness to Fitness clients, but I'd really appreciate it if you could spread the word. No one's weight-loss success should be halted by . . . other people's bad choices." She waved to indicate everyone in the supper club group. "You five have lost between fifteen and twenty-five pounds each. I hope you realize how incredible your achievement is, and I truly hope to see you at future meetings. Thank you." Exhausted from her long speech, Phoebe sank into her chair.

After Willy led the group in a round of applause for the sweet and gentle nutritionist, he opened the lid of a large cooler with a flourish. Reaching inside, he cupped his hands around a pint-sized foam cup and held it aloft before his friends.

"I'd like to help all of the folks who are doing their best to get in shape by giving them a special treat this summer. Your group has had some mighty big stumbling blocks with all the goings-on around here, so I've created a new flavor of custard to keep your spirits up as the numbers on the scale keep going down."

"What's the flavor?" Bennett asked, clearly excited by the idea of sampling Willy's custard.

"I am *so* glad you asked that question, my friend. It's a light-as-air, sweet cream vanilla with a hint of honey and a kiss of cinnamon. I've named it Sweet Lucy Light in honor of the brave and intelligent lady who I am proud to number among my friends. Without you, Lucy Hanover, things would still be right messy around this town. Not only would they be a mess, but I also wouldn't have gotten a check from those tight-fisted insurance folks. Since they finally paid up, I can start rebuilding my dream. And it's all thanks to you."

Willy handed out quarts of his new flavor of frozen custard to all. Lucy accepted hers with tears in her eyes. After one taste, James couldn't believe the treat was either sugar-free or low fat. It was simply too delicious to be either.

"It's way too rich to be a light dessert!" he protested to Willy.

"James it right, It tastes like a heavenly ambrosia of spun sugar and dreams." Gillian said, rolling her eyes as she took another bite. When Willy stared at her in confusion, she congratulated him on his brilliant invention. "What a tribute to our Lucy! The future deputy!"

"Too bad that mutt Donovan took all the credit for solving the murders," Bennett said dourly. "You did the legwork and confronted the murderer. You should be getting a medal. Instead, that louse steals all the laurels."

"I'd rather have an ice cream named for me, thanks," Lucy replied graciously. "Besides, I wasn't all that courageous. I knew Dylan wouldn't hurt me. I know it sounds screwed up, but once he'd had his revenge, he deflated. He lost his whole purpose in life. Also, James was with me, so I had no reason to be scared."

Lindy caught the secretive smiles exchanged between James and Lucy and put her hands on her hips. "Okay, you two have been grinning at each other since you got here. Do you have a hot romance brewing?"

"Maybe," Lucy said enigmatically.

Carter was too impatient to learn about the details of Dylan's arrest to allow the topic of conversation to divert from murder investigations. Stepping in front of Lindy, he pointed his plastic spoon at Lucy. "So how did Deputy Donovan steal your thunder?"

Lucy shrugged. "Simple bad luck. I had Sheriff Huckabee's number programmed into my cell phone, but Donovan picked up instead of Huckabee. Dylan assumed he was talking to the sheriff, so he just began to spill the beans about both deaths. Donovan told Dylan to stay put, or he'd be in some seriously hot water. As Donovan was driving out to Wandering Springs, he called every reporter he knew so they'd be ready with the cameras rolling when he cuffed Dylan and loaded him into his cruiser."

"Where were you and James when this happened?" Lindy asked.

James put a hand on Lucy's shoulder. "We promised to look after Dylan's dad, so we wheeled him inside. We didn't want him to witness his son's arrest, even though it was unlikely he'd understand what was happening. It was as much for Dylan's sake and for Mr. Shane's that protected their final memory. We wanted that memory to be a beautiful day in the garden. Not sirens wailing and reporters demanding to be heard."

"Of course, Donovan made as much noise as he could," Lucy said in disgust. "He tore up the driveway with his siren going full tilt and ran up to Dylan with his weapon drawn. Dylan wasn't doing anything to warrant that. He was sitting on the same bench where he'd made the call, calm as you please. When Donovan got close, Dylan stood and offered his wrists to be cuffed. Huckabee wouldn't approve of Donovan frightening the residents of Wandering Springs half to death. But like I said, it was just a matter of bad luck. Donovan was there and Huckabee wasn't."

"That redheaded limelight hog is now the town hero!" Carter spluttered. "His picture's been in every paper from here to Mississippi *and* he's getting free meals at Dolly's for a week! It's just not right."

Lucy laughed. "That kind of food wouldn't be good for my diet. Besides, I don't want the publicity. The sheriff knows how I contributed to the case. He's really starting to see me in a new light. That's what I really want — to break into the Boy's Club. I want to get in and keep climbing, and I'm going to take the deputy exam this summer. I now know that I have what it takes to be a member of law enforcement."

Carter frowned. "There's still something I don't get. How did Ronnie end up with the bottle of tainted Jack Daniel's? The one containing the drugs?"

"When Dylan first applied for the position of exercise coach, he pretended to be interested in Ronnie," Lucy explained. "He flirted. She took the bait. She offered to make him dinner at her place, and while she was cooking, he did some snooping and saw a bottle of Jack Daniel's in her wet bar. He figured he'd come across an easy way to kill her. He bought a bottle of the same whiskey in Waynesboro, where no one would remember him, steamed off the black label that seals the cap to the neck of the bottle, put the Valium inside, and glued the label back on."

"That is cold," Carter mumbled, sounding impressed.

Lucy shot him a look and continued. "The next time Dylan was invited to Ronnie's house, he switched bottles, removing her bottle from the house and tossing it in the trash. He expected Ronnie to drink the booze and die quietly at home. Unfortunately, she brought that bottle to Pete. I guess she wanted to get him drunk in order to pump him for info. She was afraid he'd remember why he knew her from TV. If that happened, her cover would be blown. We'll never know what he told her, but she must have found it threatening because she poured the leftover whiskey on the T-shirts and started the fire."

"But I saw her at the Brunswick stew fund-raiser. How did she have time to commit arson and get to the dinner?" Lindy asked.

"She was pretty late arriving," James said. "I was one of the last people in line for food and she was right in front of me." He thought back to that evening. "I remember how she made a point of speaking with Mrs. Lowndes and Mrs. Emerson. She must have been making sure the upstanding women could testify that she was at the dinner. Ronnie even mentioned the shirts to the ladies."

Carter groaned. "Pete must have recognized Ronnie from the Red Cross scam. The poor man. I wish he'd kept his mouth shut or that he'd told someone else what he knew. Instead, Ronnie killed him. Afterward, she just sat down and ate her stew like nothing happened. What a psycho."

Lucy nodded. "She made a career of hurting people. And though Dylan felt horrible about Pete, his guilt wasn't strong enough to stop him from seeking his revenge. He wasn't going to stop until he'd punished Ronnie. According to his statement, Dylan went back to her place for another date. That's when he noticed a pack of Pall Mall cigarettes on the windowsill in her kitchen. He asked her about them and she said she only smoked to calm her nerves. The *Star* had printed every tiny detail about the Polar Pagoda fire and Dylan remembered that the butts found at the scene of the fire were Pall Malls. That's when he knew that Ronnie had deliberately set fire to that building with the intent of killing Pete."

"Is that why Dylan drowned her in the bathtub?" Lindy was both intrigued and horrified. "Because he was angry about Pete's death?"

"I do." Lucy's voice was solemn. "I think her behavior sickened him. I also believe that it fanned the fury he'd been carrying around with him for years. However, he couldn't plot her demise until they'd had a few more dates. On the Monday she pretended to be unwell, Ronnie was at home making preparations for a romantic evening with Dylan. That's why there were candles everywhere."

Bennett shook his head. "But she was unknowingly preparing to seduce a killer."

"Dylan had obviously led her to believe that they were going to sleep together. He got her pretty drunk on wine and then plied her with the spiked Jack Daniel's," Lucy continued. "According to his statement, Dylan suggested they take a bath together. He never disrobed, and as soon as he saw Ronnie's chameleon tattoo, he knew that Ronnie was Stacy. He'd seen the tattoo when she was sunbathing in Dylan's yard back in Miami. It was the perfect tattoo for such a changeable person." Lucy smirked. "Anyway, Dylan was overcome by feeling of loss and rage. He thought of his family and of Stacy's betrayal and he couldn't control his fury, so he grabbed her ankles and held her under until she was still. It wasn't hard. She was very drunk."

The supper club members fell silent. James imagined they were all remembering the grim image of Ronnie's body in the bathtub.

And yet, there was one question he wanted to ask. "If Ronnie was a smoker, why didn't anyone find cigarettes in her town house after her death?"

"Dylan took the cigarettes with him the night of the murder. He was very thorough in cleaning up." Lucy dabbed at her lips with a paper napkin. "Also, Ronnie didn't have an ashtray. She told Dylan that she only smoked outside and disposed of the butts in public trash cans. Seems she didn't care for the odor of tobacco inside her house."

The group finished their ice cream and gazed at the remains of the Polar Pagoda and the darkened Witness to Fitness storefront. James could hardly believe the shocking events that had taken place in their little town over the past few weeks.

Lucy stood up and moved closer to the wreckage of Willy's former business. The caution tape set out by the fire department had faded from a bright yellow to buttery beige. The black lettering had turned a dull shade of gray. She rubbed the tape pensively with her fingertips, a thoughtful expression on her face. "You should name a custard flavor after Pete instead of me, Willy," Lucy said. "It seems like we're the only ones left to keep his memory alive. Us and dear old Fred Wimple."

Willy took Lucy's hand. "None of us will forget Pete. I'm going to build a memorial bench in his honor and place it in front of the new shop. Let's turn our thoughts away from the past and focus on long, lazy summer days. And on making new memories together."

"Hear! Hear! No more talk of murder and mayhem!" Gillian declared. "Aren't we supposed to be celebrating tonight?"

"Yeah, Willy." Bennett slung an arm around his friend. "What gives with the easel? You going to start painting like James's dad?"

"It's not a painting. It's an architectural rendering of my new ice cream parlor. The Town Planning Committee approved my proposal this afternoon." Willy flashed them a crooked grin. "Word on the street is that Mrs. Savannah Lowndes was on vacation this week, so I rushed over to the office with my plan. It was passed by just one little vote." Willy chuckled with glee. "Y'all ready to see the design for the all-new Custard Cottage?"

"Yes!" his friends yelled in unison.

Willy whipped off the sheet to reveal a colored drawing of a lavender cottage with creamy gingerbread trim that seemed to drip down the building like warm icing. Giant-sized lollipops lined the exterior walls and gumdrops in a rainbow of colors danced along the roof. A path made to look like pinwheel mints led to the double front doors painted a cheerful raspberry. Ten café tables with striped umbrellas were positioned outside, and a set of trash cans shaped like ice cream cones flanked the entrance.

"Call me Hansel," James said as he admired the sketch. "Because that place looks good enough to eat."

"I'm going to carry bulk candy as well as frozen custard and ice cream. The candy will help me pay the bills during the winter." Willy beamed at his friends. "Construction starts at the end of the month."

Lindy gave Willy a fierce hug. "This is wonderful, Willy! We're so glad you're staying in Quincy's Gap."

Willy feigned a scowl. "Well, I'd better sell a heck of a lot of ice cream this summer, because I have to pay extra for the fancy new sprinkler system."

"I hereby declare that the Custard Cottage is enough excitement for the town of Quincy's Gap this summer," Lindy cried, raising her empty ice cream cup in a toast. "We could all use some peace and quiet. After I lose a few more pounds, I'm going to spend a week at the beach. I'm going to catch up on my reading and turn my skin a deeper shade of Brazilian bronze."

"I'm studying for that exam," Lucy said and noticed Carter staring at her in unmasked admiration. She smiled at him. "Since you know so much about crime, will you help me study?"

Pleased, Carter nodded in agreement.

Bennett thumped his chest. "Carter won't have much free time, Lucy. He and I are starting a post office bowling league. It's about time someone took on those boys from the DMV. They've won the league trophy five years in a row." Bennett flexed his arm. "Now that I'm getting some muscle tone back, I'll hurl that fourteen-pound ball down the lane and smack those pins to smithereens."

"Looks like I'll have to hire someone new to work on my Pet Palaces," Gillian sighed. "It might take the whole summer to find a replacement. Your creative talent and boundless energy aren't easy to replicate, my dear friend. You don't have a twin, do you, Willy?"

Willy laughed. "Aw, don't go making me blush. And though I do have a sister, she's not too handy. She can cook up a storm when her nose isn't stuck in a book. Speaking of books, what about you, James?" Willy asked. "What are your summer plans?"

James shrugged. "I haven't thought too far ahead, but I know what I'm doing tomorrow. I'm going to drive to that big mall in Charlottesville and go clothes shopping—an errand I usually avoid at all costs." He tugged at the waist of his chinos and was able to gather several inches of extra fabric between his fingers. "For the first time in ten years, I'm actually looking forward to buying a new pair of pants."

About the Author

New York Times bestselling author Ellery Adams grew up on a beach near the Long Island Sound. Having spent her adult life in a series of landlocked towns, she cherishes her memories of open water, violent storms, and the smell of the sea. She now writes full-time from her home in North Carolina, which she shares with her husband, two trolls, and three keyboard-hogging felines. Adams loves coffee, champagne, kickboxing, 1,000-piece jigsaw puzzles, Pinterest, and black jelly beans.

Her traditionally published series include The Secret, Book, and Scone Society Mysteries; The Book Retreat Mysteries; The Books by the Bay Mysteries; and The Charmed Pie Shoppe Mysteries.

Her Indie series include The Supper Club Mysteries, The Hope Street Church Mysteries, and The Antiques & Collectibles Mysteries.

9 781958 384664